Praise for the novels of

LUANNE JONES

"Jones has created a wonderful alternate universe in
this story, and exploring it is a pleasure. This book is as
emotional as it is funny—so keep some tissues handy."
—*Romantic Times BOOKreviews* on *Heathen Girls*

"Life in the South is different from anywhere else
in this country. That fact is personified in Luanne Jones's
Heathen Girls, a tale packed full with warm vivacity and
remarkable characterization…. Her characters fairly jump
off the pages and straight into your heart. Written with an
obviously loving touch, with careful consideration for all
of her characters' actions, mannerisms, and dialogue,
Ms. Jones doesn't pull any punches."
—*Romance Reveiws Today*

"Written with sass and style and brimming with
endearingly eccentric yet wonderfully memorable
characters, this is an unabashed delight. Jones['s]…
first book, *Sweethearts of the Twilight Lanes,* was an
equally addictive blend of Southern charm
and humorous romance."
—*Library Journal* on *The Dixie Belle's Guide to Love*

"Southern humor shines in Luanne Jones'
The Dixie Belle's Guide to Love."
—*Romantic Times BOOKreviews*

LUANNE JONES

The Southern Comforts

MIRA®

MIRA

ISBN-13: 978-0-7783-2422-5
ISBN-10:   0-7783-2422-2

THE SOUTHERN COMFORTS

www.MIRABooks.com

Printed in U.S.A.

10 9 8 7 6 5 4 3 2 1

Here's to the Porchers.
The rockers and the off-their rockers,
The tea brewers, the bra-tossers,
The tale-spinners, the leg pullers,
The book writers, booksellers, book lovers,
The thong-wearers and nekkid moon dancers,
The pict-chur takers and Web site makers,
Ya'll of many faiths and places
But of a single state of mind—
Sharing life and stories from the shelter of a porch
Unseen by any eye but recognizable to all as
Home.

ACKNOWLEDGMENTS

Thanks to Joyce for the inspiration and imagination for women dancing beneath the full moon to celebrate their power. Thanks to all the members of the Southern Porch for their support and laughter.

Kathie, Kathi, Kendoll (Ken), Lovelace, Alec, Jim (my OSU Pal), Janet, Jill, Judith, Shellie, Dottie, Ron, Kay, Vyv, Nicki, Linda, Bob, Mac (that's *Ms.* Mac to y'all), Jackie, Brandon, Lisa, Linda, Pam and Gene. And if I missed anyone, forgive me!

PROLOGUE

You cannot wash away the sin of having lived a generally proper life while wearing support hose and a padded bra. Not even a silk monogrammed thong can take that plunge with you, and especially not your mother's best pearls.

No, the leap from reasonably behaved middle-aged martyr to flinging-yourself-into-life-head-on heathen girl can only be made in all-embracing, dimpled-butted, stretch-mark-bellied, gravity-ravaged glory.

Spiritually, emotionally and bare-skinned, bodily naked.

"Yee-haw, y'all, Charma Deane George Parker is finally going to do this…this…this absolutely idiotic and awesome undertaking!" I should have shouted it to the four winds, the Holy Trinity and the multitude of late lamented minor gods and goddesses scattered through heaven and maybe hell and whatever lies between that make up the greater George family theocracy. But I mostly just whispered it for my own self.

It was a private triumph after all. I was going to finally jump into the pond that had robbed me of my father, into the water that had almost swallowed me up, that had taunted me for a lifetime. Now it was my last best hope of saving myself.

This act alone could wash away the despair and desperation that had trickled slowly year after year through my being, until at last it had saturated me. I had steeped in it for too long and it had begun to warp me.

And not the good kind of being warped, either.

Not that I had started out all that true and whole and astonishing. Maybe as a baby, sure. To my way of thinking babies come out pure distilled hope and potential. Then they open their eyes and become a part of this imperfect world. No wonder they spend their first months screaming and soiling themselves.

But this, my own rebirth, this at last could rid me of a lifetime of sins gathered in the pursuit of what must have looked to anyone not paying close attention—lovers, acquaintances, and myself, for example—like a damn good life. The sin of sameness. The sin of second-guessing myself. The sin of never putting more at stake than I could stand to lose. The sin of shame over things that were not my doing. The greater sin of having no shame at all about things gentler souls would have fallen down prostrate before God, loved ones and the state of Arkansas to plead to be forgiven for, or at least to get off with time served.

For these sins I would surrender myself. I would jump. I would go down and down and trust the universe and my will to stay alive to bring me up again, renewed and ready to face the rest of my life.

The house where I had grown up among the most mule-headed and magnificent women on earth stood in long shadows not far away. Empty for now. The friends and family who had swarmed about it for the last week had taken leave—some for just a breather, some I didn't know if I would ever see again. We had buried my cousin Bess today.

She was gone. Barely fifty. Newly married. And she was…*gone*.

If ever there was a day for recommitting to life, to ridding yourself of the things that weighed you down for too long, for jumping and hoping and taking the consequences either way, this was that day.

The October sun hung low in the afternoon sky. It warmed the broadest part of my bare back. It felt strange and sexy and a little bit silly to the parts of my body that had not basked in sunlight since the more wayward days of my youth. But there I stood on the floating dock in my birthday suit.

If my mother could have seen me…but then my mother never *could* see me, not really. Not even when I stood right in front of her. But if she *had* looked out the window of our family house— and it is *ours,* my aunts Fawnie and Shug's and mine, despite the deed getting willed out of our hands—I wonder what she might think. Or why her opinion would still matter to me so much.

"God, why didn't you make me bolder? Or stronger? Or smarter? Or—" I lowered my head and my gaze fell over the southern hemisphere of my earthly vessel "—or at least a *real* redhead?"

God didn't answer.

In acceptance of His silence, I clenched my fist against the fullness of my thigh. Women should have thighs, I believe, and breasts and hips and even tummies, so I don't hold the fact that mine are ample (though not overmuch so) against the Almighty. But the way my life had drifted this past year, the losses I had suffered, not to mention dry skin and the fact that with age my arms and legs had begun to freckle? *That* I wholeheartedly held against the creator of all things good and holy…*and* freckled.

I squinted toward the road beyond the huge hedges surrounding the big old house that everyone in Orla, Arkansas, called the Aunt Farm. Time was running out.

So sure was I of my scheme to engineer my own rebirth that I had invited a certain man over for, well, *I* invited him for forever. *He* just thought it was for the night.

Either way, the time had come to fish or cut bait. To jump or…

It was not yet full-on fall in Arkansas, but the leaves had begun to change, to dry out, to be pressed by the wind against the foundations of my home and the exposed roots of trees in my yard, and to tangle in the tall grass around the pond where I stood. I flexed my toes against the rough boards of the dock as I had in childhood.

Almost forty years ago I had nearly drowned jumping into this pond. I had gone under, become disoriented, terrified and…

And then I felt my father's presence. "Jump! Jump into the water, Charma Deane! Everybody here loves you. Not a one of us would ever let anything bad happen to you. You're safe. You're strong. You're free. Jump wa-aa-ay out. Jump out past your fear."

Daddy had promised I could jump and nothing would hurt me. I believed him, and rightly so. He kept his word, and he paid with his life.

Somehow I had found a way to blame my older cousin, Bess, for that tragedy. After that it got easier to blame her more and more, and she didn't make things harder. So year upon year Bess collected the blame for the fears and insecurities that directed my choices in life for far too long.

But we had *buried* Bess today.

I had no more excuses. No one else to blame.

Now it was my turn.

Dead to the old. Reborn in the new.

Yes, it was just a symbolic gesture. To take a risk, throw myself into thin air, to fall and go under and to rise again.

Dead to the old. Reborn in the new.

God above, I wanted it to be true.

I wanted it to work.

All I could do was jump and see.

❧ CHAPTER ONE

Two weeks later

"Why do you have to jump in to the rescue every time those aunts of yours fart sideways? I swear they will be the death of you yet." Inez Calaveras scowled at me over the top of my vintage gold-tone hearse.

Yeah, *hearse.* I drive a fully restored 1974 Cotner-Bevington Oldsmobile hearse. How I ended up with it was a long story that involves love, death, betrayal and the deep, abiding, personal satisfaction of knowing wherever I went in it, I'd make a scene.

The thing didn't actually belong to me, though. It belonged to a certain *man.* Sort of like my house, which belonged to *another* man. But like my house, the hearse was undeniably *mine.*

Only one of the men was mine, Guy Chapman. And I wasn't all too sure about him some days. The hearse belonged to him. He was a mortician.

Me and a mortician. God and His sense of humor. He must laugh so hard over my life some days that He lets out a big ol' snort. My luck, I'll be standing too close one time and get sucked up by the intake. Imagine the indignation in Orla when a bunch of good people see *that* happen and think Charma Deane George Parker, infamously fabulous heathen girl and only so-so Baptist, was the first one Raptured!

That's the way it is with me, never a good thing without a backlash. Rapture and laughter and causing more righteous indignation than a decent person should, and usually because of something that sucks, too.

Wasn't jumping in that damned pond supposed to fix all this?

Dead to the old? Reborn in the new?

But everything about my life, about me, still felt…old. Especially this argument.

"Excuse me but I do not jump *every* time." With the words still hanging in the air, I took the precaution of switching off my cell phone so I wouldn't get summoned yet again and be made to look a complete *old* fool. "And by the way, we do not fart sideways in the George family, we are gracious, refined southern ladies, damn it."

"Southern ladies don't fart?" She tossed back her way-too-black-for-being-over-fifty hair and muttered a curse in her native language—New Jerseyian—then added, "So what happens when they have gas?"

"Angels come down and carry it away on little satin pillows and release it over the polar ice cap." I flapped my hands and tried to look serene to illustrate the undertaking.

"The *South* Pole, no doubt."

"Of course." I imagined tiny winged things in hoop skirts batting fans across their heaving bosoms. Then all I could think of was how Aunt Shug would love to get after something like that with her flyswatter. "Every time my aunts fart, an angel gets frostbit wings."

I believe Inez groaned at that. Then she commanded my gaze. "If those aunts of yours have guardian fart angels watching over them, then they sure as hell don't need you to cancel your plans to rush back and take care of them, woman."

"Did you just say 'guardian fart angels'?"

She didn't answer, probably because she knew as well as I did that I had only tossed it out there to buy time. What more can a person do when confronted with the unpleasant, unwavering truth just blurted out like that?

My aunts had gotten along for a long time without me around to shepherd them through. If I dashed off to the rescue, now I would be going for myself. To *preserve* myself.

I was Charma Deane, after all, saver of everything from awkward social situations to lost souls. I was the nurse, the nurturer, the mother, the daughter, the niece, *the* caregiver. My course had been set the day my father had died, and I had not wavered from it since if I could help it. I didn't know how to be anyone else, and jumping in ponds in acts of false baptism aside, it terrified me to think of trying to be anyone else.

Inez cocked her hip, stretched her arm over the hood of my hearse and drummed her orange fingernails on the glossy finish. "I say we finish what we came out here to do and let them ladies be. What do you think, Charma? Let's me and you go and find the true path to God."

"True path to God?" I pressed my knuckles into the spot above the bridge of my nose, squeezing my eyes shut. Leave who I am by the wayside and go looking for God? On purpose? It was too much. Too *damn* much.

"Shitfire, Inez. It's a bunch of lines in the dirt." My gaze followed the gravel outline of circles within circles in some farmer's field that she had read about in the travel section of the Orla Sunday paper.

"A labyrinth," I whispered, shaking my head.

"An enigma," she murmured, temptation in her tone. "A sacred spot. A pilgrimage."

Inez is a bit of a drama queen. Not like a royal queen, of course, more like some locally sponsored, riding-on-a-flatbed-float-alongside-a-bunch-of-bitchy-wannabes-with-meaningless-titles-in-a-small-town-festival-parade type of queen. In other words, she didn't hold a candle to my family in the hierarchy of women who make way too big a damn deal out of every piddly-ass thing.

"A path," I said, still visually following the concentric curves. They represented order and the basic human drive to find a way in this life to connect with something beyond your own chaotic existence. I found the labyrinth beautiful, compelling and…intrinsically hostile.

Labyrinths were things of mystery and meditation. Their history stretched back to pagan times and to the earliest churches. They stood silent, sentinels to the ages, gateways to secret societies, places for profound prayer. One did not belong on just any barren quarter acre of ordinary Arkansas red dirt.

Inez thought we should build one at the Aunt Farm.

I didn't disagree.

In fact, I thought trying to plunk one of these suckers down at my house would be a hoot. Not just because I wanted to find spiritual meaning in my life, either. But also because I knew that dumping a truckload of gravel out and fashioning an ancient design in my sideyard would literally leave my mark on the property for all time. In one more small way, I would stake my claim. And *that* would royally piss off the new legal owner of the Aunt Farm, Sterling Mayhouse.

Inez bundled her hair in her hand just at the nape of her neck and shimmied her shoulders. Her earrings bounced. Her teeth shone white against her persimmon-colored lips. I could see myself reflected in her sunglasses, pinch-faced and milky by comparison. "Walk it with me, Charma. It won't take more than an hour."

I glanced at my cell phone. I'd missed a second call from my aunts. My stomach clamped down into a cold, hard knot. "I don't have an hour."

"You have all the time you need. What's wrong with you, woman? What about that vow?"

"No fair, Inez, invoking the vow."

She gave me a "Screw fairness" look and folded her arms.

Bess and I, on the occasion of my nana Abbra's death, made this vow—on account that my whole family acted like real squirrels and donkeys that day. Also because my mama and the aunts she ended up sharing a house with later, all widows who despised my grandma, buried my nana dressed like some drunken poodle-permed senior citizen tourist. A thing like that leaves an impression on young girls.

So we made up this vow.

We will live without limits. We will love without questions. We will laugh without apologies. And whoever dies first, the other cousin has to get to Chapman and Son's Funeral Home first to do the other's clothes, hair and makeup, so the deceased doesn't go to heaven looking like hell.

I wanted to go with Inez. I wanted to fulfill the promise I had made, not just with Bess, but *for* Bess and for myself on the day I had jumped into the pond at last. The new Charma would go without questions or apologies.

But the old pull was strong. What if they really, *really* needed me this time? What if I didn't go and I could have said or done something that would have turned the tide?

Just like that, just like a bandage ripped from a still unhealed wound, it was done.

"Problem with a vow between two people involving death is that only one of them reaps the benefit of it." I didn't mean it was a benefit that Bess had suffered a protracted death by cancer. Inez knew that. "That deal is over, Inez. That vow doesn't count for anything anymore."

"Like hell it doesn't," she said, all cool and quiet-like, which was not like her at all and shook me a little. Then she leaned forward, dead serious, and added in an angry little whisper, "It's a damned miracle that Bess hasn't come back from beyond to haunt you into living up to that vow."

"I wish she could." It came out before I could think through the consequences of saying something like that. I held my breath. I should take it back. Spit between my fingers or knock wood or say a prayer to take it back. I mean, Bess was in a better place, right? It was damned lousy of me to wish her back just because *I* was feeling confused and defeated.

But I didn't want to take it back. I wanted *Bess* back. And my mother. And life as I had once known it. I put my hand over my face, exhaled, then skimmed my curved fingers back over my autumn-frizzed hair. "I could always rely on Bess to kick me in the butt when I needed it."

"Honey." Inez came around the front of the car and draped her arm around my shoulder. "If you should ever need *anyone* to kick you in the butt, send out the word. There will be a line formed in Orla so long people will think they're giving out government cheese at the armory."

"Thanks."

"No problem." She patted my back. "In fact, if it would make you feel better, I'll go on record right now to honor that vow for your cousin. I'll come do your makeup at Chapman's if you die before me."

I took a long look at my friend and resigned myself to this new reality. "Great. I am going to meet Jesus looking like a big-haired, Puerto-Rican, hillbilly whore."

"You'll look so good God won't even know you."

"And therefore might let me in by default?"

"Sure would increase your chances of getting in without a

disguise if you took up some more spiritual pastimes. Walking a labyrinth, for example."

I shook my head. "I have to go back, Inez."

"They sure do have you trained, girl."

"It's a crisis."

"It's a kid." She waved me off and moved to the passenger side door. "Your cousin Minnie's daughter showing up unannounced is not a crisis."

I wanted to agree with her, but this dull twisting low in my gut wouldn't allow it. "Abby was supposed to meet her parents in Japan with her intended and his whole family. Instead her parents, Minnie and Travis are probably just now getting off a plane in the Tokyo airport to find no intended, no family and no Abby. Because, unbeknown to them, Abby is sitting in her grandmother's kitchen asking for peanut butter to settle her stomach."

This was big. Cleaving-the-family-asunder big. I knew what Minnie would expect me to do, but I also knew…

The thing about twenty-year-old Abbra Raynes was that she wasn't one of us. We loved her. Adored her, really. But unlike my own two sons, who had grown up in Orla and around my aunts and under my family's influence, she had not spent so much as a summer weekend at the Aunt Farm without her mother's constant supervision.

All her life Minnie had been the mediator between Bess and me—the buffer. She had kept that role into adulthood with her daughter, sheltering the girl from our mouths, our less-than-Donna-Reed-like mothering styles and our…modus operandi.

According to Minnie we were, in a word, *too much*. See, even when someone tries to find one word to describe us, they have to use two. *Too much.*

Too rich. Too bossy. *Too* Southern.

Arkansas *is* southern. Don't let one of those Old South or True

South snobs tell you otherwise. So are Texas and whole chunks of Oklahoma, though they can get a bit slapdash and...*western* in their thinking. And Tennessee, where Abby was raised? No question.

But the girl missed out on a real southern upbringing. Her father, Travis Raynes, aka the least talkative man on earth, was born in California. His people still live there. And Minnie—Minnie is a citizen of the world. Half Japanese, half George, all old soul and affable spirit.

She is the best one of us. Her very existence proves we Georges have in us the stuff of the stars and streams and all things eternal and lovely, the things that guide and nourish and inspire. We could all of us have been more like Minnie, if we hadn't all been so damned determined to be like ourselves.

That's probably why, when Abby went off to college and finally got out from under all that silence and sweetness, she cut loose and connected with her inner heathen.

That only goes to show you can protect a child from the examples of her relations, but in the end blood will out. In Abby's case it outted itself à la her grandfather's (my uncle Kel) predilections. Uncle Kel married Fawnie young and turned over his life to her, whatever was left of his life that his mother and then later the army hadn't staked claim to. Years later, without warning or actual legal divorce proceedings, he brought home his second wife, Shug, from an assignment in Japan, with the bonus bun of Minnie in the oven.

Like her grandfather, as soon as she got out from under the watchful eye of the family, Abby got herself doubly involved—in her case, practically engaged to two young men at the same time. One Japanese, the real deal, about to return to some place so remote even Shug had not heard of it. The other was the son of a former Junior League president and a well-heeled judge and general big political hoo-ha. In other words, small-town Tennessee royalty. That kid was studying to be a lawyer in order to return and take over the family business of social climbing and general political hoo-ha-ing. Before her parents would give their blessing to either union, they would have to meet everyone involved.

"You don't know what it took for Minnie to consent to take this trip." It had cost Minnie emotionally. It required she reexamine who she was growing up, who she had become and who she wanted to be for the rest of her life. That's not something a person akin to a star or a stream takes lightly. "It made her deal with her own mother, for mercy's sake!"

"Hey, I *know*. Don't forget I also straddle many cultures."

"And to prove how much I appreciate your situation, I will keep any remarks about your straddling many cultures to myself."

"You are so classy." She popped open the hearse door.

I did the same on my side, and when we had both settled into the seats, I said, "It's all old money and breeding. It always shows."

"Oh, yeah, like ten minutes ago when you tried to convince me to lie down in the back of this tacky thing and pop up to wave at passing kids in minivans."

"I'm telling you, the looks on their faces would have been price-less."

"Well, maybe if we had walked the labyrinth, then gone for drinks like we planned, I might have been more inclined."

"No, drinking would have ruined it. Frightening the pee-wadin' out of little children is the kind of thing you have to do stone cold sober or it's just sad, Inez."

"That a George family motto, Charma Deane?"

"No. But maybe it should have been." I took a deep breath, or tried to, but a sharp pain at the center of my chest cut it short. Guilt. Or angst. I didn't know which, I only knew I never went too far between breaths without feeling it these days.

That's the real reason I had jumped at the chance to run home to take care of the situation with Abby. I needed to feel needed. I needed to feel something. Or maybe I needed to *not* feel. Either way, taking on someone else's problems seemed like it might do the trick. Something had to.

I had jumped into the pond and faced my fears, yet I still felt the gnawing sense of wanting to grab on to something, anything, to keep myself afloat. I had survived the water, but life after rebirth was drowning me.

"At least call Minnie and find out what's going on with her, what she knows and what plans she had for dealing with all this. Don't take responsibility for this by yourself."

"I can't call Minnie, Inez." I tore out of the tiny parking lot and onto the bumpy side road that would bring me back to the main highway. "She's in Tokyo."

"I'm pretty sure they have cell service there."

"Okay, sure, but Fawnie and Shug promised Abby that no one would do anything until I got there to talk to her in person."

"Your family." She put her feet up on the dash. I'd have yelled at her for it, but she learned the habit from me. "I swear if one of you Georges showed up at that house with a corpse and no alibi, the others would help you make up a story about how you'd bought the car used and forgot to check the trunk for bodies."

"Who told you about that?"

Her feet dropped to the floorboard, and she angled around to face me, one eye gone all squinty in some kind of warning.

I laughed. "There are worse things than intense family loyalty, Inez."

"Yeah, like intense family loyalty and being forced to choose sides."

I flicked on the air conditioning and a blast of cold air drew goose bumps on my arms. At least I told myself it was the air that caused the chilly reaction.

Inez sighed and began rummaging around in her ugly old purse. "If you're not going to listen to sense from me, then I'm afraid I'm going to have to call in the big guns."

"The wha…?" I didn't finish it because, well, it was such a ridiculous thing for her to say that it didn't deserve the kind of time and attention to detail it takes to speak in a complete sentence. And, in truth, my sons say that to me all the time—"wha…?"—when something totally lame comes out of my mouth, and just once I wanted to be on the giving and not the receiving end of it. "Girl, what are you talking about? In my circle of friends and family there are no guns bigger than me."

I threw my chest out.

"Oh, please, I've dated *men* with bigger boobs than yours."

"Guns, not boobs, Inez. They are not the same thing. If you are talking guns as body parts, anyway, it means muscles." I flexed my arm as evidence.

"Yeah? Funny, in my family we call those things grannyflaps." She prodded the soft beginning of a fleshy batwing beneath the more toned part of my upper arm.

"Bitch," I muttered, and steered the passenger side tire toward a nasty rut. "But thank you for not taking that boobs-as-guns analogy in the whole 'before long you'll be able to wear those guns in a holster on your hips' direction."

She patted my forearm. "You're welcome, honey."

I stole a glance at her. "You didn't think of that one, did you?"

"No, I didn't." She wriggled down into the seat getting all cozy. "But I *will* file it away in my memory for next time."

"Next time?" I laughed. "You honestly think there is going to be *another* time in our relationship when you threaten me with something as batshit crazy as calling in the *big guns?*"

"It was *not* crazy."

"Batshit crazy," I corrected her. I mean, is it asking too much for someone to get the terminology right? Calling in the *big guns?* On *me?*

Who was she going to call? Fawnie and Shug? I could take those two old women out with a cutting remark and wouldn't even have to spit my gum into my hand while I did it. No, Bess, Mama and Nana were all dead. I had stepped up to the top rank of the artillery.

"Talking about calling in the big guns, Inez. That's not just your ordinary wearing-your-swimsuit-and-a-tiara-to-the-Winn-Dixie crazy. That's batshit crazy. In the first place it's a cornball phrase and in the second, it's totally meaningless, because—"

"In your circle of friends and family there are no guns bigger than you."

"Damn right."

"Sounds like something your mama would have said. Or your grandma. Maybe even your aunt Fawnie."

"Fawnie?" My whole body tensed. "Oh, now there was no call to get ugly about this."

"I'm not getting ugly, I'm getting serious."

"You?"

"As a heart attack," she promised.

"How so?"

"I'm calling Guy Chapman."

"You? Call Guy? You are such a liar." I took my eyes off the road just long enough to catch the flash of the cell phone in her hand.

"I may be a liar, but I also have our friendly local mortician on my speed dial."

Inez? Guy? I tried to remember if I'd ever seen them carry on any conversation about anything but me, and that done right before my eyes. A less likely pair of phone buddies I could not imagine. "Why would you…?"

"A woman never knows when she might need to call in the big

gun." She used the tip of her nail to press the tiny keys. "In fact, if I recall, rightly, you told me the other day he had the biggest—"

"Put that phone down or I will drive this hearse—"

"Where? Where are you going to drive this hearse, Charma? What's a worse place for you than back to that house of old women and every day a new problem? Hey!" She switched seamlessly from challenging me to greeting the man in my life. "I'm with Charma and we're not at the labyrinth anymore. We're on our way to…yeah, I know you know."

My chest constricted. I tried to take a deep breath, but my lungs wouldn't have it. Why the hell couldn't the man in my life and my closest nonrelated friend be on *my* side for once?

"Mmm-hmm. I told her."

I clenched my jaw. Them talking like that about me while at the same time excluding me, it made me feel so…it made me feel out of control. And that just would not fly.

I cleared my throat and took the last turn before I'd hit the long shale drive that curved in front of my eight-bedroom monster of an old house. "Since you've got Guy on the phone, tell him to make himself useful. I'd say…hmmm, chicken."

"She called you chicken. I know. I know. I personally think you are the bravest man I know. *Also* maybe a little bit of a lunatic, unless you want to reconsider—"

"I didn't *call* him chicken, I want him to bring chicken…what was that supposed to mean? Reconsider what?"

"He wants to know how much chicken, where and when?"

"Two buckets, all the sides, extra biscuits. Aunt Farm. As soon as he can get his adorable behind out there."

"He says that's too much food."

"Tell him I'm having a family crisis. Too much food might not be nearly enough."

"Damn, girl, you're a nurse, you know you shouldn't eat like that."

"Tell him to spare me the lecture."

"He hung up, that lecture came from me." Inez tucked the phone back in her purse. "Ever since Bess came back, dealing with her illness and…all, you haven't taken care of yourself, Charma. You don't get enough sleep, you don't get any exercise and you eat like crap."

"I've always been a light sleeper." I gripped the steering wheel until the leather padding burned against my palms. "I get as much exercise as I ever did, maybe more since Guy has started staying over nights."

"And eating?"

"I eat. Holy cow, Inez, anyone who looks at my hips can tell I don't have any problem poking food down."

"*Poking food down?* You think that's healthy? Don't answer." She held her hand up. "I'll tell you it's not. Any more than it's healthy the way you suppress your emotions."

"Suppress my emotions? *Suppress?* I don't know what surprises me more, that you used that word or applied it to me! Shitfire, girl, the only suppressed thing about me is…is…I can't even name one."

"A person can fly off half cocked and full-blown smart-assed at every little thing and still not be dealing with their issues."

"Half cocked and full-blown smart-assed. I like it. Mind if I have it put on a T-shirt?"

"Charma, I am just saying that since Bess came back and dredged up all the crap from your past, how your father died saving you and the way your mother died denying you and then her dying…" As she tried to describe my life, her hands flapped and fluttered like the wings of a terrified bird. Finally she shut her eyes and pressed her fingertips against her temples. "These few last months all I have seen you swallow is grief and cholesterol."

"Oh, I've swallowed a few other things, trust me."

I *meant* my pride. *Honest.*

Inez didn't take it that way, either.

Not that I cared.

We were almost there and I had Abby to think of, after all. And I couldn't forget Minnie.

I passed by the line of trees, the last one scarred by a shotgun blast in the dead of night.

Or Mama. I couldn't forget my mama.

The huge old house I could not legally call my home loomed over us.

And I couldn't forget Bess.

"Inez, you are coming in with me, right?"

"Nope." She nodded toward her car waiting in the drive.

"But—"

"You don't need me here. This is family."

"But—"

"Save your but, Charma, and I mean that in more ways than one." She gave me a hug and patted my back. "And remember that vow, or Bess may come back to haunt you yet."

❧ CHAPTER TWO

"I know why you came here, Abby. I know what you want. But there are a few things you have to know before you decide to unpack your bags." Ten minutes later, I strolled across the front porch of the house imagining myself commanding center stage. I had walked into a situation where my choices were clear and final. Yet I had decided that maybe, if I hedged and skirted, watched what I said and saw to it that I didn't hear too much, just maybe I could…not totally screw everything up. "This is a place brimming over with new beginnings and hopeful endings. People have been coming here for those for nearly half a century."

I shifted my eyes to make sure I had everyone's attention.

Shug tucked one of her legs up under her small bottom and leaned on her hand to listen. Her fingers pushed the sun-darkened skin of her face into a thousand soft pleats over her cheek and under her eye. With her short white hair, black almond eyes and catlike smile, she looked like an advertisement for the effects of the gracious plenty of the American South on the transplanted Japanese soul. Peace. Contentment. And just enough inappropriate mischief to keep people on their toes.

Meanwhile, freshly blond-root-jobbed and bouffanted Fawnie

puffed on a cigarette and blew the smoke out of the side of her mouth. She learned to do this back in the days when people would smoke and carry on conversations at the same time—though she wouldn't have done that in public, being a woman of good taste and possessing an all-consuming ambition to appear superior to…well, everyone.

She was dressed for company, though she would deny it by proclaiming, "This old outfit? Why, I was just thinking I should give it to the Salvation Army to use as rags to polish their little brass bells."

Women who made too big a deal over everything. And I had earned my place among them.

"My daddy used to always say to me: 'Charma, your life began as music.'"

Abby narrowed her eyes and gathered her brunette hair into one hand alongside her neck. "And your point is?"

My eyes went even narrower than hers, just slits, really. I guess my voice got just that tight, too. "New beginnings and happy endings are not always delivered directly to the point, Abby, honey. In this house sometimes you will be led down a path and left to your own conclusions."

Not often, but it *did* happen. And I'd be damned if I'd let some child bully me out of this pretty winding passage I had already rehearsed in my head on the way here.

Inhale, release, begin again. "'Charma Deane,' he'd say, 'your life began as music. Some sappy song about beguiling charms I sang to Mama the night you were conceived'."

"Your parents told you about the night you were *conceived?*" Abby hit the last word really hard, less in shock than in panic, it seemed.

"Under the spell of the music, the pale summer moon and my blue-eyed daddy, my mother's life was forever altered." I held my composure, made a note of her reaction and kept on. "They married not long after that, and when I came along they named me Charma Deane. Charma for a charmed life and Deane for my mother's mother."

Abby, sitting on the steps in the shade, looped her arms over her knees. "But I still don't see…"

"My childhood here *was* charmed and lyrical, growing up the only child of Dinah McCoy—"

"Honey, the woman could'a been a model." Fawnie's cigarette left a trail of smoke from where she held it up at her side to just inches away from her lips. Her hand froze there, trembled. Or perhaps that was a trick of the white-gray ashes flickering, seeming just about to fall into her lap but instead clinging to the tip of her suspended cigarette.

"And John Levy 'Jolly' George," I pressed on.

"What a handsome man." Fawnie took a draw at last and held the smoke for what seemed a full minute.

"Not as handsome as my Kelvin," Shug took advantage of the break to add.

"*My* Kelvin." The claim of ownership from Fawnie came out tinged with smoke and raw-throated anger.

"We are not going into *that* now." I shook my head.

Everyone here knew the story, of course. Kelvin George had married Fawnette Faubus when she was just fourteen years old. Twenty years later he had married a barely eighteen and decidedly pregnant Sugi Ichiuchi while stationed in Japan. He may have neglected to get a legal divorce between the two weddings, but the blessed event of the arrival of my cousin Minami—Abby's mom, Minnie—made all that moot, and we had all been what Mama liked to call "one big by-gawd happy family" ever since.

And my aunts were not going to blow that today.

I glared at the pair.

Fawnie pouted, folding her age-spotted hands so that her wedding ring clattered against her other jewelry.

Shug smiled and gazed at Abby adoringly. Diamonds may be a girl's best friend, but granddaughters are the best revenge.

I sighed. "I saved for my parents the kind of admiration most young girls had for movie stars who died too young, characters in tragic novels and Black Beauty. They were that dramatic, that dazzling." And that distant.

"Look, I don't get all this. I just came here for—"

I held out my hand to help the girl up from the steps. "We know what you came for, Abby."

Shug nodded. "Peanut butter."

"And sanctuary." A stream of smoke whooshed over Fawnie's champagne-mocha-frost lipstick.

Abby opened her mouth, closed it, looked at her grandmother, then her...whatever the hell Fawnie was to her, then at me. Her shoulders rose and fell and she nodded, her gaze dipping downward. "Yeah. That's about it. Peanut butter and sanctuary."

"And this is our way of telling you—" I waited until she stood steady on her feet "—you've come to the right place for both."

"We've been expecting you, actually. The other ones—Charma's boys, even Ruth and Chuck's grandchildren, you know them?" Fawnie waved her hand in the general direction of Texas where her sister-in-law, my aunt Ruth, had raised Bess and her two brothers, and where the brothers had in turn raised their own children. "They've all had their time here. They've laid down their roots. We've been waiting for you to do the same."

"Just our way of saying welcome," I said.

Her eyes glimmered with doubt. "By telling me your life began as music?"

"By telling you that this is not just a house, it's our family's heritage, and just the way my father promised me a charmed life, we want you to have one, too." I studied her face a moment, struggling to catch a glimpse of her mother in her features. Her skin was too pale, her eyes too round, her mouth too full, but she had freckles.

"If this is where you tell me we are some kind of magical clan of witchy women who have the power to turn men into toads..." She paused, scowled, cocked her head, then wet her lips before going on. "Okay, *that* I could get into. But if this is a bunch of dancing-naked, giving-each-other-sisterwomen-names-because-we-are-the-keepers-of-the-secrets-of-the-heart crap, I think I'll be moving on."

Freckles and attitude. She wasn't ours, *yet*, but she was one of us.

"Stay, Abby. I promise if either one of these wild women start dancing naked, I'll personally throw a sheet over..." My aunts jerked their heads up. Neither was the dancing-naked earth-mother type, but clearly they'd be damned if they'd let me promise anyone they never would up and decide to transform themselves into one. "I'll throw a sheet over the window so you won't have to see it."

Fawnie dipped her head in gracious acceptance of the deal we had just struck, then raised her chin and said to Abby, "And while you are with us, we will do our best to extend to you all the southern comforts."

"The southern...*comforts?*"

"Oh, you know, the standards. Faith, family..." I wanted to say "home," but I couldn't offer her that, so I settled for a looser definition. "A place where they have to take you in because you belong to them."

"Good food and plenty of it," Fawnie offered.

"Independence!" Shug placed her hand over her heart.

"Being somebody," Fawnie stubbed out her cigarette, and before the butt grew cold in the crystal ashtray, reached for the pack and withdrew another.

"The right to own your own gun." Hand still on her chest, Shug went downright misty-eyed.

Fawnie tapped the end of the cigarette against the back of her hand. "Well, aren't you the sentimental little yellow-skinned redneck?"

"Watch out what you say." Shug narrowed her eyes. "I know where Dinah hid her shotgun. I get you one night, old woman."

"Yeah, you try it." Fawnie leaned in to light up, letting the flame on her silver lighter flare a bit longer than necessary. "One squeeze of the trigger and the kickback would blow your butt off the balcony."

"Yeah? Cool." Shug laughed. Her nose crinkled. "I be like the Flying Nun."

"The Frying Nun?" The flame flickered, then rose. Her thumb still crooked down over the lever, Fawnie shook the lighter trying to extinguish the light. "You've been in this country forty-seven years—when are you going to learn the language?"

I lunged to try to take the jammed lighter from her shaking hand.

"I been in this country forty-seven years. So what?" Shug beat me to the lighter. "You been smoking over a hundred and forty-seven years, you old bat, and you still almost set yourself on fire once a day."

Shug slipped the engraved silver object out of the other woman's grasp, shut it off and slammed it down on the table.

Fawnie grumbled under her breath, her dignity left intact by Shug's complete lack of sympathy.

Shug lowered herself back into her chair and exhaled. "I wouldn't care except you going to get on that damned scooter of yours and ride through the house trying to put yourself out and catch the damn curtains on fire, too."

More grumbling from Fawnie.

Shug reached out, her hand trembling, then patted the age-gnarled knuckles of her oldest friend in the world. Looking away, she said softly, "And I love them damned curtains."

I looked at Abby. "The southern comforts," I murmured.

"And while you count them, don't forget the whole bunch of real fine hootch." Shug patted Fawnie's thigh and from beneath the fine accordion-pleated skirt came a distinctly metallic clank.

Abby blinked.

"Your great-grandfather's personal silver hip flask," I whispered.

"It's a health precaution for me, of course." Fawnie took great pains arranging her clothes.

"Yeah, old woman has booze duct-taped to her wooden leg. You know God pushed her down the stairs a couple years ago and they cut off her leg, right?"

Fawnie had taken a tumble down the stairs a few years back and decided it was a personal call from the Almighty. She saw it as her sacred duty thereafter to single-handedly restore the George family name to a place of honor in Orla society. She had planned to do it by dying and having a magnificent funeral, but so far, she had failed in that endeavor.

"That's where she keep her stash now." Shug jabbed her finger at the flask, then pantomimed tossing back a shot. "First sign of the sniffles and up goes her skirt and the doctor is in."

"That's just too tacky for me to even respond to," Fawnie huffed. "Abby, precious, pardon me for saying so, but your grandmother is just plain nuts. In fact, if you ever plan on having children yourself, consider adopting, because class that low has got to have wormed its way down into the DNA."

"If I…I never said…I'm way too young to have a…" The young girl rubbed her forehead with one hand and put her other hand to her stomach. "I'm sorry I'm really hungry and not thinking right. Could I get that peanut butter and maybe some crackers or a soda or something?"

"Come with me." I had my arm around the child so fast I think I may have left marks, the way Bess used to do when she'd twist our wrists and leave what we called "Indian burns."

We slipped inside, leaving the old women on the porch to bicker and giggle.

The cavernous foyer was cool and dim. I'd gotten used to keeping it that way in the last days of Bess's life when the light had hurt her eyes and none of the rest of us wanted to look at anything but her bad enough to illuminate a whole room.

In the kitchen, I reached up on top of the refrigerator, pulled down a generic-brand coffee can and peeled back the plastic lid. I offered what was inside to Abby.

She slid the jar of locally made gourmet peanut butter from inside its hiding place. "Thanks."

"You're welcome."

She smiled. Sort of. But she didn't meet my eyes.

I took a step or two to retrieve the crackers from the cabinet, then turned and found her practically standing in my still-warm footprints. Or maybe it just felt that way.

Eight bedrooms, three baths, formal dining room, breakfast room, north and south parlors, eat-in kitchen and two balconies big enough for a dozen people to sleep on—the Aunt Farm was too damned big for any *one* family, as Inez liked to point out. Despite her dreams of using the extra space as a women's clinic or shelter or child care center or all three, the Georges of Orla had always found the place a bit of a tight fit. Maybe that was because our personalities tended to extend beyond the normally accepted boundaries of personal space, so that wherever there were two or more of us together, we were always sort of bumping up against one another, metaphysically speaking.

Late afternoon sunlight poured in through the starched white curtains. It glinted off the old chrome dinette set where generations of George women had shared our dreams and laughter, cigarettes and every kind of grief imaginable. Here Minnie and Bess and I had plotted everything from how to spend our allowances as children to the details of Bess's funeral.

Without getting too sister-mystic, this was a sacred place.

Abby shuffled her feet on the faded linoleum and nibbled a cracker that she had dipped in the peanut butter. "What's the deal about this peanut butter, anyway? Why do you hide it from Grandma and Fawnie?"

"Because it's expensive."

She cocked her head, stared straight at me and sighed, just the way her mother would have had Minnie caught me in a barefaced flimsy lie.

I licked my lips. "And I'll be damned if I will see it spread on sardines by your grandmother just because she knows it sets Fawnie off when she eats like that. Or worse, used to hold some poor unsuspecting Jehovah's Witness hostage while they put on the full Shug-and-Fawnie-pay-attention-to-me extravaganza."

Abby munched and scowled.

"They like to give the Jehovah's witnesses peanut butter because it makes it hard for them to share their views or make excuses to leave," I said.

"And?"

"And?"

"And I know we haven't spent a lot of time together, Charma, but you have to know my mom has made sure I know you. And the Charma my mother told me about wouldn't have had a problem with sardines or serving door-to-door religion salesmen to the old ladies for entertainment. What's the real deal with this stuff?"

"It was the only real food Bess could keep down toward the end," I finally confessed. At last I looked at the jar, which I hadn't had out since we'd gone to feeding Bess primarily through a tube. I took in the aroma, the unique shape of the container, the hand-written price tag smudged by who-knows-whose fingerprints. "I used to have to drive ninety miles round trip to a specialty store to buy it for her. This is her…this is the last jar."

"I won't eat it all," Abby assured me in hushed reverence.

I could only nod.

She put her hand on my shoulder. "Thanks for coming home so quick, Charma."

"I was on a spiritual quest, you know. But…" But I didn't matter here. "I had to come. You asked," I said simply, then opened my arms. "You're Minnie's little girl and you needed me."

Abby fit herself into my embrace so easy you'd have thought her my own daughter.

Of course, no daughter of mine would have been so sweet. Or so skinny. "Hmmm. Some diet you're on there, you old fat thing."

She pulled away, cleared her throat and wiped a cracker crumb from the corner of her mouth. "I'm sorry my showing up like this called you away from that spiritual quest and—" she smiled "—and two-drink minimum that you had gone after."

"Damn. You mother really has told you too much about me. You'll have to clue me in while you're here."

"Okay." She nodded. "Can I have something to drink?"

"Whatever is in the fridge, but don't—" I cut myself off before I started handing out advice. Advice implied knowing what was best for another person, and that implied knowing too much to feign innocent-bystander status later. "Don't drink the juice in the fancy decanter. That's Fawnie's special elixir. Nasty stuff."

I stepped away and began to peel out of my "spiritual-quest-and-bar-hopping outfit." It's a big old house, I'm a woman standing on the precipice of perimenopause and air-conditioning can only do so much. So since moving back in, I've kept a white cotton…thing—there has been some debate among family members if it's a nightgown or a flimsy sundress—on a hook by the kitchen door. I slipped into it, my eyes always fixed on Abby and her attempt to both consume and conserve the precious stuff in the jar.

"You look tired," I said.

"Dead on my feet." She'd hardly gotten the words out when her eyes grew wide. "I'm sorry, I didn't mean *dead*. Bad choice. I didn't mean to make light of…"

I held my hand up. "We dance around the truth a hell of a lot in this house, but we do not walk on eggshells."

She dropped her hand and exhaled.

I studied the dark circles beneath her sorrowful eyes. "Why don't you go up and take a nap in your mother's old room?"

Her gaze dipped. She set the crackers and peanut butter on the counter and brushed her hands together, never meeting my eyes. "I'd rather not, if you don't mind. Being there with all the reminders of my mom and her childhood dreams and expectations…you know."

"I do." I did know. I had decreed the door to my own mother's room would stay shut until I felt ready to go in there myself. A mother's domain, the closet where she hung her clothes, the drawers where she neatly folded away her private things, the mirror where she met her own reflection—those are places of great power for a daughter. "Okay, then take my room."

"But the house has so many bedrooms, surely…"

"Fawnie and your grandmother each have rooms." Two fingers went up. "The master is…*was*…my mother's room, and we haven't cleared it out since…"

"So that's three rooms taken." She held up four fingers on one hand. "And my mom's and yours. Doesn't that leave—" She wiggled the three fingers on her other hand.

I shook my head. "Sterling took the furniture out of those rooms."

"What? Why?"

She sounded edgy, almost panicked.

I identified with the feeling but had no insight to offer into the man's reasoning.

"Just showed up one day in work clothes, and by nightfall all the big things were moved into the attic or garage."

"He didn't throw anything out the window? Mom said it's a big thing to throw things out the windows around here."

"One lousy toilet thirty years ago." I held up my index finger, then used it to point toward the door that led into the hallway. "Sterling took the downstairs rooms. What's the fun of throwing stuff out the downstairs window?"

"Just like that, then? Attic, garage. No windows." She looked disappointed.

"Just like that. We still have small things, boxes and the closets and all to empty, but the big things are all gone." Sometimes in the long mental desert of my sleepless nights I wondered what he might cast out next. My nana Abbra's antique armoire? The ornate silver serving pieces and candelabras that glinted in the virtually unused formal dining room? My aunts? *Me?*

"I guess that's his right," she said, "with Bess leaving him the house. He can do whatever he wants, then, and you can't do anything about it, right?"

"That's what they say."

We both nodded a couple times too many, like a pair of tongue-tied bobble-head dolls. Then it got real quiet.

"If I take your room, where will you sleep?" Abby finally asked.

"Don't worry about me. I'll make a bed on the couch in Grandpa George's parlor."

Sometimes we called it the main parlor or the front parlor, even though the other parlor was just across the hallway from it, just as big. Guy called that one the fancy parlor, which was polite-speak for a girly geegaw cluttered white-on-white with gold-trimmed-everything nightmare. While Nana Abbra had lived here, both rooms had been equally well used. Now the fancy parlor sat empty, untouched by time or good taste. Everyone gravitated toward the darker, more cozy of the pair of rooms.

"Grandpa George's parlor?" Abby frowned and cocked her head. "Isn't that where Bess died?"

It was. But that fact didn't bother me. "Don't go all spooky on me, girl. If we stopped using places around here where someone had died, we'd be limited to this kitchen, the hallway and a couple of vacant bedrooms."

Bess had just been the last in a long line of Georges to meet his or her Maker on family turf. My own mama had died on the back porch. By all official accounts Daddy had met his end in the pond—though I had just recently learned that he probably drew his last breath in one of the downstairs bedrooms with my mother at his side, or perhaps over his head, holding a pillow. I'll never know that for sure until I have made an eternal change of address myself, I guess. Just like I'll never know for sure where my grandfather died. I do know it was someplace that Nana Abbra steadfastly refused to tell us about—we figured that meant the bathroom on the pot or in bed on Nana.

"Don't worry. The only things that haunt this place are the actions of the living, not the spirits of the dead." I shook my head just imaging it all. "If you can cope with that, then welcome home, Abby."

"Thanks." She set the peanut butter down then, wiped her hands on her jeans, started to turn away then stopped. "Don't you...don't you want to know why I'm here?"

"Not particularly."

She blinked at me, clearly expecting a different answer. "Not the least bit curious?"

"I didn't say that." Obviously I had my suspicions about what brought the girl here. She showed up at the Aunt Farm for the same reason women had been arriving on our doorstep for as long as I could remember. Something was missing in her life.

My whole life I had seen them, these women with their missing pieces.

Missing teeth (usually after a beating).

Missing self-esteem (beatings, yes, but also from verbal shred-dings, humiliations, a total absence of basic human kindness).

Even missing husbands (mostly ran-off kinds of husbands, but once or twice of the missing-their-heads or heartbeat variety).

All kinds ended up at the large home where Mama, Fawnie and Shug held court, and held their own with a couple of double-barreled shotguns.

I figured Abby was probably missing something, too. Like her period.

Normally I'd put forth that suspicion with all the conviction of a traveling tent revivalist hollering about the cornerstones of the gospels. But what did I stand to gain by throwing out a blind guess as fact then watching for the fallout to see if I'd hit the mark? Besides, she's made a public denial already—not that I bought it, but why pull out the rug from under the girl's pride so soon? "I'm already going against my own instincts, letting you stay here without calling your mother."

"I know."

"*That* I can skate by on because I can justify that it's your grandmother's place to make that call."

She nodded.

"But if I know what really brought you here—"

"You'd have to lie to my mother."

"Worse."

"Worse?"

"I'd have to keep a secret from her." I pressed my fist to my breastbone and tried to take a deep breath.

Abby opened her mouth, but the sharp nasal tone and blunted consonants of her grandmother's accent coming from the front hallway cut through the air instead.

"Charmika, your lover man is here!"

"Lover," Fawnie corrected, overenunciating with the same iron-fisted grace she applied to…well, everything. "Luh. Luh. Lover. Why can't you just say it right? Not that it's right you should call him that, but if that's what you want to call him…it's simple. Say it with me—luh…luh—"

"You want me to call Guy Chapman what he is? No problem."

The hinges of the front door squawked.

Shug hollered, "Hey, Charma! That man with the great butt who you sneak into your room after we go to bed at night, the one me and Fawnie thinks you should marry and we won't mind having around the house, sometime maybe with his shirt off, is here."

Abby gave me a surprised look.

I smiled. "Hey, you're not the only one in this house seeking a few southern comforts, sweetie."

I gave the hem of my gown a rustle and winked.

She opened her mouth to say something, and I put my finger to my lips.

"I don't want to know," I whispered. "In less than a year I lost my mother, Bess and I am on the verge of losing my home. I refuse to lose your mother, too."

I turned and started down the hallway.

I was kidding myself, of course, by taking Abby in without so much as calling her mother. I had lost Minnie already. I had chosen sides, and no amount of comfort would ever ease the ache in my heart.

❧ CHAPTER THREE

"C'mon, Shug, let's go set the table." Fawnie wedged her cane between Shug's knee and Guy's shin. I had no doubt she'd use every last bit of leverage she could muster to pry her counterpart away from the man standing on the porch if the need arose. Push came to shove—and that was a literal possibility, not merely a quaint saying. Fawnie could wield that cane like a kung fu master with his weapon and not so much as muss her makeup or put a dent in her hairdo in the fray.

"Give us a minute to get the plates down and then bring the chicken and yourself right along, okay, sweetie?" Shug reluctantly released her hold on Guy's arm.

"Bring the chicken and yourself right along," Fawnie parroted.

"Bring *your*self right along. Big-haired bimbo, you just…" Shug sniped at Fawnie in what we had long ago dubbed "yapanese," a mix of her native language and Southern hyperbole as they hurried off toward the back of the house.

Fawnie cut a wide swath swinging her cane, plunking it down just inches from the spot where Shug was about to place her next footfall.

"You just jealous because I'm his favorite." Shug batted the bedeviling cane aside.

"That's not jealousy." The rubber tip of the cane thumped against the floor. "It's discomfiture over how big a fool you make of yourself over anything in fly-front trousers and sporting facial hair."

"Yeah, right. If I go after anything with facial hair, *you* wouldn't be safe in your bed at night, old woman," Shug warned, then cackled and slapped the other Mrs. Kelvin George on the back. "Get it? I make a joke about—"

"I get it and I wouldn't be so quick to laugh if I were you, Miss Hasn't-seen-a-pair-of-jaw-tweezers-since-God-wore-kneepants." Any further insults were lost behind the closing of the swinging kitchen door.

And then Guy and I were alone. So alone I could hear my own heartbeat. Or was that his? I wanted to lay my hand on his chest to find out for certain. Instead I took a bag of side orders from under his arm and kissed his cheek. Barely kissed his cheek.

"They like you," I told him.

His dark eyes sparked with pride even as he brushed aside the compliment. "They'd like any man who showed up here regular to bring them food and attention."

"You make them sound so cheap and shallow." I did the hair-flip thing as best as my frazzled not-red, not-brown hair would cooperate. "How did you ever see beneath their cunning and polished veneer of sophistication like that?"

"Ah, don't be hard on the old girls, they're lonely. People do all kinds of things to stave that off, you know."

I did know. Half orphaned young. Fully orphaned not so long ago. One-time jilted bride. Divorced. Mother of boys who thought they were men and had the gall to act like it most of the time, moving out on their own and all. Caregiver to my cousin up to her very last breath. I'd known lonely.

I also understood what lengths a person might go to in order to hold off the loneliness, if only for a while. I'd been in enough church-basement socials and bedrooms of men who didn't mean a damned thing to me to attest to that. But I wasn't the one doing the talking now, and it made me wonder.

"Do you have a confession you'd like to make, Mr. Chapman?"

He laughed, but not after a slightly awkward hesitation. "I like your aunts, too. Besides, not everyone can be as discerning as you, Charma Deane."

"Discerning? Dis*cerning?* That's code for…?"

"Cautious."

"Cautious?" I practically choked on the word. "Is this pick-on-Charma day? Because earlier Inez accused me of suppressing my emotions."

"Neither one is exactly an insult, you know."

"They are to me. They are to a George. We just don't do that kind of thing. I mean, really, cautious? *Me?*"

Me, who charges to the rescue of first cousins once removed in need? Who threw herself naked into the fearsome pond? Who…

He studied me. Hard-gazed, jaw set, his body still and his breathing slow. When he opened his mouth, he did not speak up right away, but instead seemed to struggle to find the words. Finally, his shoulders eased down and his cheek twitched. "I was back in town a whole year before you came to my door to speak to me."

"That?" I leaned against the door frame, all flirty-like and coy, part Patty Duke, part Marilyn Monroe and just a little bit Aileen Wuornos—you know, that woman who killed all those men and left their bodies in ditches by the highways? "That wasn't caution. That was a rare case of me using common sense."

"Okay, point taken." This time the laugh came easy. "But what about now?"

"What about now?"

"I've been standing on your front porch for five minutes holding dinner and you haven't invited me in. That seems pretty damned cautious to me."

"No, that's…" Me trying to keep the world beyond these doors and the world inside them from blending too much, too easily.

Nothing inside these doors was certain anymore.

My whole life the one thing I had known I could count on was that in my home I was safe, and loved, and…home. Mama dying here without calling me to her side and Bess dying and leaving the house to a man she had known only a few months—a man I had been dating before her—had taken all that away from me. And I had topped it all off today with the small but cutting betrayal of taking Abby in. I could no longer depend on anything inside this place anymore.

It scared me.

Once Guy stepped over that threshold, what then?

"That's discerning," I said, a bit breathless but brave none the less.

He smiled, just a little, hung his head and shook it.

He looked adorable. And dependable. And achingly sexy. I don't know when dependable became sexy to me but it had, and this man embodied it right down to the crease in his jeans and the extra bag of biscuits and gravy in his hand. And yet I hesitated.

No big secret as to why I would do that.

I swear sometimes when I look at Guy Chapman I don't know how to draw my next breath.

It hurts that much.

Not because I am so consumed with love or because his face and body fire up the flames of uncontrollable lust in my loins. The guy does it for me, don't get me wrong. But in those brief, fleeting moments when we first lay eyes on each other, when I still have the tiniest hope of maintaining control of myself around him, of setting the pace of what will and won't go between us, it is not love or lust that tightens the emotional grip on me.

I can't help it. When I see him, like now, standing in the doorway, his hair all tousled, his head lowered and his smile all crooked and self-effacing? I want to shove him backward with every ounce of strength I have and demand, "Why the hell did you screw up my life the way you did?"

I loved this man when I was nineteen years old. Surrendered myself to him body and soul as readily and as often as possible without actually piling all my belongings into the back seat of his oxidized Bonneville and sending out change of address cards. To whom it may concern: *Charma Deane George now lives in Guy Chapman's pants.*

He was *it* for me. The end all and be all. And even though he danced all over my then delicate psyche, busted up my heart and literally changed the course of my life in a single poorly thought-out night, I never stopped loving him.

No, not even when he left me standing at the altar and ran off on *our* honeymoon with my cousin Bess. Which is the way I tell the story even though that's not exactly how it happened. Hey, I'm sure when he or Bess tells it…told it…they had their own special way of diverting any personal responsibility for all the pain and misunderstanding that young people in love can inflict on each other.

And then there is this happy ending. Happy new beginning?

He's in my life again. And my bed. And my heart, though I haven't confessed that to him.

But…all those years.

All the things that might have been.

I look at him and see the good life that never was, the children we did not have. Though come to think of it, I have to assume now he didn't want children, since he has none. As for me, I wouldn't trade the sons I *did* have with Boyd Parker. Well, never the younger one and most of the time not the firstborn. But still, we did miss a lot. Home and laughter and building something lasting. Christmases and snowy evenings and summer vacations and being young and full of possibilities and staying that way until we grew old together.

Regret is just an awful emotion. Claustrophobic and stifling. Caustic as the bile it brings to the back of the throat, harsh and bitter. And so damned hard to turn loose of.

I should grow up and get over it. And I will. I *have*. Mostly. But for one split second every time I see him, the questions ring through my mind.

Why didn't you love me enough then? How do I know you won't stop loving me even for a night—which will be long enough to finally do me in forever?

"Well?" He raised the large bag in each hand.

"Well." I sighed, then stood aside to bid him to enter the house.

Lord, he smelled good. Like fried chicken and Old Spice, all coziness and conflict. I'd have stood right there in the hallway and licked him all over but my aunts might take exception to that kind of behavior, especially if it meant their dinner would go cold.

Breathing shallowly and fighting my urges, I jerked my head toward the kitchen and led the way, glancing over my shoulder long enough to ask, "Why the hell didn't you show up for our wedding all those years ago?"

"I'm here now, aren't I?"

"As they say on *Family Feud*—not surprisingly Fawnie and Shug's favorite game show, by the way—good answer." I fixed my gaze forward and applauded his diplomacy by patting my fingers against the white-and-red bag clutched in my hand. "Good answer."

And it *was* a good answer, because if he had thrown the real reason in my face why he hadn't met me at the altar of the Rock Creek Baptist Church—that I had staged a massive adolescent theatrical production about not being ready to be tied to one man on his doorstep the night before the pending nuptials and actually jilted *him* even though I tried to take it back the next day— I'd have slapped him so hard he'd have seen Jesus. And I am pretty sure Jesus would have slapped him, too.

But he kept low key and light, so I did the same. "Did anyone ever tell you that you are one sexy, fine mortician?"

"Sexy? Maybe. Fine mortician? Hardly." He rattled the bags in his hands. "He-man provider of chicken and biscuits? Many, *many* times."

I paused three feet away from the swinging kitchen door to yank one of the bags from his hand. "Don't cheapen this meal with the reminder of all the women you have fed before me."

"*After* you," he corrected even as he leaned in to steal a quick kiss. His gaze never left my eyes as he pulled away just enough to speak but stayed so close I could feel the movement of his lips as he whispered, "As far as I'm concerned, *all* women *always* come *after* you, Charma Deane."

"I guess that's supposed to sound romantic or something, right?" I turned quickly to hide my triumphant delighted grin.

"Or *something,*" he said, his mouth moving against the back of my hair and his now-free hand reaching around the front to pull me back against him.

I swept around again, telling myself that in my little white sheath of a gown I embodied the likeness of every sultry southern siren who ever padded barefoot through a family mansion leading a man to—

Wham.

"My gizzards!" The kitchen door banged open and Shug appeared in the doorway, with not just her arms outstretched but her hands, too, and her wriggling fingers extended like an excited child's. "I thought you'd never get back here with those gizzards."

"And hearts." Guy put his hand on my shoulder and leaned in to give my aunt a wink. "I know how you do love those deep-fried innards, Miz Shug, ma'am."

"Oh, Grandma! Gross." Abby covered her mouth, horror in her eyes. "I cannot stay in here and watch y'all eat that."

Without a backward glance the girl headed for the side door that led to the back hallway and was gone.

"Don't mind her. She's become a crazy Vulcan." Fawnie snubbed her cigarette out in the brown plastic ashtray that had sat in the center of the yellow dinette set for as long as I could remember.

"Vegan," Shug corrected.

"What?" Fawnie pulled out a cigarette and laid it on top of the pack, ready to light up as soon as she finished her meal.

"Vulcan from *Star Trek*." Shug held up her hand—the one not in a death grip on the small container of gizzards and hearts—and spread her fingers in the "live long and prosper" sign, which I felt sure was not the only sign she would have liked to have given Fawnie. "You know, Mr. Spock. Pointy ears? She didn't decide to become a spaceman, she just don't eat meat."

"Either way, it's just crazy thinking. Especially if it means giving up fried chicken and gravy." Fawnie winced. "What kind of meaning does life hold without gravy for gum's sake?"

"Amen to that," Guy murmured, reaching into the bag to work free the large red-and-white bucket of chicken. He plunked it down on the table and flipped off the top.

Steam rose from the heap of legs and wings and cumbersome odd pieces that hardly seemed a part of any chicken I had ever seen.

Guy helped himself to a crispy piece without even bothering to join my aunts sitting at the table.

Just seeing the pleasure he took in that greasy, well-padded thigh did my heart good. And it didn't stunt my libido any, either. A man who eats wholly loves wholly. I truly believe that.

I smiled at Guy and gave a jerk of my head that I hoped said, "Grab some of that gravy and let's head upstairs for our own picnic."

He picked a piece of chicken from the pile and held it out to me. "Some fortification for the road?"

"Road?" I took the golden brown leg, then glanced upward in the general direction of my bedroom. "As in why did the chicken cross the?"

"As in why don't you and I blow this joint?"

"Great minds—"

A shuffling of footsteps, of something tossed to the floor, the complaint of bedsprings and suddenly I recalled I'd given my room away to Abby.

"Should be able to come up with some way for us to be alone," I concluded, and started to put the chicken leg back in the bucket.

"What?" Guy shoved a napkin into the front pocket of his jeans, and the way he was gathering together food, I half expected him to stuff a hot wing in there, too, or maybe even some mashed potatoes and gravy.

"Great minds should find a way for us to…"

R-r-ring.

The phone on the wall not six inches from Guy's shoulder cut me off.

Minnie! I glanced at the clock, tried to do the math to calculate what time it was in Tokyo, then gave up. It didn't matter what time it was—as soon as my cousin found out that Abby wasn't in Japan or at the family home in Tennessee, this was the number she would dial.

Another thud and bang from overhead, a scurry of footsteps, retching, then the flush of the toilet.

I shut my eyes, tight. Regret is an ugly emotion. If I had been more discerning, more cautious toward her staying here, I would have regretted it. But I jumped in where I didn't belong fully knowing the consequences.

R-r-ring.

That didn't mean I was ready to face those consequences.

"If one of you ain't going to get that, get out my way so I can." Shug nudged Guy aside.

Before she could say another word, I held out my hand and opened my mouth.

"If that's for me, I am not here." Guy spoke before I could.

I blinked at him.

"I don't want any dead bodies coming between us tonight," he said in a way that did nothing at all to convince me he meant that.

Shug lifted the receiver.

"I'm not here, either," I whispered before she could get the piece to her ear.

"Hey, none of that. I'm a good Christian woman, you know."

"And she can't lie for shit," Fawnie added.

"That, too," Shug concurred. "So you want me to say you not here…"

"We're gone." I grabbed Guy by the arm and headed down the hall.

The kitchen door swung shut behind us just as Shug said, "Hello?"

We hit the front door and spilled out onto the porch. Breathless, I smiled at the man and said, "Now all we need to figure out is where in Orla I can show up barefoot, in a nightgown, with a man and a paper napkin full of chicken and not raise gossip about me to a whole new level."

"Not to worry." Guy jangled his car keys and nodded toward the drive. "I have planned ahead for just this occasion."

❧ CHAPTER FOUR

"Now, this…this makes sense." I rolled my ankle to admire one of the sequined flip-flops Shug had left in the garden and I had grabbed on my way to Guy's car.

On the drive I had dug around in his gym bag and found a button front shirt to throw over my gown, tying it at the waist and rolling it up at the sleeves to make it look deliberately crumpled, casual and carefree. *Carefree*—now there was the word of the moment.

"This works." I pressed my hip to the fender of Guy's black sedan and checked out my reflection in the dark tinted window. You want to make a getaway in Orla, that hearse won't do. But a company car, when the company is a funeral home? Folks are happy to let that pass on by without too much speculation. Most people see it as respect, but I think it is fear repackaged as respect. And for some it's just common sense mixed with plain old practical superstition. Ask not for whom the mortician's sedan rolls, or, baby, it will be rolling for thee.

Anyway, I checked my hair in the tinted glass and at the same time managed to give the bed-and-breakfast we'd ended up at a once-over, as well. Prim white house, picket fence, American flag flapping gently from a post on the front porch. Cute. Quaint. Cozy. All the things you'd expect from a rural oasis—if you were the sort who thought it was cute to call your decorating style "country," only spelled with a *k* and a backward *y* at the end and you liked to put signs in your ward about being owned by your attack cat. And if you had never happened upon a real fine old historic home like the Aunt Farm.

Lord, I loved the Aunt Farm. Seeing a place like this only reminded me how much. I loved every creak in the floors and every view from the windows. I loved the richness of the woodwork, not just for the way it glowed in the low light from the antique chandeliers, but because I knew that three generations of the women in my family had hand rubbed and hard cursed that wood to make it gleam like that. I would much rather have sent my aunts and Abby out and stayed there with Guy than to end up here.

Of course, if I'd tried it, Sterling might have issued a no-sex-on-the-premises injunction and had the sheriff haul Guy away; then the woodwork wouldn't have been the only thing hand-rubbed around the place. So this definitely worked for me.

"Twenty-four whole hours without having to worry about misdirected deeds, or misdeeds in general." I whipped around to face the house and plastered on a smile. "No circles within circles, no tap dancing around the truth, no phone calls from Tokyo or road maps from the Almighty."

"Circles? Tokyo? The Almighty?" He slammed the car door.

"It makes sense in here." I tapped the side of my head. "But I'm not sure I could get it all out and do it justice."

"*That* I understand. I have something like that careening around inside me, too."

"Oh?" I stood stock still and blinked a couple times. This was supposed to communicate with him to spill his guts and/or his guilt and explain himself. He didn't.

Of course, that didn't keep me from supplying the answers for him.

He loved me. Truly. Deeply. Sacred-as-hell-forever-and-everly. And he wanted to say it but didn't know how. Though he had known how years ago. And I think he had thrown it out a time or two over the phone in parting or maybe even once in the throes of passion. So why suddenly wouldn't he be able to get those words out and do them justice?

The answer was simple: *He hated me.*

No. He didn't. That I much I knew.

He loved me but he wasn't "in love" with me. No, that's the kind of thing women say, not men.

Men say, "What's the rush?" That had to be it, he wanted to slow things down. I had loved him—and hated him—for twenty years, and he was standing there thinking that we should keep things light, be friends who now and again saw each other naked, and with their legs thrown over each other's shoulders, and see what happens. Of course, if he wanted to slow things down, why run off in such a hurry to a bed-and-breakfast and not even let me get dressed properly?

He worked his bent fingers back through his wavy hair, making the gray and silver more prominent in his wake.

The wind whipped at my gown and tossed my own once-vibrant hair across my cheek.

So much time had passed since we should have gone away together like this. So many opportunities. So many things undone and unsaid. I tried to swallow but couldn't.

I was a mess. He had a secret agenda. We could force all that into the open or we could leave it be and just…be.

He bent down to pick up my overnight bag.

I grabbed his adorable ass.

"Can't that wait until we get inside?" He glanced back at me, but I noticed he didn't move away.

"Damn, sweetstuff, for an old man you still look great from the back in a pair of faded jeans." I slid my hands up under his T-shirt and flattened both my palms against his hairy, taut—okay, tautish—belly.

He straightened and let out a soft, low moan.

"Thanks for bringing me here today." I laid my cheek against his back. "I needed to escape for a day or so, to just breathe and think. I know it's cowardly, running away just when Abby showed up and all, but I don't care, it makes me feel…free. Like coming up to the surface and finally taking that first big breath."

"Ain't nothing wrong with doing what you have to do to breathe, Charma, to grab a little freedom whenever and wherever you can," he murmured.

You should know. I pressed my lips shut to keep from blurting it out. With Bess or Minnie I wouldn't have bothered keeping my thoughts to myself. But with Guy, with *men*, you never knew. You could strike a chord letting the truth tumble out like that.

And there was always the very real chance the man didn't even know what he'd said or why it would matter to me. *Ain't nothing wrong with running off. Ain't nothing wrong with wanting to feel free, for reveling in it. Ain't nothing wrong with leaving loved ones and responsibilities behind no matter who it hurts, as long as you get what you need out of it.*

He turned and wrapped his arm around my shoulders, giving me this look that practically had steam coming off of it. Steam with just enough of boyish "tell me again I done good" to elevate his whole reason for asking me here to more than the chance to play naked Twister. But not by much.

Clueless.

The man was definitely clueless.

Clueless about how much I had loathed him and for so long. Clueless about how much I loved him now. Clueless that he had just booked himself a room at a secluded bed-and-breakfast with a crazy woman.

Poor, sweet, horny darling. I didn't know whether to jump him right there in the parking lot or slap his face and tell him to wise up.

I took my overnight case from his hand. "What the hell did you have in mind, arranging to be alone with me ninety miles from the safety of your sweet little mortuary, anyway?"

"Like you don't know."

"I don't."

"You spent all that time with Inez today and she never once dropped a hint? You never got the least bit suspicious?"

"I'm always suspicious." People destined to forever go around saving everyone have to be vigilant like that.

"You say that like it makes you proud." He touched my jaw, my chin, my cheek so lightly I could have swept his hand away with a wave. "You know not everyone considers living in a state of constant wariness a heroic trait."

"What'd you call it before? Discerning?"

"Cautious."

"Just your everyday, average act of self-preservation." I didn't have to tell this man that too many people I had loved, too many people that I would have died to protect, had, at one point or another, betrayed me. Cut me straight through, and each one in ways so unique and varied that I could not have found a way to defend myself against them. Each with a treachery not born of their weaknesses and desires but using my own weakness and desires against me. They had left scars that would never wholly heal.

"You needed to safeguard yourself against Inez?"

No. Inez was the exception, Inez and Minnie. The thought of my cousin and how I'd left her daughter back home and hurting shamed me. I shut my eyes, redirected my thoughts. "I should have known Inez was in on this, though."

"I needed time to make some phone calls and get some things from the house."

"I hope you didn't let Fawnie and Shug pack this thing, Guy." I nodded toward the overnight case. "Because if you did, I may come to bed in an orthopedic dominatrix get-up."

"Not to worry. I packed for you, went through your dresser and hand-selected what I thought you'd want for the night."

"You did? How sweet of you."

"It was my pleasure. You know how much I've always loved getting in your drawers, Charma."

"No crotchless woolen union suit with tassels on the tits?" I scrubbed my fingers over his chest.

He smiled slyly. "Nope."

"No elastic corset and fishnet knee highs?" I shook my gown by the hem, hinting at what surprises might lie beneath. "Or a flannel nightie with feather trim?"

He leaned down and kissed the bridge of my nose. "No nightie at all."

I laughed all low in my throat and husky. "What am I supposed to sleep in?"

"My arms."

"You wicked, wonderful man." I rose up on tiptoe and gave his cheek a little lick. "How fast we can we get inside and get at each other?"

"What happened to being cautious?"

"To everything there is a season."

"You did not just quote the Bible as an excuse to hop into bed and start fornicating, did you?"

"I was thinking of that song. I forgot it was from the Bible." I gave him a push for reminding me, drudging up the latent Baptist in me and putting a damper on the whole mood. "Anyway, since when have you not been a fan of getting out of sight and into fornication?"

"Since I decided that maybe there should be more to the act than just getting into and out of bed, then lather, rinse, repeat."

The wind pressed my gown against my thighs. I shivered. "This has to do with what's careening around inside of you, doesn't it? The thing you don't know how to say?"

"No, not really." He swept the back of his hand along my neck. "Maybe."

I stepped back.

He held his hand, the one that had stroked my sensitive skin, open and still in the air between us. "It may surprise you to know there's more than one thing going on in my head, Charma Deane."

"Well, you've known me long enough to know I only really care about the stuff that concerns *me*."

"I've known you long enough to know that you say shit like that because you think it's clever and makes you look cute and because you believe it throws people off the scent, keeps them from knowing the exact opposite is true." He dropped his hand to lace my fingers with his. "But in this case I don't want to talk about anything but the part that concerns you."

The way he said it made my stomach lurch as if I was on an elevator rocketing downward, then jerking up and down to find the proper place to stop. "Do I want to hear this now?"

I *didn't* want to hear it. I hoped he would intuitively understand my feelings. Not for the first time in our relationship, I knew he would disappoint me.

"I guess now's as good a time as any."

"If you'd rather…"

"No, if I don't do this now I might…I've practiced a hundred times today, what I would say, how you would react. I played it out in my mind over and over as we drove out here, as I packed the car and got gas, even when I talked to your sons on the phone this morning." He held open a small velvet box. "But I guess this isn't the kind of thing you can predict how it will go. You just have to do it and hope."

He dropped to one knee right there before me.

Tears welled up in my eyes. My throat closed. I staggered back a step and put my hand to my chest. "You…you called my sons?"

React to the ring, you idiot. That is one big honkin' diamond— from Guy Chapman!

It wasn't like I hadn't been proposed to before—one time by this very man. But going behind my back to talk about me with my boys?

"What did you say to them?"

He looked up at me and pushed the ring in my direction. "I asked them for their blessings."

I folded my arms. "And I hope they told you to go straight to hell."

He chuckled. "Actually, the younger one—"

"George," I said.

"Was all for it. John, on the other hand…"

"Hell?"

"More purgatory, I'd say."

"That sounds like him." I wet my lips and scanned the horizon. There were still some orange and yellow leaves clinging to the trees in the distance and fat gray clouds had begun to roll across the horizon. "He always has had a problem making a commitment."

"Like his mother?"

"Me?" I thumped my chest. "You have the nerve to accuse *me* of lacking commitment? *You?*"

"Me. Yes. The one here down on one knee holding a diamond." He rocked the velvet box in his hand, and the remaining sunlight made the stone glint.

I swallowed hard and thrust my chin up. "You called my…family maybe I should call yours before I give my answer."

"You want to call my brother? And ask him what?"

I opened my mouth, then poured out my heart. "Ask him why I am such a damned fool that I am not jumping at this chance to have everything in life I ever wanted."

"I see." He snapped the lid closed and got to his feet.

What are you waiting for? For God Almighty to kick you in the butt? The words Bess had spoken to me as a child trying to prod me into action, reverberated through my being.

I twisted my fingers together and stared at a bug struggling to get past a stone on the ground. "I guess the person I really wish I could talk to is—"

"Your mother?"

He *would* think of her. Not just because it felt natural for a woman to want her mother's counsel at a time like this but also because for the past eleven months he had remained in possession of her ashes.

"I was going to say Bess."

"Not Minnie?"

I drew my shoulders up at the mention of her name. I shook my head. "Bess."

"What? You'd like to ask her what it was like to live with me?" He gave an unconvincing laugh under his breath. "I'd rather you'd talk to Minnie. She's more likely to be on my side."

"Hardly." I patted his cheek. "*Minnie* wouldn't take sides. Bess, on the other hand…"

"Liked playing all sides against the middle."

Her giving the Aunt Farm to Sterling in her will proved that point all too well. And it also told me what she would have said if I could have asked for her advice. She didn't want me to have the house because she wanted me to move on with my life, not to get mired down by my aunts and a lifetime of trying to save my family from itself.

"And she would tell me to say yes," I whispered.

His still dark eyebrows crimped down over his disbelieving gaze. "Really?"

I gulped down a big breath and let it out slowly.

"She already has." I slid the box from his hand. "Does your offer still stand?"

"Offer?"

"To marry me?"

"You ready to say yes?"

"Yes."

We kissed and it was good. Not the all-consuming thrill I'd felt the first time he had asked and I'd accepted, but good.

We checked into our room and made love and that was good, too. Likewise dinner and a moonlight walk and sharing a bubble bath and curling up naked in each other's arms. All good.

Too good, maybe. I had to make sure before I could shut my eyes that I hadn't made it all up. Head on Guy's chest, I pressed my body close to his, warm and safe and loved. And lying with my eyes on the stars outside our window I had to ask, "That's it, right? You're going to go through with it. It's a done deal. For sure?"

"It's a done deal, Charma Deane." His chest rose and fell. He stroked my bare back once, then his hand fell away. "You and I are going to get married."

I listened to the quiet for a moment, to the night sounds and the heartbeat of the man I loved, and then I added so softly that I didn't think that he would hear me,

"Unless one of us backs out."

"Unless one of us…" he murmured, all groggy and compliant. "Or *both* of us…backs out."

❧ CHAPTER FIVE

I wouldn't call the ride home the next day awkward. The word I'd use? Delicate. An operation requiring skill and caution. Sitting down with raw eggs in your back pockets, that's a delicate endeavor. If you pull it off, you have every reason to feel proud, because you are flipping brilliant. If you fail at it and have to walk around with egg-goo all over your ass? Now, that's awkward.

So my goal the whole hour and a half in that car was to be able to extricate myself without causing a disaster or needing to take a shower afterward. Delicate.

"So." Guy exhaled, his gaze fixed forward and his knuckles practically white against the leather-padded steering wheel.

"So," I agreed.

"That was…"

After a few seconds to allow him to come up with a credible or at least colorful narrative of our time together, I sank back in the seat and offered a quiet, "Yeah, it sure was."

We'd slept together, but then we'd done that sort of thing plenty in the two weeks we'd been back together, not to mention the two years we'd dated a lifetime ago. It wasn't more magical or even less messy because I'd accepted his proposal. In fact, our time between the sheets was the best part of the past twenty-four hours. And I don't mean the eight hours we spent snoring like a couple of hibernating bears who crawled into their cave without their Breathe Right nose strips.

The part in bed awake and aroused, that still felt good and right and natural between us. It was the other fourteen hours and...

"Did we make love three times or four?" I rubbed one eye, not just to get the gunk out but also because doing math in my head is hard.

"Three, but we did start for four, then realized they were going to stop serving breakfast."

"Oh, that's right." That's when I had learned the sad truth about myself—given the option of throwing myself onto a short stake of pecan pancakes or fully erect and willing male member, I will chose the pancakes.

It makes sense, really. Penises can be found in abundance. They practically roam wild all over the Arkansas landscape—attached to whatever manner of man you might want to imagine, of course. Most of them are willing to rise to the occasion and fulfill your hunger. And they, the penises, don't even require a spatula—usually—to keep them in line, or an alarm to warn you when they've had a little too much heat. But whipping up a fluffy, golden-brown pecan pancake? Now, that's an art form.

And in my defense, these were really good pancakes. So good I'd had the owner of the B & B put a few in a foam to-go box for me to bring home for a late comfort snack. You can't do that kind of thing with sex, save the leftovers to have cold later to assuage your battered feelings. Sex has to be served hot and fresh to be any good at all. Another point in favor of the flapjacks.

"Okay, so three times for..." Ugh, math really does suck. Real math, that is. "Girl math," which is what Bess and Minnie and I perfected over the years to configure our *real* ages—calendars are notorious liars, y'all—"girl math" is easy.

"What are you trying to figure out?"

I was trying to figure out what to tell Inez and my family about the other fourteen hours and fifty some odd minutes that we had to fill without using the words *thorny, bristling* or *scraped across my very last nerve like a knuckle on a cheese grater.*

"I am trying to figure out…" I glanced his way and caught his face in profile.

The face I would see every day for the rest of my life. It was a good face. Time had treated Guy well, even if it had bent his nose a bit, left lines high on his cheeks and salted the dark stubble on his face with white and gray.

I could honestly say at the moment that I would rather have had this man than pecan pancakes. And that's damned high praise considering that breakfast.

"I was just trying to figure out how to tell my family our big news."

"I say don't tell them and let's just run off some weekend to Eureka Springs and elope."

"That would kill Fawnie and Shug."

"And staging a—what did Fawnie call the funeral she wanted thrown when she died?"

"Big-ass bountiful."

"Yeah, staging a big-ass bountiful wedding for you won't kill them?"

"No, it won't. In fact, it will give them something to live for." An image of my aunts at Bess and Sterling's impromptu wedding in our backyard sprang into my head. Bess in Fawnie's old wedding dress, lights twinkling in the trees, the bathtub in the backyard filled with roses and cold beer. Perfect.

But we had pulled that together so fast and under such emotional stress that aside from a few precious moments stolen here and there, no one had really taken any great joy in the planning of the event. With me, Fawnie and Shug would not just *want* that great joy from my wedding—they'd *demand* it.

"No, it won't kill them," I said, shutting my eyes to try to blot out the images of those two squabbling over everything from the color of the sugar roses for the cake to the brand of shaving cream for decorating the car. "It will kill *me*."

"Don't tell," he whispered, doing his best to sound like a ghost or my conscience, which to my way of thinking aren't all that different.

I laughed. "I'll consider it."

Then the steering wheel veered slightly and the tires thumbed up onto the Aunt Farm's long, curved crush-shale drive and I was home. I glanced up, expecting that sense of safe harbor you think sailors must have when they spot a friendly lighthouse, and gasped. "Why is there a U-Haul truck backed up to my front door?"

Guy pulled the car up a few feet away from the truck and I popped open the passenger door. "You go on. I'll get my things from you later."

"Charma, shouldn't we—"

"No! Let me handle this. If you come along, then you and this weekend and whether we tell anyone or not will become inextricably tangled up in whatever other bullshit nonsense is going on here." I didn't think I actually said "whatever *other* bullshit nonsense" but I wouldn't swear to it, especially given the look on Guy's face.

Then he smiled. He always knows when to smile and take that kind of crap and when to call me on it. When I *need* calling on it. And sometimes he did both.

He leaned toward the open passenger side door and yelled out, "You thought there was some chance that our engagement wouldn't get forever tied up in some kind of bullshit nonsense with your family?"

I should have jumped back in that car and run off and married him on the spot. He could laugh when a lesser man might have tried to pull that white-knight-charging-to-my-rescue crap or, worse, try to talk sense into me.

But I was in full force, ready to fling myself fully into the defense of my turf, and I did not need Guy Chapman or anyone getting in my way.

I turned and ducked to speak to him inside the car. "Please, Guy, go on home."

"That *place* is not my home," he said softly.

Me and a mortician who didn't want to *be* a mortician. The owner of big, old, established funeral home that did not consider the mortuary where he had been raised and now resided as his home. Sometimes God threw me a bone.

"I know, but much as I'd love to listen for the umpteenth time to you bitch about what your brother did, leaving you high and dry when he ran off with the embalmer and forced you to come back to town and save the family business, frankly I don't have the patience for it today." I never had had the patience for it, and the look he gave me said he knew as much. I sighed and kissed my fingertips and wriggled them in his direction, like that ridiculously sweet gesture would make up for my total lack of sympathy for his situation. "Just go. I don't want you to stick around here. There might be a scene."

"*Might* be a scene?"

"Thank you for making my point." A real kiss this time, but so quick I don't know if I hit his lips or his earlobe, and I was gone. Two steps away it hit me that I'd left my pancakes, but going back for them now would make me look wishy-washy, something I just could not afford as I marched in to battle.

"Abbra Georgette Raynes!" I shouted above the roar of Guy taking off. I gave the side of the small-size rental truck a *whap* to add weight to my pronouncement, the way the roll of thunder or a drumbeat in a movie foretells pending danger. "I agreed you could stay until you worked things out, not move in! How dare you show up with a mini-moving van full of—"

"It doesn't belong to Abby."

"Johnny!" As long as I live, no matter how mad they make me, no matter how rotten the relationship between us, I cannot imagine a time when my heart won't literally leap at the sight of one of my sons. "Who invited you here, and how fast can you hit the road?"

Tough love. That's what Inez called it. To me it was just...love. I'd never known that love could be anything but tough. That's the way of all things that come at a high cost. Tenderness does not last. Toughness does. I learned that from my own mother and grandmother, and I taught it to my child in turn.

I leaned back and cocked my head to study him.

He sat sprawled all out as if he had landed himself in a saggy old beanbag chair instead of Fawnie's favorite white wicker rocker. One long leg stretched across the painted floorboards and the other foot had kicked up to rest haphazardly on his knee. His whole posture said "I don't give a shit." He had on secondhand cowboy boots, probably just because he knew it would set my teeth on edge.

His father always wore cowboy boots—with tin boot tips that he told everyone were hand-engraved silver. The big lying phony. Johnny's father, that is. And, well, probably Johnny as well.

I nudged the sole of my boy's boot. "I don't suppose you have the money you stole from me?"

"I didn't steal money from you." He leaned forward and clasped his hands between his knees. He did not meet my eyes. "You gave me your car to do with what I wanted. I wanted to sell it."

"I *traded* cars with you because yours was a piece of shit and you needed reliable transportation to get you to the big-time important professional-type job you dropped out of law school to—"

"You seem to get around all right." He cut me off, his hardened gaze moving from the hearse, to the drive where Guy's car had sat moments ago to the U-Haul.

I stepped back and put my hand on the porch rail. I didn't need the steadying effect so much as I wanted to remove myself from the expression of anger and pain in my child's face, and the rail kept me from going too far. I forced myself to hold my ground verbally. "I *traded* cars with you because I knew you'd need decent wheels for your new job. You really *did* have a job, didn't you?"

"Yes, I really did have a job. A dream-killin', sell-your-soul one to a company saddled with some other man's name and some other man's dreams for four bucks above minimum wage, one where you come home too tired to eat or fuck or do anything but stare at the TV until you fall asleep on the couch, then get up and do it again and again."

"Well, at least you told me the truth about that."

His father had never told the truth about much of anything, especially about holding a job. The man worked—he worked on getting other women to sleep with him, but *that* he didn't lie about so much. Orla is a small town. My family was big news. It wouldn't have done him much good to lie about that, anyway. That's probably why both my sons moved to Tulsa to go to college and build their lives. In Tulsa the living, and the lying, was bound to be easier.

"You quit or get fired?" I crossed my legs at the ankles.

"I took a few days off."

"Do they know about it?"

He looked at me, and it broke my heart that I couldn't read anything in his eyes but that he looked just like his daddy.

The way I got Boyd Parker to let me name our son after my father instead of calling him Boyd Junior was to tell him that ninety percent of the men in prison had been named after their fathers. I don't know if that statistic is strictly true, but Boyd could count more than enough no-account so-and-so juniors among his friends to sour him on taking the risk. That alone should have prevented me from having a second child with the man, but he had this power over me that to this day still holds a strange and mysterious allure. Namely, my family hated him.

And anyone my family hated I figured had to have something going for him. They'd loved Guy, after all. So there was Boyd, this dark-eyed Arkansas Adonis in a muscle shirt and mullet, and when he grinned—the man did not smile, he grinned—he had this single dimple on the right side of his face. It gave him this lop-eared lone wolf pup quality. Crooked and vulnerable enough that I wanted to save him and yet cocky enough that I wanted to sleep with him. A lot. So I married him, which I thought would let me accomplish both.

He remained unsaved in every way imaginable, and for a great deal of our marriage I slept alone. But I had been seven months pregnant when he had proposed and couldn't afford to be picky.

Johnny was Boyd's spitting image—sans the mullet. I did have *some* influence on the kid, after all. But he had his father's eyes, his father's dimple and his father's pain-in-the-ass attitude.

I forced out a long breath and folded my arms. "I'm not getting any younger waiting for your answer, young man."

"Are you kidding? Doesn't girl math let you subtract years off your life for time spent in the company of worthless men?"

"Of course it does. That's just common sense." I swept my gaze over him, looking for signs he'd been ill or not eating right or had come to his senses and wanted to apologize for the way he'd been acting lately. I saw none of those things. Nothing.

Nothing but the kid I still prayed for every day of my life, that I still missed seeing across the breakfast table, that I would go to my grave believing and desiring the best of and for. I went to him and brushed back his hair just like when he was a little boy. "But I never once said *you* were worthless."

He jerked his head away, only not really, just made the show of doing it. "How could I be worthless after all the money you've spent on trying to make something of me?"

I love both my boys, but there is no use hiding it: my firstborn gets under my skin. My youngest, George, and I, we are like good old friends. We can sit together each reading a book or watching TV or working a jigsaw puzzle in total silence with sweet unspoiled ease. But the oldest, the baby I named after my daddy? There is no such thing as ease between him and me.

"You were already *something* before I invested a dime in you, baby boy." I held out my hand.

Someone else might have opened her arms. Might have made herself a welcome place for her child to surrender and pour out his wounded soul. And Johnny's soul was wounded, I knew that the instant I laid eyes on him.

Someone else might have seen that and decided she had to offer reconciliation. I couldn't. And even if I could, he wouldn't have accepted it.

He gazed into my open palm.

"You'd better be reading my future, because you're out of luck if you're looking for money in that hand," I said, only a little bit joking.

He put two fingers to his temple and narrowed his eyes on me, not on my hand, on *me*. "You will cross paths with a tall, troublesome stranger."

I curled my fingers closed. "Who comes riding into town in a U-Haul?"

"That's not my doing."

I turned toward the truck again. "It's not?"

"And I'm not the stranger in this scenario."

It wasn't Abby and it wasn't Johnny. I folded my hands together, and the enormous diamond I had just accepted dug into the side of my fingers.

Confidences. Cousins. Carats and kids. I was juggling chain saws here and somebody wanted to throw a pineapple into the mix. I hated pineapples.

The only thing I hated worse was…

"Hey, Charma." Sterling Mayhouse strode out onto the porch like he owned the place. And since he did, it created a decided chill up my spine when he met my gaze, unwavering, and said, "Looks like you made it back in time to help me unpack and settle in."

❧ CHAPTER SIX

"This is why you cleared out those three bedrooms, isn't it?" My borrowed flip-flops slapped over the polished hardwood for one, two, three full steps before I kicked them off and charged on barefoot. Even I couldn't pull off home-grown hellfire and well-earned righteous indignation with my feet giving off sounds like someone smacking around a wet fish. "You cleared out nearly half the bedrooms in my family's ancestral home so you could move yourself in."

The tall man with the tumbles of dark blond and sun-streaked curls turned and flashed his brilliant capped-tooth smile. "Hi, honey, I'm home."

In another lifetime I'd have laughed at that. Not because I found it particularly clever or endearing but because I found the man saying it both those and more. He was the kind of man you think you could easily despise and/or carry on a passionate but meaningless affair with for oh, one night to roughly…the rest of your life. Overeducated, under-employed, living off a trust fund while not seeming all that trustworthy his own self, he was blue-eyed, blond and blessed with a sense of humor about himself. Think Paul Newman in *The Long, Hot Summer,* only more vulnerable, less sweaty and definitely not the same loin-stirring sight without his shirt on.

And soul-sick.

Did I mention that? Because nobody could look at this man just a few months shy of celebrating his thirty-fifth birthday and not see that right off. Like just about everyone who ever ended up at the Aunt Farm, he carried in him a hurt so deep that only time and love and a bona fide miracle could ever heal it.

But we were fresh out of miracles here, and somehow, deep down, I think he knew that. That's why he hardly flinched at all when I tipped back my head and gave him the best damn piece of advice I had at my disposal.

"Sterling Mayhouse, this is *not* your home, and you are making a potentially painful mistake trying to force your way in and use it as such."

"Strictly speaking, Charma Deane, you are right. This place has not been my home." He turned to press his back against a door and raised his knee to hoist the box in his hands up higher against his chest. "But it is now. It's also my law office."

"*What* office?" He had a law degree, I knew. I'd seen it in his bedroom closet about a year ago, when he'd tried to use it to impress me into sleeping with him after our first date.

"My law office," he repeated.

A law office! In the *Aunt Farm?* Oh, God was having a big barrel of yucks over that one, for sure.

"Where are you planning to put this office?" I demanded, taking off after him as he headed down the hall with his secured load.

"In the back bedroom."

"The linen room?" For as long as I could recall, my mother and my aunts had collected linens. Bed linens. Kitchen linens. Bath linens. Linen napkins, linen hankies and a whole lot of things that weren't really linen at all. No woman ever left our home without sheets and tablecloths and tea towels and, if they so desired, envelopes made of silk scarves intended for holding gloves and secreting away old love letters. Whatever a woman might need to dress her home in something that would reflect who she was, something she could call her own, we had it in the linen room. It was an old-fashioned concept that had its roots in hope chests and needlework tucked into sewing boxes going back hundreds and hundreds of years.

"Not anymore," he said.

I scowled, which I usually try not to do because it not only looks bad, it creates wrinkles. But what the hell I was engaged to a man who had seen me every which way but hanging naked from a trapeze by my knees—you have to preserve a *little* mystery in a romance, after all. What did I care about a few frown lines? And Sterling here had me all worked up—and not in that Paul Newman kind of way—here about his intentions. "What did you do with all those years' worth of collected sheets and tea towels and tablecloths?"

He tipped his head, just ever so slighty, and that wise-ass darling smile of his slid a bit to one side. "Your aunts are boxing them up right now."

"They are helping you in this sacrilege?" I felt slapped in the face at the very thought.

"Go see for yourself." He plunked the box down inside the side door to the kitchen on top of a small pyramid of boxes—a virtual monument to a truly bad idea and to the power of anyone of the male gender to get my aunts to go along with just about anything.

In a couple of thunderous steps I was at the open doorway of the back bedroom. I stood in horrified witness to the carnage taking place inside. "You are! You two are actually participating in this sacrilege!"

Fawnie and Shug stood at opposite sides of the room, each holding a side of a white chenille bedspread with a colorful peacock pattern in the center.

"Charma, lamb! You're back!" Fawnie did not look up from her task. "How was your getaway?"

"Tell us the juicy parts first." Shug beamed at me

I just stood there, barefoot and incredulous. "What are you two doing?"

"Folding. This sucker so big and heavy, it takes two of us to make it even." Shug walked slowly toward her counterpart, looking like a child bearing the cumbersome train of a make-believe princess.

Fawnie snatched away both edges and held them against her chest, oblivious to the fringe snagging against her chains and pearls. At least she didn't have a cigarette, or they'd have had a barbecued peacock on their hands. And it would have served them right, I told myself. The traitors.

But then Fawnie never smoked in the linen room. No one smoked in the linen room. My mother had ordered it so decades ago, and even though she had died this past New Year's weekend and we had now been almost a year without her, her decree remained in full force today. That was the kind of power Mama held over this house.

I was her daughter. Surely I had some kind of residual bossing-around credentials?

"Y'all stop this nonsense this instant!" I commanded, hands on hips and toes curled hard against the cold, dusty floor.

Shug walked down to the folded end of the bedspread and lifted it. They stood there holding the thing between them like a hammock and Shug turned to me. "Didn't you get any nookie last night, sweetie? You awfully grumpy for someone just come back from sharing a bed with a hot-blooded man."

I grabbed my left hand with my right, then remembered I'd stashed my ring in my pocket. Good. No need to give the old gals reason to veer further off course. No need to let them use the fact that the act of matrimony would make what happened in this house no longer any of my damned business as an excuse for diffusing my clout around here.

"Maybe she's constipated." Fawnie gave the spread a shake to flip the fringe together. "She always did tend to seize up when she traveled. Charma, honey, you need some prunes?"

Clout? Power? I was kidding myself. Mama may have garnered respect and control around here, but I never would. Unless I charged in and took it for myself.

"What I need is for you two to learn to lock the doors around here at night and not give all kinds of vermin-disguised-as-lawyers and car-stealing offspring free rein of my home." I crossed the threshold and glanced around at the boxes marked by content, the nearly emptied closet and the built-in dresser with its drawers left hanging open, things still in them.

"*Your* home?" Fawnie smoothed her gnarled hand over the square of folded fabric draped over her arm.

"*His* home, Charmika." Shug moved behind me to one of the open drawers, patting my back as she went. She turned, glanced toward the open bedroom door, peered out, then smiled at me, winked and said real loud, "The house belong to the lawyer man now, sweetheart."

I crossed my arms and engaged in no such silliness, meeting her square in the eyes and saying, even louder, "Only if you give it to him without a fight."

"We too old to fight." Shug waved off the idea, then dove in to pull a stack of embroidered towels from the drawer.

"Bullshit." Too old to fight? These two? They would go to their graves in full battle regalia.

Fawnie placed the bedspread into an almost full box, then trailed her hand slowly over the nubby pattern. "Besides, we kind of like the idea of having a man around the house full-time."

"Bingo." Full battle regalia for these two would include pearls and perfume and full falderal of a femme fatale on the prowl.

"Besides, that Sterling? He's nice. He take care of us." Shug plopped the towels into a box and flipped the cardboard flaps shut.

"But he—"

"He loved our Bess." Fawnie made a wobbly slashing motion with her hand as if to say, "That's it, that's all, end of discussion."

I clenched my jaw. No one cut me off in my own home, especially not by invoking as savior the name of someone who had, when it suited her selfish desires, showed no hesitation to destroy or disappoint every person she ever cared about—except Sterling. Sterling, Bess had only had time to dent a little before her death.

"But even Bess didn't always have other people's best intentions at heart," I argued. More diplomatic than my norm given my feelings on the matter, but still strong enough to strike home.

"There are certain protections in place." Fawnie reached her hand out as if meaning to grab up a pack of cigarettes. When her hand fell on the table beside her and found nothing, she snapped up her cane and held it in both hands instead. "Legal protections. Checks and balances."

"You mean Aunt Ruth?" I tried to imagine my father's younger sister in the robes of blind justice crying out for equity and reason to prevail. The best I could do was to see the perpetually tanned and unnaturally toned seventy-year-old in a spa robe with a towel turban falling over her eyes, calling out for a gin and tonic from pool boy in her froggy-throated Texas accent. "You're relying on *Aunt Ruth* to provide balance?"

"That's what the will provides," Fawnie announced, her words oddly stiff and uncharacteristically carefully chosen. "Ruth has final say on what happens to the George family mansion."

"Which is fine because Ruth don't want this place," Shug muttered. "She won't kick us out, and Sterling can't do nothing without her no matter what tricks he has up his briefs."

"You mean what's *in* his briefs?"

"Oh, see, you act all high and mighty, but you think about what's in that man's briefs, too." Shug tee-heed, her shoulders shaking without her making any actual laughing sound.

Fawnie shook her head and rolled her eyes.

I sighed.

I loved my father's sister, Ruth, and I think she truly loved me. We had formed a special bond as she and I became the ever-vigilant caretakers for Bess in the last stages of relinquishing her life to bone cancer. But Ruth had no love for her sisters-in-law, and had never gotten over the fact that they had taken over the family home from Nana Abbra and made it their own.

Ruth had thought nothing of keeping it a secret that my grandmother had willed the family home to her. She had, in turn, quietly given the deed to Bess and Bess had left it to Sterling, with the codicil that he not be allowed to sell the property without Ruth's consent.

Nothing, not even the basics of food, clothing and shelter, came without complications in my family. No wonder my aunts put such store in any small comfort they could find, from fine linens to fine-looking young men.

And how could I begrudge them that? No, this fight was mine and mine alone now. But I couldn't help firing off a parting shot as I headed out the door. "I think you have a little too much faith in family, Aunt Fawnie, and too little fear of the American justice system."

❧ CHAPTER SEVEN

"Sterling?" I met him in the hallway and jerked the gooseneck desk lamp out of his hand. "You. Me. Now."

"Now?" He said it low, intrigued but not intimidated, and a bit too flirty for respectability.

His response gave me a flutter, or a chill, not sure which. Something, that sense of foreboding, that prickling up of the hairs on your neck or the watery glub in the pit of your stomach that says, "Maybe you should think this through." But when in my life had I ever stopped to think anything through? Why would I start now with my home and happiness hanging in the balance?

"Now," I said, all no-nonsense and pushing forward no matter what.

I glanced in the direction of the front parlor. I made a quick check of the hallway and the open door to the back bedroom where Fawnie and Shug's voices still chattered along as if they hadn't quite noticed my leave-taking. I narrowed my eyes toward the kitchen where Sterling had been headed. Surely there was someplace in this sacred place of sanctuary where I could stomach standing and talking for five lousy minutes?

"Out here," I said finally, pushing past him, down the hall and out into the screened-in back porch.

"Here?" He stuck his head out the back door. "You sure?"

It was a reasonable question given my history with this spot, but I forged on until I stood far enough away from the door that we wouldn't be heard in the house.

The unforgiving coldness of the concrete floor stung the soles of my feet. Carrying the smell of algae and wet earth, the wind came in gusts through the tarnished old screens. Warped and worked loose by years of neglect they moved in and out with every breeze so that the very walls around us seemed to be breathing.

The limbs of the tree at the corner of the house scraped against the sagging gutters, and weeds had begun to overtake and hide the path to the pond. Bamboo furniture from the 1960s lined the walls, the once fat cushions squashed down by years of women flopping down on them on hot evenings when they couldn't sleep and children dragging them off to build forts on rainy days. And near the center, facing out toward the pond where my father had died, sat my mother's rocker.

Mama had sat herself in that simple maple rocker one evening just after Christmas while I was off visiting my sons. With Bess as her confederate, she had hidden the fact that she had stopped taking her heart medicine, stopped following doctor's orders and had saved up enough pain medication to finally and forever complete the wall she had always kept around herself by dying in the dark, alone.

"You okay?" Sterling asked, the slick sole of his loafer skimming the single step that led down to the porch floor.

"Do you care?"

"Three rooms, Charma. Three lousy rooms. You act like I've backed a wrecking ball up to the main chimney and am working the levers to set the thing swinging with my own two hands."

"Don't be ridiculous." I gave him a slow once-over. "I know good and well you would never get your hands dirty operating heavy machinery."

"Yeah." He looked at his palms, then stuffed his hands in his pockets and stood there looking at me, waiting.

He'd lost weight. *More* weight. He'd lost some during the worst weeks of losing Bess, then gained a bit back when all the friends and family descended with their hams and Jell-O salads and scalloped potato casseroles with cornflake toppings.

"You're not eating right," I told him.

"Right back at ya," he murmured.

I wrapped my hands around myself and my fingers sank into the soft flesh of my upper arms. "I guess it shows on both of us."

"On you it looks good." He smiled, but his eyes did not light up the way they used to.

I nodded.

"Charma Deane, I…" He took a step toward me.

"Why are you doing this?"

"Don't be cross with me."

"Answer my question." And I was cross with him. More cross than I'd have ever been if he hadn't said that because…because seeing him like this, humble and hurting, it damn near killed me. "Why are trying to take the Aunt Farm away from us?"

"Three rooms," he whispered, holding up three fingers. "You'd begrudge me three rooms?"

"Three rooms in *my* home, Sterling. Hell, yes, I *begrudge* you them." I wadded the fabric of my neckline in my fist. "You know how hard we worked to keep this place. Hell, it was your legal wrangling that kept it in Fawnie and Shug's hands when Bess wanted to evict them. And now you…you…"

His broad shoulders rose and fell. He did not hold my gaze. "I am only trying to carry out Bess's dying wishes."

"I know," I said softly, and went to his side. I touched his back, ran my hand down his arm, took his hand in my own and positioned myself in front of him, bending low so that I could look into his eyes as I said, "But you did not really know or love Bess long enough to understand her wishes, dying or otherwise."

His eyes glistened with tears that he did not shed. His jaw hardly moved and his voice came out quiet, harsh and shredded as if he had to drag the words over jagged rocks to get them out. "Are you saying you don't think I really loved Bess?"

I took both his hands in mine and studied them. Immaculate and strong. Large hands that could not possibly hold all the responsibilities he had been handed.

"I'm saying that I think that what you have in mind here—" I tipped my head up to put my face before him. My eyes were moist and my lips dry but I compelled myself to finish "—are your *own* wishes, Sterling."

He nodded and caught the beginnings of a sob in the back of his throat, turning it into something between a cough and a shuddering breath. "Okay. I can accept that. Fair enough. Maybe I am thinking as much of myself as I am of my wife."

"Your *late* wife," I whispered. Hard for him to hear, probably more than it was for me to say, but I had to do it. He had to hear it. "You just want to be here in this house to keep her alive, I think. To try to hang on…just a little longer. Don't you?"

"Do I?"

I brushed his cheek with my fingertips. "Yes."

"Or maybe…" He edged in closer until I could feel the warmth of his skin on mine.

I felt the man he had become and the boy he was struggling to hold inside reaching out together, looming over me and reaching…

He slipped his hand behind my neck and held my head firmly in place. His mouth closed over mine. Hard. Hungry but for something more than sexual gratification. Needy and scared and melt-me-to-the-bone hot.

We had kissed before, of course. Nothing more than a kiss. But those kisses…were *nothing* like this.

I worked my hands between us to push him away. But I didn't push him. I flattened my palms to his chest, tipped my head back and moaned as his lips moved down my neck and up to my jaw, then found my mouth again. It was just the two of us, no aunts, no kids, no other lovers.

He murmured a name. *Mine?* Or had he said…Bess?

And just that fast the world righted itself and everything and *everyone* came sharply into focus.

I wriggled free of his grasp and gulped in air as if it were water.

"What the hell was that?" I swiped my knuckle across my lower lip.

"Don't ask me to leave this house again, Charma Deane" was all he said.

"Because it's yours," I said, narrowing my eyes to both keep him in focus and to try to keep anything beyond him from demanding my attention. The house was his. Bess had been his. And if he wanted it that way, he had just suggested without using a word that I could be his, too.

This was not the boy I had known a year ago who had tried to impress me with a law degree in his bedroom closet. This was a man. A dangerous man. A man who had learned about love from my cousin Bess and wasn't afraid of me or anyone. He had nothing to lose.

"It's mine. This house is mine, Charma."

I drew in a breath and the odor of the pond and of the dying leaves filled my nostrils. I glared at him, turned, then started for the door.

"Oh, and don't get any ideas about you and Inez putting a labyrinth on this property or building a woman's retreat."

Labyrinth and a woman's retreat. Those were the last things I wanted, the last things on my mind right now. Until he brought them up, and suddenly all I could say was "I'll do what I damn well please."

"Not here you won't."

"Don't count on that, Mayhouse. It may just happen yet. And if it does, we can name a wing after you—since you're the thing women need to retreat from in the first place."

"A lawyer?" He chuckled.

"A man," I said coy-like, teasing to make it obvious I wasn't trying to come off like some women's channel movie heroine.

The chuckled deepened. He shifted his loafers on the concrete. "You don't even know what a man is, you're in love with a memory."

I swear my mouth hung open for four full seconds before I could shake my head, blink and ask, "*What?* I cannot believe you just said that to me. You been staying up all night watching Spanish soap operas again?"

"*Un poco.*" He held his thumb and forefinger finger a half an inch apart.

I laughed and in doing so knew the man had scored another point on me. Damn him.

"A memory, Sterling?" I reached around to fish my new engagement ring out of my back pocket. I flashed it for him then slid it in place on my left hand. "You of all people accuse me of *that?*"

His gaze followed my movements. He sneered, slightly. "I was in love with a real person who is now nothing but a memory. You are in love with the idea of Guy Chapman, Charma. Of finally winning him and knowing for sure that Bess won't steal him or ruin it. It's your final triumph over her."

"You don't know what you're talking about."

"I know Bess hurt you and I know that you never really forgave her, not even in death."

"I did so." *It was Guy I hadn't forgiven.* Wisely I kept that part to myself.

"Then why didn't you let her talk to you about it? Why didn't you let her get her feelings out in the open so the two of you could face them and fight it out and truly forgive each other?"

I took a step backward and braced my arm against the door frame. "I didn't do anything that required her forgiveness."

"Except force her to carry the responsibility for *your* pain to her grave." His expression did not accuse me. He simply said it and left it there for me to do with what I would.

"I never…" Of course I had. It was one of the sins I had hoped to wash away. It was a sin I could not rid myself of that easily. I bowed my head.

"Everyone makes mistakes. Everyone strays from the path. Sometimes the burden of the secret kept does more damage than the misstep," he said.

"I never wanted to do anything but *save* Bess."

"From what?"

From me not loving her.

And Sterling was telling me now that I had failed.

I pressed my hand to my forehead and shut my eyes tight until colors formed behind my lids.

"You are a coward, Charma Deane Parker. You rush off and get yourself hip deep into every cause that you can find, but way down you are terrified of making one wrong move. And you're doubly terrified of accepting that people you love will make wrong moves, sometimes by mistake and sometimes by design. Because of that, you can't move at all."

"Oh, I can move, mister, and I suggest you do the same before I—"

"What? What act can you threaten me with?" He came to me and placed his hand on my shoulder, gentle but all control and coolness. "Charma, you don't even have the gumption to go to the funeral home and collect your mother's ashes."

"I don't need a pile of dust and bones to remind me of my mother. I carry her with me always." I pumped my hand over my chest. *Thud-thud.*

"Like a thorn in the side." He took my fisted hand in his, worked my fingers free, then touched the tip of his middle finger to my cupped palm just as doubting Thomas might have done to Christ. "Just what every good little martyr needs."

Before the kiss, before…the truth he'd spoken here, I would have slapped the crap out of him for that. Instead I tugged my hand free and tucked it behind my back. "For all you know, I *do* have Mama's ashes. You don't know everything I do."

"I know *this* thing. Chapman told me so this morning."

I held up my left hand and wriggled my ring finger.

"Chapman was with me this morning."

"Not Guy. The other one. The brother."

"Loyal?" My fingers stilled. "How could you have talked to Loyal Chapman? He's—"

"Back in town. Met him at the funeral home just a few hours ago when I went to pay Bess's final bill. He gave me a few things that belonged to her and asked me if I had the legal authority to receive the ashes of one Ms. Dinah McCoy George before they had to dispose of them."

"Dispose of? *Mama?* He doesn't have the right to do that!" I took another step and found myself in the kitchen and slowly something flowed back into me. I stood straighter and smiled cockier, adding, "Or the balls."

Sterling followed me into the room, his own smile not quite so hard now. "I can't speak to his testicular situation, but he does have the right, as co-owner of Chapman and Son's Funeral Home."

"Co-owner?" I laughed. "No-o-o, sir. He all but bankrupted the place, then took off with the person who did their embalming. Guy had to come home and…and reassure everyone that a Chapman still had the reins of the business just to keep the doors open. Everyone in Orla knows that."

"Everyone in Orla doesn't know squat."

He had me there. I checked the clock on the wall. "If I call Guy on his cell, I might catch him in time to warn him that his brother is in town."

"Guy knows."

"Guy can't possibly know."

"According to Dathan, he and his wife had a nice long talk with both Chapmans yesterday."

Dathan would know. The young man knew everything that went on at Chapman and Sons. He was, after all, the real moritician behind Guy's pretense of running the place. *If Guy knew that, why didn't he tell me? Had he tried?*

"He had warned me that he had more than one thing careening around inside his head just before he proposed." I sounded defensive.

Sterling picked up on that. "Maybe that was what had prompted his rush to propose. His brother is here to take things off his hands, and Guy is ready to blow town again."

Only this time he wanted me—and not Bess—with him.

"I guess that's not so hard to understand." Sterling made some vague hand gesture. "If a man loves a woman, he wants her with him."

If a man loves a woman. My mind overemphasized the first word, because standing here now watching the scene replay in my thoughts, it dawned on me: Guy had never said he loved me. I had thought that was his big next move, to tell me that he loved me. But he hadn't. He had asked me to marry him, and I had assumed that meant one and the same.

"Of course, men marry for other reasons, too. God only knows what kinds of reasons they have for proposing."

With Sterling's parting words I had begun to doubt everything I had just proclaimed as truth.

Could Sterling be right? Could I only want Guy to finally win out over Bess? Did Guy only want me because he wanted out of Orla and it felt right to take me along? Despite our long history, we'd only been together again for a couple of weeks. Did I really know the man at all? He had lied to me before—more than once.

I wanted to run, but where could I go? To the couch where I planned to sleep tonight? The couch in the parlor where Bess had died? To Min's room? The living memorial to hope and innocence and the cutting reminder that I was participating in deceiving her? To Mama's room?

Maybe Sterling was right about that, too. This was not my house. It belonged to too many people crammed into too few room crowded with too many possibilities.

I could go out to the pond, but why? A person could not keep baptizing themselves and pretending the gesture continued to hold any real meaning. Besides, if I jumped in today with the weight of the world on my shoulders and those better-than-sex pecan pancakes lying like river rock in my gut, I'd sink straight to the bottom. And I didn't have one lick of faith that I would have the strength or the will to struggle to the top and swim for the shore.

So I guessed if I was going to jump and die, I might as well jump to conclusions and head to the place all good people go when they leave their earthly homes behind.

❧ CHAPTER EIGHT

"You are not going to believe the shit Sterling is trying to stir up!" I hit the back door of the mortuary with all the energy of a tattletale home from school with fresh dirt on her worst enemy.

Maybe it was because it was the first time I'd been alone in days, or maybe the very act of driving the hearse that carried Bess to her final resting place to the funeral home storing my mother's ashes had jarred me back to my senses, but the trip over to Chapman's had restored my perspective. Sterling was the enemy here. First and foremost in the growing list of people I loved with my entire being but was righteously pissed off at, and who in return were rightly and remorselessly pissed off at me. Bottom line? I needed someone on my side again, and I figured a man lays out five grand for a ring and hands it to a woman he has only been sleeping with for two weeks, that man is a good bet to not sell you down the river.

I have been wrong about that kind of thing before, though.

"Hello? Guy?" My hastily thrown on flip-flops skidded over the uneven linoleum floor of the cramped kitchen. "Dathan? Anybody?"

Dead silence. An apt description in more ways than one.

I froze.

I held my breath.

I listened.

Nothing.

No TV or radio softly buzzed away in the background. No gurgle of coffee warming in the pot. Not even the hush and rustle of mourners milling about in the front rooms. Nothing. This wasn't the sort of quiet afternoon stillness I'd grown used to living in a largely vacant old house with two aging women.

This was…wrong.

How I came to know what was wrong or right for a small-town southern mortuary I can't say exactly. It's the kind of thing you just know. Especially if you have a family like mine, where they buried people young and often. Not that they buried and reburied people, but that we lost Uncle Kel and Daddy and Nana all in a short span when I was young so that the funeral home setting was not foreign turf to me. Or to anyone I knew.

Around here, people chose funeral homes with the kind of care and allegiance that people in cooler climates reserve for churches or country clubs. We're Chapman people, the Georges, and we always will be. I'm sure my mother, in her need to maintain control over every last detail, had it written in her will that she would only allow Chapman's to handle her cremation. That's how Guy and Dathan got away with the charade for so long of Guy being the hands on mortician in the place when, in fact, Dathan did the real work that involved the bodies, everything from accounting for their gold teeth and jewelry to getting them dressed for their final farewells. And his wife, Rebecca, that pretty little thing, was a third-generation mortician and did the embalming. Even in this day and age, for white southerners of the old school, to know dark-skinned hands had wrestled Grandpa's Mason ring from his gnarled finger, sealed shut the eyes of Great Aunt Celia, or worst of all from an Old South point of view, touched Mama's naked body, might have rocked this fine old family business to its very foundations. Luckily, steadfast Chapman people didn't ask who did that kind of thing, as long as a Chapman, even one as reluctant and ill suited to the role as Guy, greeted them at the door, showed them into the office, expressed sympathy for their loss and helped them pick out the proper caskets and bereavement accessories.

I stood and listened again for the sounds of the bright young staff that Dathan had brought in. Nothing. The quiet click of someone at the computer processing all the mandatory paperwork. Nope. Even the creak of someone walking around upstairs in the sleeping quarters. You could have heard a pin drop.

The heavy door between the kitchen and the butler's pantry drew me across the room. Standing there, I could visualize the layout of the entire first floor, the chapel—the office, the three viewing parlors, the large foyer with a large pedestal for the guest book and smaller one for the display of urns. Everything would be dark, even on the sunniest of days, and the walnut paneling and carpet in a shade they called "evergreen" did nothing to lighten the surroundings or the mood.

I inched toward the door with cautious, precise steps. If anyone had seen me, I suspect I might have looked as if I half expected to step in something wet and squishy at any moment.

I took a long, steadying breath. The place smelled…musty. As always.

Antiseptic. Also the norm.

And perfumed—recently sprayed with something meant to suggest roses.

I wrinkled my nose. All together the mingling of odors left me anxious and shimmering with a sensation I couldn't name.

I glanced at the table and noticed a pair of discarded latex gloves. By them, an opened packet of antacid. No glass. But there was a teakettle sitting a wee bit askew atop a cheery-red-and-yellow oven mitt.

Ooky.

That was what I felt.

My whole life I have watched *The Addams Family.* Sung the theme song and snapped my fingers in all the right places but I never really appreciated that term, *ooky,* until this very moment.

"What was that?" A voice carried from the other side of the door.

No more than a few flutters that might have been footsteps came in answer. Then a sound not decisive enough to be *clunk* and too brief to be a *clatter.* A click. Clearly a click. With all the finality of metal against metal.

This was ooky. Definitely ooky.

I licked my lips, then curled my fingers around the doorknob. The chilly brass pressed into my damp palm. This was the point in slasher movies where I'd turn ugly on the characters and start rooting for the bad guys to hack them to bits just to keep that level of helpless stupidity out of the gene pool.

"Don't open the door, you idiot!" I'd want to scream at the movie screen. "Run!"

Addams Family. Slasher films. Too much child of the media there, I gave myself a mental scolding. I might have grown up on that stuff, but it had only entertained me, not formed me. It did not define me. I had role models bolder, smarter, sassier than anything Hollywood could concoct. I was a George woman, after all. I need only ask myself, "What would Mama do?"

Or Nana Abbra.

Or my aunts.

Or…

I raised my head and looked around me.

"Or Bess," I whispered.

Just saying her name aloud here in this place where Dathan and Rebecca had prepared her body, the place where twenty years earlier I had first learned she had run away with Guy, I could almost feel her presence.

Bess would not have hesitated. She never did. Neither did I, generally.

You are a coward, Charma Deane Parker. You rush off and get yourself hip deep into every cause that you can find, but deep down you are terrified of making one wrong move. And you're doubly terrified of accepting that sometimes people you love will make wrong moves, sometimes by mistake and sometimes by design. Because of that, you can't move at all.

Sterling's accusation had played through my head more than once on the mad dash over here, and now it all but nailed my flip-flops to the floorboards.

"Shiiiit," I whispered, stretching it out to an extra third syllable for emphasis.

I was in Guy's place of business and his home, and something was up. What was I supposed to do—get spooked and run off? If I did that, I'd never know what was going on.

"Screw Sterling," I muttered, and promptly wished I'd come up with another fate to wish on my new housemate. I pressed my lips together. "What does he know about me? What the hell does he know about anything?"

I said it out loud just in case Bess really was here and might want to give me an answer. None came, so I had to make the decision on my own.

Armed with only my wits and the burning desire to get myself stuck into just about everything concerning everyone I had ever known, I turned the knob and flung open the door.

"What the—" Dathan Daniels' large hand gripped his shoulder where the door had swung into him. The darkness of his skin and warmth of his gleaming gold wedding band made an odd contrast to the stark whiteness of his customary starched white shirt. "Oh. Oh, hello, ma'am."

In the dim light of the confined space between the living quarters and mortuary proper, I couldn't see the young man's features, but I didn't have to. They were always guarded, except in the company of his wife and the co-workers he had personally hired. Such was life in a small town when you carried a big secret.

"Sorry if I startled you, Dathan. And how many times do I have to ask you? Please, call me..."

"Charma Deane Parker, you sorry little slacker ho." Loyal Chapman had always held that if I had truly applied myself, I could have been one of the all time greatest sluts and seducers of southern men ever to come out of Orla and the surrounding counties.

Taking second place only to him.

"Promise me you are not really going to squander your potential on my brother, *again*." He folded me into a fleshy embrace.

I patted the back of his crumpled gray suit jacket.

He pulled away, and his dark tie clung to my bare arm. "Sorry," he said, his sausagelike fingers working over the knot and pressing down a wayward wrinkle in the black-and-maroon fabric. "Damned cheap loaner. I left town in such a hurry that I didn't have time to pack a proper one."

If Blanche DuBois had been a balding middle-aged mortician, she would have been Loyal Chapman—iron-willed frailty, badly lit deception and all.

Yes, Loyal was gay. But not *fabulously* gay, not in the style of the contemporary stereotype. He looked more gender ambivalent optometrist than queer eye, though no one would ever mistake him for a bubba or a good ol' boy.

Mama and the aunts always referred to him in hushed tones

as "genteel" and "a lovely man who certainly knows how to treat his mother."

That's how most folks around town thought of him. A throwback to a sweeter time, a true gentleman and let's face it, someone about whom they did not want to know too much. He was a mortician, after all, and a damned fine one. The very nature of his work was to do things that nobody wanted to hear about. He was the fellow in town entrusted with everyone's skeletons, real and the kind best hidden in closets, so who were they to begrudge him a few of his own skeletons—or closets?

No, if a man kept his private life private, did his job well and was kind to his mama, most people would overlook just about anything. Even in a last-notch-between-redemption-and-damnation-on-the-Bible Belt bit of Arkansas like Orla.

Especially in Orla, where nobody wanted to upset Loyal and Guy's mother by discussing anything as awkward and ugly as the truth about her baby. To her dying day, Maimie Rose Chapman told people, "I don't know why some girl doesn't snap up my Loyal and have a dozen babies with him. He'd make such pretty babies with the right girl, don't you think?"

To which any person who had been raised properly would reply, "But, Miz Chapman, *who* in this town is good enough for your boy?"

Miz Chapman would nod her agreement, and even the best of Baptists could walk away relieved that they had neither had to lie nor lay waste to a frail old lady's last delusions.

No such pretenses went on with Mr. Chapman the elder, who knew both his sons for what they were and treated them both with equal indifference. Perhaps when you spend your days divesting your neighbors of their clothing, their gold fillings and their essential bodily fluids, it is hard to stay impressed with the vanities of the living, even of your own flesh and blood.

"I think you look real nice, Loyal." I glanced a kiss off his sweat-dampened cheek.

"I think you're the best liar in all of Arkansas." He kissed me, too, except he missed and left a sweat smudge on my earlobe that made me shiver.

"*I* thought you said you locked all the doors." Guy came in and scowled first at me, then at Dathan.

"I'll take care of it." Dathan slipped into the kitchen and back again with the kind of lightning-speed discretion I've only seen practiced by career morticians and highly compensated mistresses.

"Now no more trash can blow in," I said to the man I was going to finally marry…someday…maybe.

Loyal headed into the dark-wood-paneled front lobby of the old funeral home.

"It's not trash I'm worried about, Charma." Guy stood against the door. His eyes narrowed down to a laser beam death ray on his brother. "It's trouble."

Guy nabbed me by the wrist and planted a greeting kiss on my temple. No sweat, no smudge.

I brushed his cheek with my fingertips, then turned his head to force his gaze to meet mine. "You used to consider *me* trouble."

He smiled more with his eyes than his lips. Fine by me. I loved those eyes and I had plans for those lips.

Before that still small voice—and I don't mean God—could tell me I was trying to erase the feel of Sterling's mouth on mine, trying to chase away any doubts that brief incident on the porch had aroused, I decided to do a little arousing of my own.

"Kissing? In the funeral parlor? Isn't that bad luck?" Loyal asked Dathan. "Or worse, *bad manners?*"

"You're a hell of a one to talk about bad manners, Loyal." Dathan took a tone I had never heard him use with anyone. Hard. Angry. Threatening. "Especially to someone who found you and a certain ex-employee playing strip hide-and-go-seek in the casket room and chapel."

"Shitfire, Loyal!" I couldn't help it—that pulled me right out of the moment with the man I loved. I blinked and gripped Guy's sleeve in one hand. "Not the chapel!"

"We didn't do the actual deed in there," Loyal said as he turned toward us, his face pleasant as a church lady at a basement potluck dinner asking if we wanted more sweet tea or perhaps a slice of pie. "But we had to include the chapel because it has all the best hiding places. Not to mention the accoutrements."

Dathan shook his head and warned me, "You don't want to hear this."

"Velvet drapes." He crossed his wrists. "Gold rope tie backs. Tassels."

"Don't say another word." Guy shut his eyes.

Just standing next to him, I could feel his jaw clamping down so tight I thought he might just crack a molar.

"We have enough to handle keeping anything else gruesome or unlawful from happening here today. I'd rather do without thinking about what's gone on here in the past that might have cost us our license and our reputation, thank you."

"Gruesome and unlawful?" I thought of the latex gloves, the strange smell, the silence. I glanced at the visitation parlor, then toward the heavy front door kept in perpetual shadow by the porch and the dark awning over the walkway. I twisted Guy's cotton shirt in my hand. "What the hell is going on?"

"The embalmer," Loyal said.

I cocked my head. "*Your* embalmer?" I was damn sure he didn't mean the current embalmer, Dathan's wife.

He held his hands up as if he were doing nothing more significant than refusing a refill of his coffee. "Not anymore."

"What happened?"

"Oh, you know, honey, *men!*" He rolled his eyes.

I narrowed mine.

He heaved a sigh and looked away, clearly feeding me a line meant to obscure more than enlighten me. "Well, he never was any damned good, was he? Y'all knew that. I should have suspected as much when he had me take out all kinds of loans and things against the business. Once we'd gone through all that money and had to resort to what I believed to be honest work? Well, then his true colors showed, and they were…not pretty."

Had to resort to what Loyal *believed* to be honest work? What was that all about? I wondered.

"Don't ask too many questions, Charma." Guy gave his brother a look that suggested Loyal might have already said too much. "There's a lot more at stake here than a lover's quarrel."

"Lover? Why, Guy, that's the first time you've ever referred to one of my partners as my lover. Your influence, Charma?"

"Yeah, she's turned him into a real pussycat." Dathan stole a glance out the front window.

"No." Loyal sank down to sit on the stairs directly facing the huge front doors. "Of course. I should have realized it was *you* who had that effect on him, Dathan."

The young man took a step backward and almost knocked over an urn. "Hey, I never…don't drag me into your family situation."

"*Drag* being the operative word?" Loyal gave an uncharacteristic flourish with his hand, then sneered at both men. "I just meant that after a lifetime as an educated, upper-middle-class white American straight male, my brother has finally learned what it is to have to hide who he really is. He suddenly knows what it means to never let his guard down, to always wonder when people might discover his deceit and turn on him just for being himself."

There was no bitterness in Loyal's words, but an unkind, cutting edge. And hurt. Always hurt from one brother to the other, always the unspoken accusation that one had gotten the only thing either of them craved, their father's respect and love. Loyal assumed Guy had it by doing nothing more than following his natural sexual preference. Guy had always assumed Loyal had earned a place in the old man's heart by following in their father's footsteps and doing it so well. They were both wrong and they both knew it, but years and years of jealousy had settled like dust into every exchange between the brothers, and this one was no different.

"My brother *is* changed. A little. We can thank your presence in our family's funeral parlor for that, *Mr. Daniels.*"

He intended the formal use of mister and the surname as a high compliment, and Dathan, young as he was, understood that and accepted it with humble grace and a nod of his head.

Guy did not take it so nobly. "We are still potentially in some deep, deep shit here, Loyal."

"Why?" I asked.

"I got a letter." Loyal, framed by the sweep of the green-carpeted stairway, looked the very portrait of an old-style son of a fine southern family. Then he pounded his plump fist to his chest and let out a window-rattling belch.

"What did you do? *Eat* the letter?" I asked.

With his fingers pressed to his lips, I expected a mortified apology from the man, but instead he wiped the corner of his mouth and said, "Finally. And no, I didn't eat the letter, I ate the leftover pancakes Guy brought home. I hope you didn't overdo on those, Charma. They are time bombs."

I put my hand to my stomach and wondered if the heaviness I'd felt all day—not to mention my strange behavior, from sensing Bess nearby to kissing Sterling—could be blamed on breakfast.

"And the letter?" Loyal's upper body jerked slightly, with a less volatile burp than before. "That might as well have been a letter *bomb!* Let me tell you."

"*Don't* tell her. What she doesn't know…"

Won't hurt her.

The man had kept too much from me over the years to dare finish that thought.

"Leave her out of this. No details. No sharing." Guy looked at Dathan, then Loyal, but not at me. "She can't be held accountable if she doesn't know what's going on."

"Oh, please, we're in Orla. *Nobody* knows what's going on, but that never stopped anybody from putting somebody in a world of hurt over it."

All three men looked at me, and I could tell they wanted to agree with me but weren't sure what I had actually said.

"Oh, hell, just tell me," I demanded.

Guy held up his hand in surrender.

Loyal sighed. "I got a letter from the embalmer saying he was being investigated by the authorities."

"What authorities?"

"City. County. State." Dathan's shoulders hunched up, his face tensed. "Sons of the Confederacy. Nation of Islam. Red Hat Society."

"Shit," I murmured, then looked at Loyal, all big eyes and disbelief. "I know some of those Red Hat ladies, they will cut you."

"He's not joking, Charma." Guy placed his hand on the back of my neck.

I took a breath, not a deep one, but as much as I could, and put my hand to my throat. "What the hell is going on?"

"I got this letter," Loyal began again.

"So I heard. Maybe you should save us all a lot of time and just let me read the damn thing."

"You can't read it." Loyal raised his hands and wriggled his fingers. "Fingerprints."

"*Fingerprints?* What about some footprints on your saggy old butt?" I wiggled my toes in my truly awful footwear.

"She could wear the gloves," Loyal suggested.

"No. No gloves. No steaming it open again. No spraying the envelope with disinfectant to cover up the scent of your perfume." Guy slashed his hand through the air as he laid down the law. "I don't give a damn if you want to play this out for all the drama you can, Loyal. We are not involving Charma."

The gloves, the smell, the unlocked door, the silence to try to make it seem that no one was home. They wanted it to appear that no one had been able to pick up the mail with the mysterious letter, so no one could… "What are y'all hiding from, exactly?"

"The embalmer," Loyal said, as if I was immeasurably stupid for having to ask.

"Why?" I asked, and again the look came at me. So I turned to Guy and repeated myself. "Why?"

"A couple months ago, after Loyal and his friend went through all the money they took from Chapman and Son's…" Guy shot his brother a searing look.

Loyal gave a lukewarm smile in return.

"…they decided they could get work in a new place, running a mortuary for a man they met on the Internet."

"We did not meet him on the Internet. We met him at AA, where I was just going to provide support and because the Al Anon meeting down the hall had got too catty for words." Loyal rolled his eyes. "Some people think they are so superior just because they've never used their loved one's one month sobriety chip key chain as a cocktail marker."

"Your embalmer was an alcoholic?" I asked Loyal.

"Yeah," Dathan answered for him. "A practicing alcoholic with a criminal record and people in this town felt better about him touching their departed loved ones than me or my wife."

"Anyway, we *met* him at AA," Loyal went on. "We *checked him out* on the Internet, and everything seemed on the up-and-up. In fact the whole time I worked there, everything seemed pretty normal."

"Normal for a couple of embezzling queer undertakers putting their lives in the hands of a man they met at a place where you promise to keep your true identity from everyone." Dathan scrubbed his hand over his shaved head.

"Anything can look bad if you cast it in a harsh light," Loyal protested, and in a look I could tell he hadn't had any part in whatever skullduggery had taken place. Like most people in the town where we had been raised, he believed what he wanted to believe, knew only what he needed to know to keep the world as he wanted.

"This doesn't just *look* bad, Loyal. This *is* bad." Guy checked out the window again. "And if we aren't careful, this could destroy everything Dathan and I have worked so hard to build this past year."

I tried to put myself in Guy's shoes, which I would have preferred to the ones I had on, hands down. "That's why you didn't mention to me that Loyal had come home?"

"This is no longer Loyal's home," Guy and Dathan both said at the same time.

"I was not involved in any of this." Loyal stood. "Like Guy, I was just the front man there."

"I thought you were pretty much a back door man," Guy muttered.

"Don't be crude." I elbowed Guy in the ribs, but he anticipated the movement, caught my arm and kissed my neck quick and light.

"Guy and I, whether he wants to admit it or not, serve the same function," Loyal explained. "I know the business inside and out, the paperwork, the way to make a sale without seeming callous, to give comfort. I have the connections, all that stuff here in Orla, but beyond this place, all that skill and influence fell off a bit."

"Influence I'll spot you, but skill?" Dathan folded his arms.

"Handling the bereaved is a skill," Loyal argued, then cast a cool eye on the younger, buffer, better mortician in the room. "So is lying to them about who you are and what you do."

Dathan swallowed hard enough to make his Adam's apple more prominent.

"Anyway, since I left Orla and Guy came here, we have lived oddly parallel working lives. Like him, instead of the force behind the funeral business, I became just the guy who puts his best face forward. No more a part of the actual business than the hostess who seats you at Kaye and Buddy Mon's Island Supper Club."

"Minus the great hair," I said, thinking of Kaye, who owned a salon across the street from the only supper club within thirty miles of Orla. One of the perks she offered her hostesses was free hair care. Buddy Mon offered them other things that they mostly refused, but you could tell the ones who didn't by their bad perms and frost jobs from hell.

"Minus *all* the hair for me." Loyal ran his hand through the limp, thinning dark strands on his head. "But the point is, if you get a bellyache from a bad shrimp cocktail there, you blame Kaye or Buddy Mon or whatever high school dropout they have behind the counter. You don't blame the hair or the hostess."

Guy shook his head. "Unfortunately, where the law is concerned…"

"The law?" This time *I* looked out the window, sure I'd see a police cruiser pull up any second now. "You three don't actually think you can pretend not to be home and the police will just go away and give up?" I reached for my purse, then recalled I'd left it in the kitchen. I took a step in that direction. "Maybe I should call Sterling."

"No." Guy held me in place. "We don't need to get Skippy the Wonder Lawyer involved. And we're not stupid enough to think

we can elude the police, much less the feds and the Red Hat
Ladies, by just pretending we're not home while we try to think
of what to do next."

"Then why are you—"

"Can I tell her that much?" Loyal asked.

Guy shut his eyes and nodded.

"We're trying to avoid Garrett."

"Who?"

"The embalmer," Dathan said. "You didn't know him?"

"I made it a practice to avoid Chapman's this past couple years
until…" I looked at Guy and decided not to bring up the deaths
in my family and remind them that I still had to collect Mama's
ashes. "Why are you avoiding the embalmer?"

"Because besides the letter, we got an e-mail, and then a fax with
all the proper state paperwork asking us to take delivery of—"

Guy cleared his throat and held his hand up. "She doesn't need
to know."

"But I *want* to know," I protested.

"Trust me, you don't."

Dathan shook his head to underscore Guy's assessment.

"We're just trying to find a way to stay clear of anything connected with Garrett and my former employers." Loyal spoke
slowly, seeming to choose every word from a jumbled box of
possible verbs, nouns and modifiers. More than once he paused
and glanced at Guy for the go ahead as he pressed on with his tale.
"We figure if he drives all the way over here to deliver…"

Again Dathan shook his head.

I wanted to scream at them, *What?* Deliver what? Drugs? Phony
death records? A pizza?

"My idea is that if he comes to make this delivery, but he can't
because we're not here to receive it and don't seem to have gotten
his letter, he'll go back to…where he came from. I know him, he

isn't the type to work hard for anything. He'll think we're all out on business and won't stick around, and we'll finally be shed of him."

"There. Now you know everything you need to know." Guy put up his hand to keep his brother from saying more.

"I don't know squat."

"Exactly." Guy brushed back my hair, then applied gentle pressure between my shoulder blades to head me toward the kitchen. "Now, just go before anyone says anything else and suddenly you have information that might cause the police to want to speak with you because they think you're a potential witness...or a victim."

My spine went rigid. I looked back over my shoulder at the three men.

Loyal sort of winced sweetly.

Guy gave me another nudge.

Dathan pleaded with me first with his eyes and then with the simple words "Please, just go on now, Miz...Charma Deane."

That did it. I nodded and gave Guy's forearm a squeeze. "I'll call you later."

I wanted to say more, about how I wished this police business they were anticipating wouldn't ruin Dathan's chances of finally, openly running Chapman and Son's and maybe tell Loyal it was good to see him again, and it would all work out but knew it wouldn't ring true. These three men obviously believed that they stood to lose everything, and no amount of feminine platitudes would make that go away.

I slipped into the kitchen, collected my things and headed out the door, checking to make sure it had locked behind me.

Stealth was called for here, but also speed. I had to get going before anyone saw me and could say so. One thing about the big gold hearse—it sure made it hard to skulk around unnoticed. I hopped in, stuck the key in the ignition and revved off in reverse.

Thump.

My heart snagged high in my throat.

What had I just hit? I was out of the driver's seat in mere seconds, my hasty getaway thwarted, I thought.

But there was nothing.

Nothing in the road.

Nothing under the tires.

Nothing to do but get back in and drive like hell.

I got in, but I did not drive.

One glance in the rearview mirror and suddenly I knew exactly what the embalmer wanted to deliver. And despite all their machinations to foil his efforts, Garrett had found the perfect place to leave the goods.

❧ CHAPTER NINE

"A corpse?" I couldn't get out of that hearse fast enough, and it seemed easiest to head straight for the front door. Knowing they wouldn't answer if I just knocked, I hammered on the door, then bent to speak through the brass mail slot to make sure the guys understood the immediacy of the situation. "A corpse? That's what your friend wanted to deliver to you?"

"Well, hell, Charma Deane, I am a mortician and this is a funeral home—what the hell did you think we were hiding from? A candygram?" Guy swung the door open and had me by the hand, yanking me inside.

"Shh." Loyal pushed against the door with his full weight and clicked the lock in place. "Charma, honey, don't get yourself worked up over—"

"Over a corpse? Don't get myself worked up over a corpse?" I stumbled forward into the foyer.

"Would you stop saying *corpse?*" Smooth as any dance move, Guy swept me along into the office. A spin. A side step. He only lacked a cha-cha-cha to complete the effect, and suddenly my bottom plunked down on the leather cushion of a straight-backed chair.

All three men stared straight at me.

I turned to Loyal first, because he seemed the most likely to spew forth a full confession if pressed even in the slightest. "This embalmer friend of yours wanted to deliver a corpse?"

"He's no friend of mine." Loyal patted my leg as if I was the one who had things all confused and turned around. "That was my first mistake, I think. We should have been better friends before we started making big plans together."

"Friendship before embezzlement, always a good idea," Guy muttered.

"Both of you just shut up." I demonstrated my expectations by pinching my thumbs and fingers together. "And tell me what's going on."

Dathan chuckled.

Guy rubbed his forehead. "Charma, don't play guessing games about this."

"*Guessing* games?" Could the man be *that* clueless? "Do you really think I would run in here flushed and blithering about bodies as a ploy to try to assuage my morbid curiosity?"

His expression confirmed what he did not say.

"Okay, you have a point. I would do exactly that kind of thing if I got it in my head it was the only way to ferret out an acceptable explanation for what's going on here, but—"

He bent at the knees and put both hands on the arms of my chair. "Just leave it be and walk away, Charma Deane."

"Walk away?" I leaned forward until our noses almost touched, just to make sure he got the message that I was not fooling around here. "I may *have* to walk, because right now my car is occupied."

He did not flinch or wince or back down so much as a hairbreadth, just asked, with quiet determination, "By?"

"You tell me." I pointed toward the back of the house to mean the alley where I'd left my hearse. "I'm usually the curious sort, but even I think twice about unzipping an abandoned body bag."

Guy stood. He swore, but with his teeth so clenched that even with my own extensive filthy vocabulary I wasn't exactly sure what curse he'd used. I didn't care; given the circumstances, I totally agreed with him.

"What do we do?" Dathan had gone around behind the desk and began flipping through stacks of paperwork tucked neatly into file folders.

"What can we do?" Guy shook his head. He rubbed the heel of his hand over against his temple, then let out a weary sigh. "We have to call the police and let them handle it."

"We can't have the police come here! We'll have to show them the transfer papers for the body that we were faxed earlier. They will recognize the name of my former employers on the cover sheet." Loyal turned to me to make the case. "The second I saw that name, and of course I knew what the papers were, I knew they wanted us to accept a body. A John Doe, or so they say, but after what they did and Garrett knowing it all and playing me for a fool by keeping me in the dark…"

"Loyal, focus," I commanded.

"They will investigate us. They'll have to, just to put people's minds at ease. There will be scandal!" Loyal said "scandal" all hushed and hissy. "And you know this town, honey, just the hint of scandal and it's all over but the vilification."

"Scandal," I whispered to myself, trying to take it all in.

"Scandal," Dathan echoed softly, finally working free a file from the stack. He slapped it onto the center of the wide cherry desktop and flicked it open to show newspaper clippings inside.

I could not read the words, but the photo on the top story was of uniformed men gathered around what looked like an open grave.

"Not necessarily." Guy held his hands out. His eyes shifted back and forth as if he were scanning every info bank at his disposal for some way to crawl out of this manure barrel smelling like a rose, or at least as close as the artificial floral scent preferred by Loyal.

"Dathan and I haven't actually done anything wrong."

Clearly to get his rosy ending, he might have to throw his brother into the barrel and hold him there to take the shit for everyone.

"Neither have I." Loyal curved one hand over the other and rested his mouth on his knuckles. It was a pose I remembered from childhood when kids would tease and taunt him.

It clawed at my heart then and it still did all these years later. Loyal was just a big kid bullied by the world. When he was young, he could run home to the mortuary where he created his own world, where he was good at something and good *for* something. And, at least, his mother loved him. But now that was all gone, and not even his brother seemed to care what became of him.

"I didn't do anything wrong," he said softly into his hand again.

Guy studied his brother but did not contradict him.

I don't know what I expected. That Guy would go to Loyal and tell him they'd work it through together? Not in this universe.

I wanted to get up and go to Loyal, but what would I say to make a difference? He didn't care if I loved him or not. I loved everyone. It was only the love he could never win that he thought would save him. And it dawned on me in thinking about that, that until he gave up that impossible goal, he would never ever really be happy. The same for Guy.

I felt as helpless as Loyal looked.

"I just trusted the wrong man." Loyal drew his shoulders back at last. "Fire and damnation, y'all, I am *not* the only person in this room guilty of *that* sin."

Nobody said a word to that. Nobody looked anybody in the eye.

The leather cushion under me sighed as I repositioned my fanny, and for a few seconds that was the only sound in the room.

Finally, Dathan closed the file in front of him. "You make the call, Guy. I'll grab a gurney and collect the body. That way Charma can be long gone before the police arrive."

"You're not seriously going to—"

"Just like that?" I cut Loyal off. "You expect me just to drive off and leave all this unresolved?"

"There's nothing to resolve," Guy muttered. "You have no part in this. You should go home now, and I'll call you later with the details."

This had proved to be one hell of a day. I had kissed a man I both loved and despised, made a much closer acquaintance with a dead person than I had planned for and I had gotten engaged to a total stranger.

"You're kidding, right?" I asked.

Guy reached for the phone.

"Wait." Loyal snapped down the bar with two fingers. "You may not have broken any laws, but you have lied and deceived people with the charade that Dathan drives the hearse, gets the bodies and someone else—I don't know, they don't honestly think it's *you,* do they?"

Guy shook his head. "I don't know. No one ever asks. I mean, shit, Loyal you've been in the business longer than me. Do people usually ask who is doing the actual hands on embalming?"

"No. No, never. That's why in this business reputation is everything. They don't want to ask that stuff, they want to believe they can trust you. Like I said, you didn't break any laws, but you can't stand here and say you never tampered with that trust."

In the small, small world that was Orla, Arkansas, people were pleased enough to pretend that Loyal never married because he couldn't find the right girl. They were proud enough to do business with Chapman's and Son's only because they could still deal directly with one of the sons. They were petty enough to rather have believed the George women ran a whorehouse than admit that too many women in town needed a place to hide from abusive men. In Orla, appearances ruled.

"You make that call and we will instantly be connected to a mortuary that defrauded its clients. Even if the cops don't investigate us, how long do you think it will be before the newspaper does? Or a TV station following the trail? Or just plain folks around town who will suddenly begin asking all those questions nobody ever asked before?"

Guy looked at Dathan.

The young man looked at his own hands.

"It will be the end for Chapman and Son," Loyal went on. "The end of everything Dad built, of everything I worked most of my life to preserve. Not to mention make every sacrifice of this past year of your life, Guy, meaningless."

"We haven't done anything wrong." Dathan's dark eyes blinked in slow, measured calm. "No reason to pick today to start, not with a body working up a nice stench in a hot hearse a few yards outside our doors."

I stood. "You cannot make a huge dramatic—and frankly icky and disturbing—statement like that and think I will just walk out and mind my own beeswax now."

Loyal relinquished his hold on the phone and moved around to stand by my side. "You're such a goddess, Charma Deane."

"Yeah, the Goddess of Beeswax." Guy held the receiver to his ear for a second, then began punching in the number for the police. "Go tend your hive."

He had hit all but the last button when I threw out my shoulders to command his attention. "Do you want your ring back? Because if you are under the impression that you can speak to me that way, then maybe we had better just part right now and pretend we never even met."

My pulse measured out the beats he seemed to need to make up his mind about that. One. Two. Three. Fo-o-u-r.

"Is this the way it's going to be?" He hung up the phone.

I respectfully withheld my victory dance.

He sat on the edge of the desk, his head down but his eyes on me. "Every time I do something you don't like, you plan to threaten to break up with me?"

"Pretty much." I came to him and leaned against him thigh to thigh. "Until we're married. Then I'll have whole new avenues for threat making."

"I can hardly wait," he muttered even as he kissed my forehead.

Damn, I loved this man. Almost enough to tell him to run like hell and get as far away from this mess of a person he'd promised to marry as possible. To take the dead body with him if he must, but just get the hell out. But like that heroine in the slasher movie and me, Guy Chapman didn't have it in him to turn his back on a potentially life-shaking adventure.

I put my back against my beloved's chest and focused on his brother. "Now, Loyal, tell the Goddess of Beeswax what exactly is going on."

He didn't have to say much. The newspaper clippings told of wrongdoing at a mortuary halfway across the state, of new graves dug on top of hundred-year-old plots, of tests finding multiple DNA samples in the ashes of cremated loved ones and the funeral home suspect of pocketing kickbacks and overcharges. It was heart rending.

I thought of Mama's ashes kept here with such loving care, even more than I had shown them. And of Bess's funeral and burial in our family plot in the place where my mother should have been put to rest.

Her funeral had gone so far to introduce people to the idea of accepting Dathan as more than just "the man who drives the hearse." People my age and younger weren't so much the problem, but then, they weren't the ones whose dying wishes and prejudices had to be considered, were they?

"Guy will fare the best," his younger brother said with a sigh, sinking into the chair where I had been seated. "He has an actual skill that extends outside the burying business. Dathan and I, it's all we know."

"He's right. Guy can just go back to work. It's not like that hasn't been his goal all along." Dathan leaned back in the chair behind the desk and propped his ankle across his knee.

"Like hell I can. I'm fifty years old, with a two-year gap in my résumé. I am not going to just dance my way back into a top-tier sales job."

Loyal smiled at his brother. "So you'll marry the first unsuspecting virgin to throw herself on your volcano of love and move out to the Aunt Farm and turn it into a bed-and-breakfast or…"

"First, I may be a failed whore, but I am hardly a virgin, and volcano might be a bit—"

"Charma, please." Guy laid his forehead against my shoulder.

"Anyway, Sterling won't allow it."

"To hell with lawyer-boy. *I* won't live in another man's house, especially not one who got that house *not* by his own hard work but by marrying Bess."

What did that mean? Was he jealous of Bess and Sterling? Self-doubt colored my tone when I chimed in with my opinion. "Yeah, the sleazy dog, inheriting a house through love and marriage when he should have come to it the old-fashioned way—waiting for his parents to die."

"Hey, I earned my part of this house and this business," Guy said.

"Me, too," Loyal added.

"Is this getting us anywhere?" Dathan asked.

"I have to make that phone call." Guy pushed me away, gently but still the sudden absence of him had a jarring effect.

"I'll go collect the body." Dathan stood.

"I'll go back to clearing things out around here. You don't expect there'd be much use in having a yard sale to help keep us from total bankruptcy, do you?"

"That's it?" I watched in total disbelief. "Y'all are just going to roll over and give up?"

"I don't call doing the right thing giving up, Charma, honey." Guy was at the phone again.

These men were the sorriest excuse for schemers I had ever come across. In fact, they were so poor at it, I had to wonder now how many people in town actually knew exactly what they had been up to all along, with Guy just putting on a front. Probably half the town knew everything and the rest suspected it, and only these clowns thought they had everyone fooled. If they did, that meant the town wanted to be fooled. They just needed someone from this end to keep up the pretense.

"What if there was a way to do the right thing and not give up?" In that split second I had asked myself again, what would Mama do? Or Bess?

Well, Bess would have pulled the body out by its feet and left it lying in the alley for somebody else to deal with. But Mama? Mama was never afraid to take the law into her own hands, and since so many local officials found themselves in her debt for one thing or another, she could well afford to do so.

I didn't have my mother's connections or reputation, but I did have her name and her nerve. And my family.

Your family. I swear if one of you guys showed up at that house with

a corpse and no alibi, the others would help you make up a story about
how you'd bought the car used and forgot to check the trunk for bodies.

In Orla appearances ruled, and nobody could pull off the appearance of finding a dead body out of the blue like a George. I had to do this. In fact, I was the only person here who could. "What if I just drive that body over to the station and turn it in?"

"Charma, we are not talking about a lost wallet here." Guy sounded gruff and forbidding, but he did stop punching numbers on the phone pad.

"But if I take it over *there,* away from *here,* and you all never even set eyes on it, then—"

"Then you might just be considered an accessory to the crime." Dathan folded his arms.

But Guy hung up the phone.

"Crime?" I made a rude sound. What a bunch of amateurs. "No one said anything about crime. So far all the incidents have been in *interring* bodies, not in accepting them for preparation. Right?"

They exchanged glances, head nods and muttered affirmatives.

"Unless…" Suddenly I wondered if the embalmer was a mob nickname, not an occupation. "Should I be asking y'all how my passenger died?"

"Only if you want to collect a new death story for Fawnie and Shug." Guy laughed, a little, but enough to prop up my wavering resolve.

"Oh, I love those girls." Loyal relaxed enough to sit again. "How are they doing? Tell them to invite me out to tea soon, because I sure do have some great new stories to tell about…"

"Loyal." Guy slashed his finger across his throat.

Myself, I'd have gone for the tick-a-lock gesture, the pretending to seal your closed lips with an invisible key, but Guy really seemed to want to drive the point home. End of conversation.

"Charma, we only have a basic transfer form, with the rest to accompany the body, we assume. I mean, these people aren't in trouble for following the rules too closely or caring too much about those in their care. We could be getting into anything, or it could all be totally on the up-and-up. But just the whiff of impropriety will bring speculation and people sniffing around..."

"Please don't say whiff and sniffing around when, even as we speak, I have a dead person potentially stinking up my only means of transportation."

Guy put his hand on my back. "Are you sure you want to get involved?"

"If you're involved, I'm involved. That's what this means." I held up my left hand and rolled it slightly to make my ring sparkle in the light.

"No, *this* means you have more heart than sense." He kissed my raised hand. "Go get yourself a glass of water, then we'll call the police."

"Water, my ass. It'll take something a lot more substantial than water to entice me to sit on my butt and watch while people I care about lose everything."

"Nothing more to be done, Charma," Dathan said.

"Bullshit." I grabbed my keys out of my purse and took off toward the front door.

"But what if they detain you?" Guy strode along beside me, matching me flip for flop.

"I live under the same roof as a pretty damned good lawyer." It would cost me dearly to buy Sterling's help, but there was nothing else to be done. "If the need arises, he will bail me out. Please, let me do this for you, Guy." I put my hand to his cheek, then looked beyond him to Loyal and Dathan standing in the office doorway. "Let me do this for all of you."

And it was done. Just that easy. Just as easy as jumping off the dock into the water and going under.

"Okay, Mr. Corpse," I told whoever was stretched out in the black bag in the back of my hearse. "Let's you and me go for a little ride."

I chatted with him—or her—the whole way over, not forgetting my manners and thanking him—or her—more than once for not actually stinking up my ride too much.

And then we reached the low white building with the enormous brick sign proclaiming it the office of the Orla police. I cut the engine. I took a breath. I stole one last peek in the rearview mirror and said to my charge, "Oh, and by the way, when you reach your final destination, would you mind putting in a word with…"

God?

No, I had never felt the need of a go-between between me and the Almighty. What I needed was a man-made miracle, or rather a woman-made one. "Would you mind gathering up the women of family who have gone on before me and telling them I could use a little help?"

❧ CHAPTER TEN

Sterling came down to the police station to save my sorry ass for hauling that poor deceased stranger to the station's steps. As I suspected, it didn't take much lawyering to get me off the hook with local law enforcement at said station. That justified things in my mind since my actions had saved Loyal's sorry—by extension Guy's and Dathan's not-so-sorry—asses.

Sterling didn't know about that last part, because being a better lawyer than he had been a friend, he didn't ask. But afterward, back at the house, in his as-yet-unpacked and unproductive office space and despite the very little effort it took to square things for me, he laid down his terms. He wanted his pound of flesh, as it were, for all that ass-saving.

"No turning this place into a bed-and-breakfast. No women's sanctuary. No multigenerational Kennedy-esque compound." He shoved a piece of paper across a compact cardboard box marked B. Halloway-Mayhouse, Personal in Guy's handwriting. "No negotiations."

I'd rather he'd have taken that pound out of my ass, even if it had meant I'd sit funny for the rest of my life. But I signed my name at the bottom of the page and the deal was done.

Fawnie and Shug and I could continue to live in the place my grandfather had built to house generations of Georges, the place where I had grown up, where every event of any significance in our family life had taken place. We could live here, basically as Sterling's guests. The rest of the family, including Minnie, Bess's brothers and any of our offspring, were welcome for holidays, summer visits and short emergency stays. He'd thrown that last part in because even he didn't have the heart to toss skinny little Abby out, and Johnny, well, he saw it as some kind of olive branch to let my son stick around.

My aunt Ruth and uncle Chuck, Bess's parents, had free rein of the place, of course. A sweet gesture and a safe one since we all knew they would never avail themselves of it.

That's what we *could* do.

"You can *not* turn this place into any kind of business." Sterling signed his own name to the papers, then looked them over one last time. "It is a home, and I intend to keep it that way."

I thought about pointing out that his law office violated his own edict, but that was the kind of thing a girl might need later, so I kept it to myself.

"But surely you can't object to Charma roping off a piece of land for a labyrinth." Inez sat on the arm of Fawnie's chair. Sterling had asked her here as a witness to the proceedings and probably because he wanted to make this one point perfectly clear with no room for broader interpretations.

"No labyrinth."

"We can't even draw circles in the dirt below our windows and walk around looking for God?" I met his gaze.

The doorbell rang and he stood but didn't immediately head in that direction.

"No labyrinth," he repeated.

"Fine," I said in the same sharp monotone he had used. And it *was* fine. I didn't think I was up to the spiritual responsibility of having a path to inner peace out back alongside the bathtub my daddy and his brother had left down there a couple of decades ago when they remodeled Nana Abbra's bathroom. As far as I could tell, God hadn't gone anywhere since the world began and I knew where and how to make contact should I so desire.

The bell rang again.

Sterling folded the papers and tucked them inside his suit jacket. "Let me get it, ladies."

"After all it's *his* house." Fawnie sniffed, fingering the cigarette she'd been forbidden from lighting in any room occupied at any time by Sterling.

"To give y'all some private time," he said, backing out of the door.

Wise man. If he had turned his back on that crowd just then he might have found a knife in it—or a high heel still attached to a certain seventy-something lady's artificial leg.

"Don't have no regrets about this, baby-girl," Fawnie told me even as she reached under her skirt and snapped something loose.

I had only been fantasizing about that death by fake-leg thing, but suddenly I tensed. "Me? You and Shug are the ones that made a deal with the devil straight away. Packed up decades' worth of collected linens and let him stuff them up in the airless attic. All because you thought it might be nice to have a man around the house."

"We did that for Bess," Shug argued. "He's her husband. He's missing her. You don't know what it is to bury a spouse, Charmika. It takes some time. We knew he wouldn't want to stay here permanent. We just wanted to make it easier for him until he decide to move on."

"You're the one got it put down in writing. Made it about more than trying to heal an impossible wound. You made it an issue of pride with him. Wound a man's pride, that's the kind of thing sometimes never heals." Fawnie pulled free my grandfather's silver hip flask, unscrewed the lid and offered me the first swig. "But like I said, don't have no regrets about it, all right?"

"Is this that nasty sloe gin crap?"

"No. I gave that up after we lost our Bess. I confess I imbibed a bit more than usual toward the end—for my nerves."

Shug mouthed the addendum right along with Fawnie.

"And now it reminds me of watching her passing and…and…" She held the flask out to me.

"It's premo sippin' whiskey in there now." Shug, acting as lookout, leaned out to check the hallway. Voices drifted toward us but nothing distinct. Still she made a "hurry this along" sign by creating circles in the air with one hand. "So don't make a pig of yourself with it."

I took the flask and raised it in a solemn toast. "To everyone present, seen and unseen. No regrets."

How could I have regrets? I had jumped. I did not hesitate but dove in to rescue someone I loved. No one said there would never be consequences and I was all right with them.

This put life back on track for us all. I could live with the new rules.

I took a swig. It burned all the way down, then slowly, slowly warmed me from the pit of my stomach outward.

"Nice," I said.

"Share," Inez urged.

"It just feels so right here with my family and with you, Inez. I mean, really, were we ever anything but guests in this house, anyway? We always knew that Nana—"

"Share the booze, sugar, not your feelings." Inez snatched the flask away. "I still have dreams for this place and it will take a hell of lot more than sippin' whiskey and whimsy to make them come true."

I swallowed and the whiskey still clinging to my tongue and throat scorched all the way down. "*You* have dreams for *my* house?"

"You just said it ain't your house." Shug took her turn and let out a satisfied *aah* when she had finished. She handed the silver vessel back to Fawnie. "I'm with Inez. This house deserves to have dreams. To be dreamt about. This is the only home I ever have as a grown-up."

"You're a grown-up?" I teased, looking at one of the most grown-up women I had ever known. "So that's what one looks like."

"Check your mirror, maybe you find one there someday, too. If you ever stop being a big kid and trying to keep everybody else happy all the time." Shug scowled and shook her head. "I say we all do big-time grown-up thing and don't lie down and roll over and let that lawyer take our house away from us, even if he is very yummy man."

"Lie down, roll-l-l over and…" Fawnie looked at the flask, then at her counterpart who had never mastered the pronunciation of the letter *L* then at Inez. "Shitfire, Shug is right. I say no way do we let Yummy Man say what does or does not fly in *our* home. Ladies?"

She lifted the flask much as I had, but not to make a toast. She wanted to seal a pact.

"I'm in." Inez stood, her tangerine-colored shoes skiffing over the wooden floor. I got the idea she would have liked to have crossed swords in the center of us all like the Three Musketeers straight from the wrapper of the candy bar. But not being armed at the moment, instead she held out her crooked pinkie.

Shug hooked on. "Me, too."

Fawnie had to give her big ol' ring a twirl to keep from jabbing the others, then she, too, latched on. And they all looked at me.

I know I had asked my wayward corpse to put in a word so that the women of my family would join forces to guide and assist me. I had meant the women who had passed over, though, not the ones just a few blasts-from-the-flask shy of passing out. That's what I get for not being specific enough.

I had done the right thing. I had taken swift and bold action and all it had done was lead me to another edge, another loved one asking me what Bess had asked years ago when she tried to help me overcome my fear of the pond. *What are you waiting for?*

"I can't," I said. "I signed my name. That has to mean something, y'all."

Inez took it better than I thought. No invoking of ancient curses, no threat of visits from tough guys from Jersey. Just a cold, hard snake-eye look and the command, "Promise you won't tell Sterling what we're up to."

Shug wagged her finger. "Yeah, no consorting with the enemy."

"Consorting?" I tapped my thumbnail to my lower lip, hoping I didn't appear panicked that Aunt Shug knew what had passed between Sterling and me on the porch.

"Oh, now, I hate to think of that precious man as the enemy." Fawnie made like she just might withdraw her finger from the knot.

"We'll call him the opponent," Inez announced. "Opponent is good. Honest. Like in politics or court. They're always throwing that around, my worthy opponent."

"Or like in a boxing match." Shug threw a playful punch at my shoulder. "Only the idea isn't to whup his ass so much as to come out on top."

"Boxing, that's so primitive." Fawnie frowned.

"Don't go acting all prissy on us, old woman." Another punch in the air, this time in Fawnie's direction. "You like the idea of coming out on top of that young man as much as any of us."

Consorting with Sterling, coming out on top of him. The

whole undercurrent here made my face burn in mortification, and mortifying me is not an easy thing to do.

I groaned and covered my eyes. "Did y'all always talk this raunchy when Min and I were kids, or is this a new thing?"

"Shug was always this way," Fawnie volunteered, her nose tipped up.

Shug tried to imitate the pose. "That from one of the two women teach me most of the English I know, especially all the dirty words."

"Charma?" Inez turned her upper body toward me. "What do you think?"

"I think they were always wild women. After I moved out I guess I just didn't hear it anymore so I thought they had mellowed in their old age."

The two of them cackled at the very thought.

"You have so much to learn about getting older," Shug warned.

Inez raised her linked finger and with it my aunts' hands square into my line of vision. "What do you think about our pledge here, Charma?"

"I asked for Sterling's help, knowing it would come with strings. I can't go back on my promise to him now."

"If you can't be for us—" Inez inched inward to close in the circle of women "—just swear not to be against us."

"*That* I can do." I hooked my pinkie on to theirs.

And in that instant lightning flashed.

Shug squeaked.

Fawnie swore.

Inez appealed to the Mother of God in Spanish and then staggered backward.

Okay, it was not lightning. It was the flash from a camera, but it had felt as bright as lightning and just as dangerous, especially in the hands of my grinning oldest son.

"What are you doing?" I asked Johnny, trying to rub the spots from before my eyes.

"I'm doing…what I do, Mom. I wanted to tell you earlier but we, and by we I mean *you*, got sidetracked and ran off." He slouched one shoulder against the wall just outside the office and looked at me with those lost puppy eyes. "I've decided to take time off from work to try my hand at freelance photography."

"He's going to one of them paparazzi," Shug shouted at the top of her lungs as if she thought the bright light had rendered us all deaf instead of half blind.

"You are?" I tried not to make a face like I just got a whiff of dead skunk and cabbage, but I couldn't help it. "Paparazzi?"

"Yeah. And I'm going to get my big break sneaking in and taking pictures of the loony shit that goes on around here." He rolled his eyes then looked down at his camera. "I'll be rich, I tell ya, rich."

"Very funny." I thought about grabbing the camera and flipping open the back to expose the film just to show him how deeply I appreciated his sense of humor. But I decided I couldn't be that cruel. And besides… "What is that? A digital camera?"

"This old thing? Are you kidding? Jeez, Mom, I found it in Grandma's closet."

Still standing at the doorway to the office, I reached out toward the black-and-silver object, but my hand stilled inches away. "You went in Mama's closet?"

He shrugged, then met my eyes, daring me to pitch a fit about it.

I pulled my hand back. He wouldn't get a scene from me. Not over this. He had loved my mother, and if being among her things gave him comfort, that was between him, his memories and the shoe racks. "When?"

"Last night after I got here and you were gone and everyone else was asleep."

"And when did you get the idea of becoming a freelance photographer?"

"Yesterday, after you got back and I said to Aunt Shug the only way I'd get to see you would be to take your picture and she said I should take photography up for a living."

I'd have honed in on the pathetic attempt to get a rise out of me by claiming maternal neglect, but I'd loaned the kid my car and he'd sold it. So naturally I was far more interested in exploring this new source for absolutely stupid ideas. "So, you're taking career advice now from Aunt Shug?"

"Stop picking on that boy," Shug called out.

"Photography has a way of capturing the soul." Inez held her hands up to form a frame around her made-up face.

"Well, that's good because I think y'all should be captured." I stepped into the hallway.

"Charma? Are you coming or not?" Sterling moved and suddenly his body blocked the light that had been streaming down the hall from the open front door.

"Oh, that's right. He wanted me to tell you that you have company." Johnny slumped against the wall again and motioned toward the front of the house.

I laid my hand on my son's arm. His big, hairy arm. Seemed like only a year ago he was three feet tall and he and his brother were tearing around this house like…like the pack of heathens Nana Abbra had always accused me and Minnie and Bess of being.

I leaned in to speak into his ear without having to look at him and be reminded of how old and at the same time totally immature I felt when I asked, "It's not the police, is it?"

"No." He straightened up and blinked at me with what I swear was a newfound kind of respect in his eyes. "But if you want to tell me why you think the police might come looking for you…"

"Charma?"

"I'll be right there." I stepped away and looked at the overgrown kid looking back at me. "You okay?"

"Go," he said. "Your boyfriend is waiting for you."

"Oh, for heaven's sake, it was just the one kiss. That hardly makes Sterling my—"

"I meant Guy Chapman, Mom." He cocked his head. His black hair tumbled over one eyebrow. Humor replaced the respect, or maybe just joined it. I knew John wasn't crazy about this engagement. It wouldn't take a mother's intuition to know he would embrace the possibility of someone other than him or George coming between Guy and me. "Maybe I should start stalking around here with my camera. Sounds like I might dig up some pretty interesting dirt."

"You just be glad that it isn't the police at the door." I wagged my finger, trying to pull off the brave, unruffled act even as I turned and headed down the hallway. "I can still report you for stealing my car."

"I didn't steal it. You gave it to me." He let me get a few feet down the hallway before hollering out, "You're the parent here, you should have known better."

"I will next time," I lied with the same light and airy tone I might have used to say "kiss my fanny" or "call when you get there," and I waved over my shoulder.

The flash went off again, and I had no idea if he had taken a picture of me, the others in the office or just pressed the button in some kind of smart-ass gesture.

And I didn't care. Very much. Not when I saw Guy standing on my front porch with his hands in his pockets and the most defeated expression I had ever seen on his handsome face.

❧ CHAPTER ELEVEN

"So after all the plotting and machinations, the police ended up calling Chapman and Son's to collect the body?" I sank into Shug's wicker chair while Guy leaned against the railing on the front porch, arms braced at his side and legs outstretched.

He nodded. "We have a contract with the county."

"I knew that." I'd found it out the night I had gone to help Inez deal with the dead guy in the bushes outside the home of one of her midwifery charges. Yeah, it sounds a little like a bad mystery series, but honestly, when you get into other people's business as much as I do and when you are intimately involved with a mortician—or even someone pretending to be a mortician—you have to expect your share of stray bodies lying around.

I sank farther into the seat. "So I took the body to the police for nothing?"

"No, your part actually helped, a little. The plan started out good. We knew they'd call us, of course, and then we could tell them we didn't want to take the body because of the connection to an ex-employee who was in legal trouble and they could then call the police in that county and we'd all be in the clear. Except…"

"Except?"

He rubbed both hands over his face and swore between his fingers. "Charma, turns out the embalmer didn't want to *deliver* a body. The embalmer *was* the body."

I gripped the arms of the chair and rose out of the seat to go to him.

He held his hand out to stave me off.

I dropped back down and the wicker creaked beneath my shifting weight. "I don't completely understand."

Guy turned to face the curved driveway.

All around us the world went on about its business. The air smelled of smoke and green wood burning. Someone nearby had built a bonfire last night. It had been a nice night for it, cool enough to say that fall was here but not so much you needed a jacket or sweater outdoors during the day. Clusters of yellow leaves still clung to the branches on the trees closest to the house, but over toward the hills in the distance the foliage was long gone, creating a backdrop of nothing but lifeless gray and brown.

In his white shirt, Guy's shoulders made an imposing outline in contrast to the autumn pallet. He hung his head and groaned. "It's ugly, Charma. Damned ugly."

"I can imagine, what with Loyal's connection to…" Again the news drew me up from my seat. "Oh, my word! Loyal didn't have anything to do with Garrett's death, did he?"

"No." A head shake. A pause. He looked down, then out toward the hills again, adding softly, "Suicide."

His brother's lover had committed suicide. Guy was too damned good a man to hear something like that and not be moved. He was more than a little concerned about Loyal, about his state of mind and how he might react to both the news and finding himself tied inextricably to it.

"Suicide," I whispered, falling back and finally drawing my

knees up to my chest, my bare toes curled over the edge of the cushion. "Are they sure?"

"Supported by physical evidence, including the shotgun, the gunpowder burns, the missing back half of his head and a note. Pretty cut-and-dried. Pretty grisly."

"Not *pretty* at all." My heart went out to the stranger. "How much pain would you have to be in to find death by your own hand a blessed relief?"

"I don't know." His voice sounded stretched thin and maybe a bit shaky.

"How's Loyal taking it?"

He shook his head. "Not good. Not…"

"Not like a Chapman?" I suggested. I couldn't imagine anything more mortifying to Guy than to see his brother fall to pieces, carrying on and showing his emotions. Guy would not have known what to do with that.

Death did not have that kind of power over Chapmans. Even when it absolutely should have.

"He's taking it *too much* like a Chapman." The answer came quietly.

"What?"

"He keeps saying how much he's let Dad down. It's like that's all that matters. He's not even grieving for his…you know."

"Friend."

"Lover." He did not turn to face me. He made no great show of emotion other than the stillness and power of his softly spoken words. "Hell, Charma, if this had happened to me—that is, if it were you lying in a morgue somewhere—I don't know. I don't know what I would do, but the last thing on my mind would be how it would affect Chapman's, or what Dad would have thought."

"Yeah, but you gave up trying to win your father's approval a long time ago, Guy."

"Did I?" His shoulders rose and fell.

Everything went still for a few minutes except for the occasional flap or clatter of something knocked about by the breeze and the ever-present sounds of the pond. Or maybe I imagined those because my thoughts went there and I wondered what it might feel like to dive in and watch the water overtake you, then to surrender yourself to inevitable eternal peace instead of pushing upward and struggling on. I wasn't thinking of doing myself in so much as trying to envision why anyone would be drawn to such an act.

"Suicide," I whispered again.

"It makes you sort of think about Bess, though, doesn't it?"

"Bess?" I struggled to make the connection.

He turned around and folded his arms low across his body. "You know, when she came home and just gave up like that."

I didn't know which surprised me more—that Guy had found another reason to mention my cousin, meaning she was on his mind again, or that…

"How?" This time I did get out of the chair. I was halfway across the porch before demanding that he explain himself. "How can you in any way associate Bess refusing cancer treatment to putting a gun barrel in your mouth and squeezing the trigger?"

"Both were choices made out of pain, desperation, and having lost any hope that things would one day get any better."

God help me, I'd never thought that about Bess. Or Mama, because standing here with it spoken out loud so clear now, I could see it applied to her, too. Pain, desperation and having lost all hope.

"I had told myself that Bess made her choice out of strength," I said softly, each word an effort to get out.

"That's the deal with you and Bess, Charma." Now he turned, his face grim. "You always saw her as the strong one. But really, it was you."

I pulled my shoulders up like a child huddled inside trying to protect herself from howling wind or the sounds of an approaching a thunderstorm.

"She came back here to die so that you could lend her the strength to do it." Guy put his hand on my back. "So you could keep everyone else around her strong."

I thought of Sterling's accusation that she had forced Bess to carry the pain of Charma's disillusionment to her grave. "Do you think I let her down?"

He cocked his head, his eyes shifted. "By allowing her to die without a fight?"

I had meant by not working things through with her, but now that he mentioned it…

I exhaled slowly and mentally added one more misstep to my list of things to feel guilty about for the rest of my life. Suddenly the pond, the peace, the surrender with no more thought of struggle felt…well, it didn't feel so horrific. That thought alone should have scared me, I suppose, but it only left me pensive.

"I don't see where anyone gets off thinking I am strong, Guy. Surely you don't see me that way?"

"I sure as hell don't see you as weak, Charma." He gave a humorless laugh and shook his head.

"Sterling does. He says I'm a coward."

"A *coward?*" His tone all but called the young lawyer an asshole for even having suggested it. "Would a coward volunteer to drive a wandering cadaver over to the police station to help out the man she loved?"

"I do love you, you know." I gave him the perfect opening to say it back to me.

"Yeah, it's the one thing I *do* know today, Charma."

I waited.

He rubbed his eyes and shook his head again.

Give it up, Charma Deane. You know the man loves you. Be happy.

"But my playing chauffer to your poor body-bag boy doesn't prove anything. Personally, I think that kind of behavior falls less under the carved-in-stone banner of bravery and more under the squiggly hand-lettered heading of lunatic or…" My hand froze in mid-scrawl of the imaginary label I was trying to file myself under. "Wait one minute. This man killed himself and then packed himself up neatly into a body bag and hopped into my hearse?"

"Obviously not. He killed himself at the other mortuary. In the embalming room, actually."

"Embalming room?" Sure beat the hell of strip hide-and-seek for things that went on in your mortuary you wouldn't want anyone to know about. "Then you wouldn't have thought there would be any reason to haul him across the state to Chapman's."

"Unless you were the staff of a business already under close scrutiny. Someone there got the bright idea to bring him to us to try to deflect any bad publicity."

"Any *further* bad publicity."

"Any *further* bad publicity, yes. Too bad they didn't know about the letter."

"The one he wrote to Loyal?"

"That one or the one he wrote the local D.A. A full confession, a last purging of all his sins, and I mean *all* of them."

"Did he…did it mention Loyal?"

"Mention? If you mean indict as a co-conspirator in fraud, health violations and abuse of a corpse, then no." Guy's forehead scrunched up so much I felt I was actually seeing a headache being formed. "He named names, though, sparing nobody. Who in positions of power took money to keep quiet about their practices. Who knew about double selling plots. How he cremated more than one body together to cut costs. And who knew nothing about it because he was 'the sweetest man and most generous lover' that Garrett had ever known."

"Loyal must be devastated."

"And humiliated. I mean, there is no one in this town save a few dear old widow women who don't *know* about Loyal, Charma. But to have his ex-lover kill himself, then as a final act of love and gratitude out Loyal in a way that would not just draw national attention but also become part of public record and probably entered as evidence in multiple lawsuits?"

"Poor man."

"Which one?"

"Both of them."

"Yeah." He nodded, then looked at me and offered the faintest of smiles. "On the bright side we all immediately thought how much Shug and Fawnie would love that story."

"No. No. They only truly love death stories where justice ultimately prevails and someone gets what's coming to them. One that hurts someone they love? It will break their hearts, Guy."

I imagined the women I had just left in the office toasting their impending triumph over Sterling's big plans. These were the strong ones, the protectors of everyone weaker than them—and who wasn't weaker than Fawnie and Shug? "No, that story will not make it into their repertoire, unless of course Loyal rises above it and…"

"Charma, don't you get what I'm telling you here? There will be no rising above anything. Chapman's is a part of all this now."

"But you'll be all right, Guy."

"How?" He walked the length of the porch away from me before twisting just his head to ask again, "How will I be all right, Charma? The business had barely gotten back in the black since Loyal and Garrett nearly bankrupted us. We can sell some things, of course, but back when Loyal and Garrett were living the high life Loyal has taken loans against a lot of the assets we owned outright, including the home and land it sits on."

"Oh, Guy." I shut my eyes. Six months ago I had been motherless but not homeless. I had been loveless but not sexless. My relationships with everyone but the man standing before me were intact—not necessarily good but intact.

Slowly it had all fallen apart. Like a bad game of musical chairs, one by one the things I had counted as always being there for me to rest on had been yanked away. Mama. Trust in my son. Bess. My home. Now the future I had counted on with Guy.

And the music played on and I had to figure out how to keep moving.

"Everything's not lost yet," I forced out in a damned cheerful lilt. "You have to wait and see how it all shakes out before you can—"

"Shakes out?" He pushed his bent fingers back through his hair. "How about this for shaking out? My father's business based on sixty years of trust and an impeccable family name is now linked to duplicity and deceit and disrespecting the dead."

"Chapman's didn't do any of that, surely people will know—"

"People love a good story, Charma. Chapman's did nothing wrong is not a good story *and* a story we both know is not strictly true in proving that we didn't do anything akin to the goings on at Loyal's ex-employer, everything we have done all our methods of operation will be exposed under investigation, and they won't have any reason to keep quiet about it."

"About that—you didn't do anything *wrong*, Guy, you just let Dathan do the work he was trained to do."

"And never told a soul."

"People will understand."

"Not people in Orla, they won't. No, Charma, face it. It's over."

"Wh-what's over, Guy, exactly?"

"The ruse that I ran Chapman's, the charade that Dathan just drove the ambulance. Our standing in the community. Our ability to earn any kind of a living. Life as we knew it." He slashed his hand through the air and let out a long breath. "Over."

❧ CHAPTER TWELVE

Over. That night I heard the word over again in my mind.

Shitfire. Could it be that simple? Could a person have done all the right things and scraped along and sacrificed and because of someone else's ill-timed transgression, it was over?

I knew the answer.

I just didn't like it.

"God? I thought that by now I could finally coast a little. Not on morality or motherhood or any of that important stuff. Well, no more than usual on those, but on having to constantly shape and reshape my life just to keep it all together." I lifted my face and my hair fell back between my shoulder blades. I buried my fist in the folds of my white gown—the one I keep by the kitchen door in case I feel too lazy to go upstairs and change out of my regular clothes or in case *the* change sneaks up on me all at once and I have a hot flash or whatever. I probably looked a fright, but then I figured my Creator had seen me worse, so went right on addressing him. "I just thought that by this point I'd have mastered all that. That the bumps and blowups along the way would no longer lay waste to my beliefs or threaten to fracture my whole sense of self."

All my life I had always counted on those things—God and

myself—to get me through. With some pretty serious backup provided by friends and family members, of course. But lately I found I no longer knew *what* I could rely on. I had no sense of trust. No path laid out before me. I could take no comfort—southern or otherwise—in knowing that someone always had my back. I felt middle-aged and over the edge, hanging on to a limb that could not hold my weight and all alone.

Thoughts like these had driven me from my usual restless bouts with trying to sleep out into the night. I'd tried sitting on the back porch, in Mama's rocker, but a chill overtook me and I couldn't stay.

Outside, my feet found the familiar path worn from a thousand footsteps through the grass between the back porch and the pond. Bess and Minnie and me, Mama and the aunts, even Nana Abbra, had come this way time and again over the years. Here we swam. We slathered on baby oil and worshiped the sun. We laughed. We shared our souls, and sometimes, when there was nothing else left to do, we would simply look out over the dark still water and remember.

Each of us sought something different. Each sought something universal.

Peace.

Hope.

Happiness.

No, not happiness. That asked too much.

Joy. The sudden unexpected surprise of joy—biting, intense and not likely to last but worth chasing all the same.

That's the real reason I had jumped into this pond. I had believed that by facing those fears I would find my joy again. I would be new and filled with wonder, even if only for a few bright, brief moments.

Was that all behind me now? Had I grown old enough that

nothing would surprise me like that? Disappoint me, yes. Baffle me, often. But surprise me with joy?

"Is that over, too?"

I listened for an answer. I couldn't say why but I thought one might just come.

I stood on the dock and searched my surroundings. Nothing unusual. And yet I couldn't shoo away the sensation that I was not alone. No chill this time. More like heat at the center of my chest and radiating through to my toes and fingertips—the indomitable suspicion of an intent gaze burning right through me. Probably a raccoon or possum.

Or the twitchy untethered spirit of a departed loved one.

We do not believe in ghosts in the George family. For one reason we are Christian to the core, if not always to the world. We know what awaits us, and frankly, none of us have ever been the types to loiter around after a party is over—especially if we knew a better party was going on down the way.

Up the way?

Anyway, the Lord promised us He'd gone ahead to prepare us "many mansions." I can't picture a single one of my relatives who would pass up the chance for laying claim to that kind of prime real estate in favor of sticking around to share a drafty old house with those of us still here.

And in point of fact, the still living Georges did not *want* our loved ones hanging around. That's why Fawnie insisted we always cover the mirrors whenever she decided to up and die on us. More so for people who were seriously sick.

We covered the mirrors the last days of Bess's life, and I am sure Bess did it for Mama. Bess could be a horrible bitch about some things, but she would not risk having my mother get stuck in the hall mirror instead of heading off to heaven. No, even Bess knew that if Dinah McCoy George was in the house, even to haunt it, no other woman would ever rise to the position of queen bee. And Bess wanted to be queen bee, if only for the short time she had left.

So, stories of ghosts and hanks and spooks and such were just never a part of our reality or our repertoire. Those things, reality and repertoire, do tend to be two distinct and different animals. I mean, if we had to limit our repertoire to hard reality, our house would fall silent for months at a time with not one interesting thing to talk about. Not that interesting things didn't happen to us all the time, just that, well, if you put your mind to it, you could always find a way to make the truth just a little bit better.

I scanned the far side of the shore, though I didn't know for what.

Fog had crept in with the cooling air of autumn. Dying grass had thickened the shoreline and moss had overtaken the concrete slab left over from the time Daddy and Uncle Kel tried to set down a permanent dock. They should have known nothing in this world is permanent. Nothing here was meant to last.

The dock never got finished. It was on that jagged bit of concrete that Daddy had hit his head and lost his life trying to save me from drowning. Nothing lasts.

"It's over," I whispered to the unseen entity I felt lurking all around me.

Dead to the old. Reborn in the new.

Had I said that aloud? Had I heard it? Or dreamt it?

I stepped forward as I had the day I jumped in to rebaptize myself into what I had thought would be a bold new wonderful life. My toes hung over the edge of the water. The dock dipped forward under the shift in weight.

I caught my breath.

Jump.

"Why?" I whispered. "Jumping didn't prove or *im*prove a damned thing."

Something shiny flashed in the water.

A fish.

A frog.

A reflection.

I leaned farther out to try to see—and suddenly the sky filled with a bright and blinding light.

"Shitfire and save matches! John Parker, I swear I am going to pry that camera out of your hands and throw it into the deepest part of this skanky pond!"

Johnny laughed.

"You wasted your film, you know. That puny flash won't even make a dent in the darkness."

"Oh, I don't know. There's a full moon." He stood at the end of the path to the dock and looked skyward. Then raised his camera in one hand as if he were shouldering an ax or some other implement of destruction and came onto the rickety raft of wood and rusty nails. "And I've been messing around with the aperture and all the pretty, shiny knobs. You never know how things just might turn out."

"Well, amen to that," I said, and cast him a look that said "I am talking about you, mister." At the same time I couldn't help thinking about Guy and me and Sterling and aunts and Inez and her labyrinth and Abby and Minnie. "You never know just how things might turn out."

He smiled.

"Damn you look like your daddy when you smile," I said even as I laughed under my breath.

"Compliment or accusation?"

I shivered and folded my arms around myself. "Just an observation."

"Most people say I look like you."

"When you scowl, or sneer, or shoot hellfire from your eyes or put on like you're better than someone else, or get sloppy drunk and tell people how much you lo-o-ve them and only want the best for them regardless of what it means for you, *then* maybe you look like me."

"Then maybe I look like you a lot of the time." The kid wasn't drunk or shooting hellfire at this actual moment, but I saw his point. He did crap like that far too often these days.

"Then you should smile more," I said, offering my sage advice.

And he did. Then he stepped forward and slipped out of his jeans jacket and put it around my shoulders.

"Couldn't sleep?" he asked.

I shook my head. "You?"

"Haven't tried."

I gave him a quick once-over. "Just coming in from a night on the town?"

"What town?" He chuckled.

But in truth he had grown up here and still had plenty of friends around and about that he could drop by to visit. Some he could get into trouble with, by either getting into backrooms of bars with no-account pals or bedrooms, I supposed, of old girlfriends. Anything that might generally sully the good name—okay, the not-totally-infamous family name of George—Johnny would likely be up for it.

"Actually, I was on my way out," he confessed.

"Aha!" I knew it. "What kind of mischief do you intend to inflict on Orla at ten o'clock at night?"

"You don't want to know," he said.

And I didn't, which only proved to me that I had crossed some kind of threshold into a world where I chose comfort over curiosity. Pancakes instead of penises. Honoring contracts instead of inciting conspiracies. Path of least resistance and all that.

"Did you hear the phone?" John asked.

"Just now?" I turned toward the house. The kitchen light shone out through the back porch. So did a light in the downstairs bedroom Sterling had taken over for his office.

"No. It rang just before I came out here." John jostled the camera in his hand so he could draw my attention back to his message. "That's *why* I came out here to tell you that I took this call and I—"

I thrust my hand up between us to cut him off. "Son, I may seem the most progressive mom in the world, but I could live the whole rest of my life without hearing about one of your booty calls."

He put his own hand up, his palm flat to mine. "Don't worry. That conversation is never going to happen between us, Mom."

"Cool." I let out a sigh.

"And for future reference, don't ever use that expression around me again."

"Off-putting, was it?"

"Enough so that you are in serious jeopardy of never becoming a grandmother."

"Oh, don't be silly." I ruffled his hair and slid his jacket off my shoulders in preparation of sending the kid off for his nefarious night out. "I still haven't ruined your brother."

He laughed and accepted the jacket back, choosing to hold it in his folded arms rather than put it on—as if he wanted to hug it and by extension me close to his chest for a minute or two. It was a small gesture, and being male he probably didn't even know he'd done it. But it was the kind of thing that made a mom questioning the purpose of her life and looking at a hazy future for herself go all warm and weepy.

I studied him, and the fog seemed to gather around his shoulders and form a halo around his head.

I blinked and it went away.

"You okay?" he asked.

"I'm just tired and…" *Hallucinating.* "It's been a long day."

"Well, go in and get some rest. You're going to need it."

"Why?"

"That phone call was from Minnie." He moved away and the whole dock rocked.

I laid my hand at the base of my throat and commanded my pulse to slow. *Deep breath and let it out slowly,* I repeated silently.

I drew in the smell of dank earth and weeds, of Johnny's after-shave and cigarette smoke. Johnny didn't smoke, but Fawnie's ever-present odor permeated everything. Funny I hadn't picked it up on him before, not even with his jacket right under my nose and around my shoulders.

"Where is she?" I asked about my cousin.

"California. It took them a few days to rearrange their flights once they got to Japan and realized Abby wasn't there. They plan to be here tomorrow afternoon."

I nodded. What was one more piece of bad news at this point?

My son retreated onto the shore, raised his camera and snapped off another shot.

"Johnny!"

"Sorry."

In that moment I decided that when he lied he *did* look more like me than like his father.

"Do me a favor and stay out of your grandmother's closet from now on."

"What do you think? I'm going to go in there and start trying on her shoes or grab that old shotgun, load it with buckshot and—"

"That old shotgun is a tool, son, not a toy." I repeated the lesson I had learned as a child. No child had ever been allowed in Mama's closet while she was alive, so I guess I hadn't driven home that point to my son. "And I dare say it's already loaded and not with buckshot."

"Really?"

"Did you ever know your grandmother to do anything half assed? If she had a shotgun, then she intended to be ready to use a shotgun. And if you doubt me just ask Guy Chapman what happened when he showed up here after jilting me at the altar."

"She shot him?"

"She shot *at* a tree that was a few feet from him. If she had wanted to shoot *him,* he wouldn't be around today to make my life so…"

"Miserable?"

"Miserable. Right." I shook my head and laughed a bit before adding, "And wonderful."

"Bet it scared him shitless." Johnny couldn't hide his bona fide glee at the thought.

"Your grandmother did not need artillery to scare any male shitless."

"See, that's why I went into her closet."

"For the shotgun?"

"For the story, Mom. Grandma was about nothing if she wasn't about her stories."

"True enough." In fact her stories were all she was about, all I had left of her—all I *ever* had of her.

"And from the day you called to tell me she died, you never said another thing about her."

"Didn't I?" I supposed I hadn't. I had a discussion or two with Fawnie, who gave me some insight into why my mother kept so closed off. But I hadn't discussed Mama's death or her life with anyone in depth.

"It was like she fell off the face of the earth."

"In a way she did," I said softly.

"But she made a pretty big impression while she was here, Mom." He rolled the camera over in his hand. "So I went into her room to see if I could find her again."

"Did you? Find her in there?"

"Maybe. A little. I do know that holding something in my hands that she held in hers feels good. It feels right."

I wound my fingers together and hunched my shoulders up. "Then I guess I won't throw the damned nuisance into the skank pond."

"Nuisance? Me or the camera?"

"Either one."

"You're all heart, Mom."

"Like fire I am." That was part acceptance, part desperate denial. "Honestly, right now I feel like all raw nerve. So get your sorry self out of here with it before I change my mind."

He started to leave, then turned back around to ask, "What are you going to do?"

"I think I'll try to get some sleep."

"Do that. You look like crap."

"Just like your daddy," I muttered.

"I mean you look exhausted."

"I am. I haven't felt this drained since you and your brother were babies. Or teenagers."

"Don't wait up for me tonight."

"I won't." In fact I could practically feel myself sinking into my familiar old mattress and pulling the warm, soft blankets up over my head.

"After all, Minnie is coming tomorrow."

And lying awake worrying about how a person could have done all the right things and scraped along and sacrificed and because of someone else's ill-timed transgression, everything could be over.

❦ CHAPTER THIRTEEN

I took the stairs slowly, hoping that with every step I would find myself lifted from the melancholy of my exhaustion and the wariness that still lingered in my soul. Had something else been out there? Something besides my smart-mouthed son, that is.

"Maybe a deer," I murmured, then started to yawn then...didn't.

Something at the top of the stairs caught my eye. I froze. The door to the master bedroom was open.

Johnny must have not latched it entirely when he'd gone in to get the camera, I supposed. But still, finding it open like that after so many months of it being closed tight and locked out of my thoughts, it made me shudder.

"Mama?" I leaned in and called.

Silence.

I didn't expect anything else. I think.

Georges do not *do* the ghost thing.

But I confess I did grip the stair rail a bit tighter than usual. I held my breath. I inched my upper body forward, I tried to peer into the huge moonlight-flooded room. I swear I saw something move. A shadow? Probably a curtain shifting softly in a draft. Still, it made me want to move on. So I swung myself around and aimed my feet toward the door of my childhood bedroom. In a few hurried steps I would be inside and safe.

"Hey!" Abby's gasp reminded me that I quite literally didn't even have my very own place to lay my head anymore.

"Sorry, sweetie, I…" I began to back out, but something about the figure huddled on the bed held me there. Poor kid. And she was just a kid. I'd really left her to her own devices way too long. Yeah, my world had begun to crumble all around me, nothing new there. For Abby, this life-screws-with-your-best-laid-plans deal was totally new, and scary and overwhelming. To hell with my own problems and with my illusions that if I made all the right moves I could manipulate the situation to keep me in good with Minnie. Abby was hurting and I was here now.

"Are you all right?" I asked, moving into the room at last.

"Yes." She pulled her knees to her chest, sniffled and turned her head away.

"Give it up, girl, you are an even worse liar than your mother." I swept fully into the space and, knowing just where to find them, yanked a tissue from the box hidden under a pile of mail I hadn't bothered to open since Bess had died.

She yanked a tissue free. The whiteness of it stood out in the dark room, stark as the raw timbre of Abby's voice when she said, "Maybe you could give me lessons in lying."

"I deserved that." And then again I didn't. I hadn't lied to the girl, or to her mother. I'd just… "I suppose you feel like I welcomed you here, then just up and abandoned you to the mercy of your grandmother and Aunt Fawnie."

"That's hardly true."

I perked up. "It's not?"

"Naw. You didn't actually welcome me so much as make a speech at me, give me some peanut butter and…and I can come up with a thousand words to describe my grandmother and Fawnie. But *merciful?*" She honked into a tissue, blubbered out something between a sob and a laugh and finished, "Not one of them."

I ran my hand along her long, soft hair. Not having girls, I was not adept at comforting them. Yeah, I'd been a school nurse, but they didn't like me to play school psychologist. In fact, in the last few years before I gave it up entirely, I had to be so careful, even in Orla, of everything I said, everything I did. Don't hug the kids. Don't ask too many questions. Don't give advice. That came at me from all sides: the parents, the teachers and oftentimes the kids themselves.

Being a school nurse had really been about people rejecting my help as much as them needing it. How screwed up was I that this was the profession I had chosen and hung in with until my family inheritance allowed me to retire early?

Georges were not big on comforting anyone, anyway. Big shows of sympathy taken too far quickly morphed into pity. Pity was a stone around the neck. It dragged people down. It wasn't tolerated.

In our defense, Abby should have known that. She even noted that I had given her that big old speech about the basic human comforts we would gladly extend to her, Shelter, a sense of belonging, a sense of self, the right to bear arms, booze. Crying towels and sympathy not included. That was the deal. That was our offer.

And what the hell else *was* there to offer her? Something sweet? Hell no. Despite all the clichés about women and chocolate, I have never met a female yet who really confuses a satiated belly with a satisfied heart. No, even the best chocolate was nothing more than that waxy stuff you can buy to hold you over when you lose a filling in your tooth—it will plug the hole but it won't heal the ache.

I sat on the bed and twisted around so the back of my shoulder brushed the back of hers. Close enough to lend support but not so much that I intruded. I handed her a fresh tissue. "The old gals putting pressure on you?"

"Relentlessly."

"Really?" I'd asked it absolutely expecting first a denial, and second, the realization that things weren't so bad around here, then a hug and "all better."

"Fawnie? *Your* grandmother?" How could that be true? Fawnie and Shug were life-long rescuers of women in distress. It was in their history. I glanced out the window to the tree bearing the scar of the day Mama fired a round at Guy with her shotgun because she thought he'd done me wrong. Standing up for their sisters, even when they were their daughters and granddaughters, was in their blood. "Giving you a hard time?"

"Yes, relentlessly. *And* they're so sneaky about it, too. Bringing me tea and baking my favorite cookies. Changing my bedding every day with linens straight off the line, so they smell all fresh and comforting."

That sounded like my girls. "The bitches."

"You laugh, but when they do all that for me and I know that I…" The space between her finely arched eyebrows crinkled. Her eyes pinched shut and she compressed her lips until they paled. She looked oddly much as she had as a newborn, but now when she finally turned loose a sob it came in quiet, crashing waves, not in an infant's piercing wail.

"Oh, sweetie, maybe if you got some rest?" I plumped the pillow and for an instant considered laying my head down on it—just for an instant.

"No. I can't rest another minute. I've rested and let them pamper me until I can't stand it anymore. And none of it helps. In fact the nicer everyone is, the harder it all becomes." She started to dab her eyes, then let her hand drop away instead. "I've let all of you down, and the longer I wait to do something about it, the more I know that I can't wait."

Usually I considered the Raynes family's plainness combined with just a touch of Japanese lineage would have given the girl an exotic appeal. I never saw much of our family in her, but then, that kind of thing took time. I suspected that the curve of the hips and the bent but not quite twisted personality—those would all come out with age. And that was the thing that struck me now. The girl looked so young. She looked her real age, probably, but her real age was so very young.

"I just can't wait much longer," she murmured again.

And I had to say something then. "You think you want to have an abortion?"

"You...knew?" Her eyes grew wide. Her lower lip trembled. "But I never said it out loud, not in this house."

"Give me some credit. I am a nurse, and a woman. And a mother. And I'm certainly at an age where I recognize rampant hormones when I see them."

She flopped back on the bed. "I made such a big mistake."

"Coming here?"

She rolled her head to the side, her face away from me. "Getting pregnant."

I plucked at a strand of her hair. "You had help."

"*Too much* help."

"Too much?" If I had said that regarding either of my pregnancies, I would have meant that I had too many aunts and cousins giving me advice. This was not Abby's problem. "Okay, so...two boyfriends...what? Two possible fathers?"

She nodded.

"Have you told him? Uh, *them?*"

A shake of her head. "I couldn't."

"You can and you should." I sat straight-backed. A flutter of movement drew my eye to the mirror above my vanity and I turned to peer at the image of myself framed by strings of beads, felt hats, perfume bottles and my small wooden *kokeshi* doll.

That doll. I could not look away from her. Her serene Asian features made such a contrast to my haggared appearance. From her spot of honor next to my Love's Baby Soft music box, she admonished me to speak, even if I knew the girl did not want to hear what I had to say. "And you have to tell your mother."

"Mom would never forgive me."

My gaze went again to the *kokeshi,* the symbol Aunt Shug had given us to remind us that we owned our own souls. "Once she holds that baby in her arms…"

"For the abortion."

"Yeah." I dropped my gaze to my lap. "I know."

"She thinks of it as murder. She thinks it's *all* murder, morning-after pill to late-term, no difference. She's very hard line about it, you know."

I couldn't help but think of all the babies Minnie had miscarried and how that had shaped her feelings on the already emotionally charged issue. "I know."

"What do *you* think?"

I could never do it, but it should stay legal for other people was how I used to answer that question. All the while in my heart I wanted to scream, "Don't do it! Babies are so wonderful, so much potential and love and hope. You can't just scrape that away and pretend it never existed." Abortion had to leave a scar of some kind, I believed, and all of us enlightened, progressive or just silent types who never acknowledged that had not done our sex any favors by pretending it didn't. That's what I really thought. But reality and repertoire, two different animals.

"The real question here is what do *you* think?" I deflected the question because I could not choose between my heart and my head where Abby was concerned. I did not want her to abort her baby, but I also did not want her to resent the baby she had, or the women she felt forced her to have it. "Could you live with the aftermath if you chose this path?"

She shook her head. "I have to, that's all there is to it."

I laid my fingertips to her wrist and could feel the steady thrumming of her pulse. "Abby…"

"But somehow I think…I believe…I hope that if it's done soon enough, if it's done quickly and quietly enough, that it will somehow be a lesser sin, you know what I mean?"

I nodded. Funny what we can convince ourselves of when we want something so badly. Or don't want it. "How far along are you?"

"I don't know."

Ding! A red flag popped up in my mind. My own pulse kicked up. "You missed your period, though, right?"

"Six days late. I'm never even six hours late."

"But with the whole arranging to haul your mom and dad out of Tennessee to Japan against their will to meet a fellow you aren't sure you want to marry—and his non-English speaking family, that put a lot of stress on you, right?"

She rolled her head toward me and everything about her said, "Duh!"

Every course I had ever taken, plus most course material I had ever taught in public school for girls-in-the-cafeteria-boys-in-the-auditorium puberty-education days said that extreme stress could play havoc with a girl's cycle. Like that whole chocolate-soothes-a-broken-heart myth, I had never known a woman yet who in reality stopped menstruating because her life was overwhelming. In fact, most women I know, if that were really true, would never, ever, ever have another period again—period. But still, it was medically possible and there were other reasons why a healthy young girl might be a week or so late as well. Maybe this was merely some horrific gynecological thing and not a baby. "You haven't been to a doctor?"

Her big eyes fixed on me. "I haven't even peed on a stick."

"Let's do this right, then. Stick, doctor, then…"

"Okay. I get it. We'll do it your way." She sat up and buried her head in her hands.

"Abby?" I eyed the indentation of her body in the piled-up duvet and it beckoned me. I so wanted to sleep. To just put all of this day and the day before out of my mind. But first I had to deal with the day that lay ahead. "Do you know your Mom is going to be here tomorrow?"

"Shit."

"Don't worry. We can get Inez to bring a pregnancy test out in the morning." This may have just been the moment for which I had befriended that woman. As a midwife in training and as a woman who did not have a lot of baggage in Orla, she could waltz right into the drugstore and buy that sucker and not cause a ripple. If I did it—waves so enormous you'd think four-hundred-pound Tiny Watson had done a cannonball in the bank fountain. "That way we will know what we're dealing with before your folks get here."

"Okay."

"So try not to lose any sleep over it tonight, okay?"

"I'll try not to lose sleep over that, but I can't promise I'll sleep much, anyway. I hate to say it, but this mattress of yours, Charma, it's…" She made a rocking motion with her hand.

"I know." I ran my hand along my hip line. "Form-fitted for me."

"Maybe you should try your mom's room…no wait, Johnny is in there."

"I bet he looks cute sleeping in all those pink ruffles and Cinderella memorabilia."

"Eh. It's good for his tortured artistic soul."

She smiled. "Actually, last night I went down and slept with my grandma. She always sleeps so well. It's soothing just being around her."

"Yeah, what do they call that?"

"The sleep of the innocent?"

"I was thinking more about how Dracula had the power to put people to sleep so he could suck their blood."

Abby laughed, or maybe she cried. Her shoulders shook, she made sounds. It was a toss-up to my ears.

"Anyway, tonight it may be the sleep of the intoxicated," I said.

"She hasn't been in Fawnie's leg liquor, has she?"

I cleared my throat.

"Maybe if I had some of that I could sleep, too."

"You really shouldn't, you know, because..." If I answered that she'd remind me about her plans, and I didn't want to hear it again. I punched the mattress. "This bed really is sort of lumpy."

"Yeah."

"Guy has complained about it, too, but it doesn't really bother me. Maybe because I'm sort of lumpy myself."

"Bet Guy doesn't complain about that." She smiled wistfully.

"If he did I would gladly point out that his feeding me pancakes doesn't help with my de-lumpification."

"Are you two really going to get married?" She brushed her fingers over my bare left hand.

"I have a ring in the downstairs bathroom that says we are."

"I bet you're so happy, you know, to have found each other again."

"Is that what we did? I hadn't thought either one of us was ever all that lost, just too lazy to put forth the effort to find each other again. Too lazy or too pigheaded to admit any wrongdoing on our own parts."

"Do you have regrets?" she asked so softly I almost thought it might be that unseen spirit I'd felt at the pond speaking.

"I don't believe in regrets." But then there were a lot of things I did not believe in that had become so much a part of my life that I scarcely went a day without dealing with them. "But, yes, I have a few."

Lost time. Lost opportunities. Christmases. New Years. Birthdays that wouldn't sting so much because we were growing old together.

"Not having children with Guy?"

"Children?"

"Yeah, don't you wish…"

And that's when I realized the truth.

Abby didn't want to get rid of her baby. I don't know why she had chosen that path, maybe the baby's father, whoever that might turn out to be, would expect it of her. Or maybe she thought if she made the child go away, then the disappointment her parents felt in her would go away, too, eventually. But with a baby as a constant reminder…

I wanted to grab her and shake her and order her to never make a decision that could alter her own life so irrevocably based on what she thought would please someone else. Not even your own mother, and particularly not a man.

But that was totally the wrong thing to do. Speaking the truth to her in her vulnerable state would turn me into the enemy.

It would turn me into her mother.

No, if I ever hoped for Abby to listen to me, I had to keep my big mouth shut.

Deep breath. Only I couldn't. Just a few shallow huffs. Pressure built behind my eyes. I sniffled and wondered—can you catch a cold from handling a dead body?

And suddenly I could imagine my nana Abbra hollering at

Min and Bess and me as children in an imaginary scene, "You girls come away from that corpse and for heaven's sake don't touch it, you don't know where it's been."

Not that we had all that many spare corpses popping up around here, but if one had, I know that's what my nana would have said. "I swear you girls act no better than heathens, poking at dead people you don't even know like that."

"Charma?"

My mind snapped back to the moment, well, wandered back more like. "Hmm?"

"I'm just taking the basics with me to stay in Grandma's room, if you don't mind, and leaving most of my clothes and things in here, okay?"

"Oh, sure, hon. I won't need the room after tonight."

"Where you going?"

"Nowhere." I blinked, then realized what I'd said. "I meant I just wanted to spend tonight in here. I'm so awfully tired all of a sudden, I just want to tuck myself away and be alone, you know?"

"I do."

Except Abby couldn't be alone, not completely, not with a child growing inside her and the responsibility of all the women of her family bearing down on her.

"Charma." She paused in the doorway with a toothbrush in one hand and a robe draped over her arm.

"What, hon?"

"Thank you."

"I didn't do anything."

"I know. That's why I'm thanking you."

"You're pretty sure you're going to do this, aren't you?"

She didn't answer, just slipped out the door and shut it between us.

This already sad day had just grown unbearably sadder. My

heart ached, proving it hadn't completely broken after all. There had still been room for just a little more hurt in it.

I tugged at my collar, ran my hand around to the back of my neck. Sweat dampened my hair. I went to the window and pushed it open in hopes of getting fresh air, but beyond the rooftop nothing stirred.

I reached under the old mail again, whisked free another tissue and patted it under my chin. My head angled, I caught a glimpse of painted wood in the disarray on the dressing table. The *kokeshi*.

Just two pieces of fitted wood. The larger, the body, was more egg-shaped but flat on the bottom, the head round with a smaller knob of a hairdo painted black and wearing a sweet, serene expression. She was smooth except for the pitted paint here and there and the random nicks and gouges we all pick up after more than forty years on this earth. I stroked the plain markings on the kimono with one trembling fingertip. "My soul."

Aunt Shug believed the *kokeshi* dated back from a time when Japanese peasant women drowned infant girls because they could not afford to care for them. They kept the simple carved figures to hold the child's place in their family and remember the little girls lost forever to expectation and circumstances. I could still see Shug as she told us the story, her face softened in anguish at the very idea of making such an unthinkable sacrifice.

Bess told us that was just plain bullshit, that the dolls were just cheap souvenirs. Still, at the end of her life, she had tolerated the doll being in her room. Min even slipped it into the coffin before they closed the lid one final time.

It seemed only right.

Our *kokeshi* represented our souls. And Shug gave them to us to remind us that we, unlike far too many women, had control over our own destinies, our own bodies. Bess certainly had that control right down to her death. Mama, too.

Now, it seemed, Abby stood ready to take up the tradition.

I wondered if Abby was carrying a girl.

A daughter.

Min's *grand*daughter.

Since I would never know for sure, I decided it must be so. Don't all babies start out female?

Tomorrow, I decided, I would get on the Internet and try to track down a *kokeshi* for Abby's never-to-be-born daughter. A simple wooden doll with a sweet face and painted kimono. A *kokeshi* to hold a place in our family for the baby we would never hold ourselves.

And who was I to judge, anyway? What kind of mother had I been? What kind of anything had I been? I stared into the dark mirror and confronted my own face. My own fate. My own failure. Yes, a failure at just about everything I had ever hoped would bring my own salvation. As a daughter, a wife, a mother, a fiancée. I had given up my only avocation, school nurse, to come to the Aunt Farm and save my family, and now the farm was gone, too. I had struck a bargain with God, done my bit and…nothing.

Had I failed God or had he failed me?

I had tried my best, given my all. And *I* had failed.

I don't know if the tears started then or if I had been silently crying for a minute or two. It didn't matter. I pressed my own *kokeshi* to my cheek and let it all out.

I am an ugly crier. My face goes red and scrunches up. Snot flows. I snort and gulp and blubber. It's the kind of thing I try never to do in front of anyone. Ever.

So alone there, with my soul cupped in the palm of my hand, I lay down on the bed, curled up like a child and cried what was left of my heart out.

❧ CHAPTER FOURTEEN

"Not tonight!" I awoke from a deep but restless sleep in full rage at the Almighty. "After everything else today, damn it, why do you have to pick tonight to give me my first hot flash?"

I threw the covers off. Sweat drenched my cotton gown. My skin boiled.

"Not fair," I muttered, then looked heavenward and shouted, "And not funny!"

I swung my feet over the edge of the mattress, and just that fast the bed felt six feet tall. The familiar floorboards of my childhood refuge rolled, loomed close, then dropped out from under me completely. Everything spun around me as if I'd just hopped off the Tilt-A-Whirl at the county fair. I tried to look at the clock, but the numbers throbbed and swam. I blinked but could not make them stop.

Whoosh-whoosh. I could actually feel the blood coursing through my veins. Only instead of the normal ebb and flow, it had the reckless force of a river crashing over the rapids. My heart beat hard. Fast and hard. It beat like a fist against a brick wall, impotent, useless.

My head hurt.

Probably dehydrated. Just need a glass of water.

My feet hit the floor. My knees wobbled. The heat surging through my body disappeared in one flush of sweat, and when I placed my hand on my forehead my skin felt clammy and cold.

"Take a breath," I reminded myself, because my brain didn't seem up to the task of running the most simple of functions. My lungs expanded, I coughed.

Without really knowing how, I found myself walking, staggering toward the door, then into the hallway. The cool darkness took me in, emboldened me. Everything would be okay.

There was no place in this house I did not know. No light could illuminate my way better than my own familiarity with every nook and nuance. So I shuffled off down the hall. In the bathroom I would put a cold rag on my face, meet my own gaze in the mirror, find my center and restore myself with a simple splash of water.

My arms and legs went leaden, then tingled.

"Water?" I rasped. But water was no cure for what was happening here.

In that instant I knew I was in big, big trouble.

The fingers on my left hand flexed. I only knew that by watching them, not by *feeling* them. And that's when I knew.

I was having a heart attack.

In case of… Don't panic… Call… All my years of medical training evaporated. I needed help immediately. Where was I?

Upstairs. The Aunt Farm. *Alone.*

"Fawnie? Shug? Sterling? Abby?" Asleep. Downstairs. Downstairs, lost in their own pain. Not here, that's all I knew. Not close enough to hear my call.

I couldn't do the stairs. I'd break my neck. That would give my aunts a great story.

Fawnie: "The silly girl broke her neck while having a heart attack! We'll never know which killed her first!"

Shug: "Went ass over teakettle the whole way down and ended up with her nightgown over her head. Not a pretty sight, I tell you. But I sort of think Charma would have liked knowing her final act was to moon me and the uppity old lady here."

I decided to spare myself the further indignity.

Across the stairwell and down the hall, in Min's old room, Johnny slept. Or maybe he was still out catting around somewhere, dissuading drunken people all over Orla of any high-held opinions they might have of his mother.

Either way, if I struggled to get to him and died on the way he would carry that "if only" the rest of his life.

"No." No, I had lived my whole life with the burden of feeling I contributed to my daddy's death. I would crawl out on the roof and die shouting at the moon before I'd foist that off on my sweet eldest boy.

"The roof…the moon…" That was my hope for salvation.

For the first time in eleven months I forced myself toward the master bedroom in the old house, knowing the door was open, not locked as I had usually demanded it be. My nana and grandfather's room, the room my mother occupied for forty years—there lay my only hope.

Yes, it took my own impending demise to make me breach that threshold, and then only in one final act of desperate self-preservation.

I pushed my way in; in fine health it would have taken me no effort at all. I did not stop to take in the surroundings but headed straight for my goal. Mama's shotgun leaned against the back wall of her closet, the butt wedged into her shoe rack. The barrel was wrapped discreetly in the folds of her full-length mink.

The coat fell against my arm, over my bare shoulder. It seemed to want to pull me in but I thrashed and fought and pulled the gun free, knowing Mama would have had my hide hanging right next to her mink for showing such disregard for the danger of my actions.

"Done in with her own mama's shotgun in the master bedroom, rest her soul." Shug would *tsk,* then a gleam would come into her dark eyes. She'd wiggle her fingers and make her tone go all wavering to jack up the spookiness of it all. "Her ghost haunted that room from that day to this."

Gun free, I stepped out of the closet and almost fell backward.

"Fell off the roof in a state of piqued frenzy," Fawnie might offer with a slow shake of her head.

I could live with either of those scenarios. Or die with them. They had a certain style and mystique that I wouldn't have minded having tagged onto the end of my life story and told again and again.

My hand closed around the gun. It was damned heavy and cold, but not as cold as I'd always figured a deadly weapon would have to be. It felt okay in my hands, and even though I hadn't fired any gun for years, I knew I could do this. With luck I wouldn't even shoot off a part of my own body in the process.

One shot was all I would need to summon help.

It seemed ages since I'd left my own room, but in reality it couldn't have been all that long. Minutes, probably, everything happening all at once, each thought distinct, yet so brief. I stood there, giving myself a moment, giving the pressure and the panic time to subside. One thing I didn't want was to pull a drastic dramatic stunt—even by George family standards—by mistaking indigestion or the onset of menopause for impending death by heart failure.

Now, *there* was a story that would follow a person to the grave.

So I waited. It didn't take long.

Whoosh. Whoosh. Whoosh. Bigger and bigger, each pounding beat so fast one seemed to actually overlap the other. And the lightness. They do not preach this at you in the horror stories about the warning signs of heart attack—the euphoria. Calm detachment affected by, I suppose, a lack of oxygen or maybe a lack of fear.

For the first time in forever I moved beyond everything that had held me down—my grief, my fears, my failures. I detached. I was free.

So this is how it is at the last moment, I thought. *This is how I will die, that answers that question once and for all. Hmm. Interesting. Not scary at all, just...this.*

Then my pulse kicked up again. I waited for it to subside, but instead it grew in both rate and power. It rose in a crescendo so hard and fast and palpable that I imagined it extending beyond my body, echoing out in great waves like ripples in water. It filled the room, penetrated the walls and went out and up until it blurred the very stars in the sky with its intensity.

I, Charma Deane George Parker, was one with the sky and the stars and on my way to the ever after.

Funny, I had leapt into the water hoping for this kind of clarity and beauty. I had been afraid to die then, and now I was dying and reaching for the sky and I felt...not that bad.

Except for the nausea and the crushing pain. And the regrets. Abby was right. I did have them, but not about not having Guy's babies. I had my babies. What I hadn't had was time, with Guy or Mama or Daddy or...Or myself this past year.

And now I was going to die.

Unless I moved now. I started for the big French doors at the back of the room, the ones that led to what Nana Abbra called the "sleeping balcony" even though she never allowed anyone to sleep there. Mama and the aunts and loads of ladies sometimes slept there in their oyster-colored slips and pastel baby-doll nighties on hot summer nights. My foot sank into the thick carpet and I could not lift it again. My knees wanted to buckle under me, I could tell. The French doors and the sleeping balcony were just too far, across Mama's room and beyond my reach.

So I turned and propelled myself the few feet to the window that opened onto the side yard. I forced up the old frame: it complained but lifted enough to allow me access to the steep gable over Grandpa's parlor. I shut my eyes and lifted my head to feel the damp heat of the still November night. In the distance I could hear the thick grassy *glub-glub* and the swish of the pond. The creak of the old dock that I had flung myself off of in hopes of finding renewal.

"Dead to the old ways. Reborn to the new."

"Who said that?" I looked around me. I could not get a focus on anything but the view beyond the window frame. I shut my eyes until they burned with tears.

"Dead to the old ways. Reborn to the new."

"Bess?" I swear I thought I heard my dead cousin's voice.

Was it too late for help? Was she calling out to me? Bright light, I thought, I should look for a bright light. Actually, what I really wanted was a cold drink.

"Dead to the old, born in the new."

"Shut up!" I shouted to Bess. I hoped it was Bess, and not, you know, Jesus. Crap. I may have just told the Prince of Peace and Savior of Mankind to shut up.

"The cycle goes on long enough it doesn't even mean anything anymore, does it?" No, the voice was too familiar, too damned smarmy to be heaven sent. "None of it means anything, Charma, unless…"

The world around me spun, then stilled. My heart raced, then stopped.

Everything went quiet and for a second a great calm overcame me. Only for a second.

But that was all I needed to climb out onto the roof of the house where I was raised, lift my mama's old shotgun up and squeeze the trigger.

❧ CHAPTER FIFTEEN

"You should get down off the roof now, Charma. Charma Deane? You should get down off the roof."

I did not turn toward the voice so much as jerk my head back and up so that I spoke to the trees, the stars, and whatever wind had carried the voice of my cousin here so she could guide me. Or so she could get yet another shot at being a big pain in the ass. "Why don't you just push me, like you pushed me into the pond for my own good when we were kids?"

"Well, if I had a corporeal body, I just might. And when are you going to let go of that tired old story about me pushing you into the pond? I did it so you'd get over being so scared of the water, you big wussy."

"Maybe now you can push me off the roof to get over my fear of hurling through the air and landing face-first in the dirt." I'd say it was a gut reaction to blithely carry on a conversation with the disembodied voice of my dead cousin Bess, but the only reaction my guts had at that moment was for me to inch along to the edge and empty my stomach into the bushes below.

"Charma, now, this is enough."

"Like you ever had any clue what was enough and what went

too far. I never let you set my boundaries when you were alive. When *we* were alive." Thought I'd cover all bases, there. "I don't intend to start now."

"You have to get inside now so they can find you and help you."

"You've come here to help me? You?" I was so dizzy and the voice was so persistent. One shoulder pressed to the side of the window, I slid down slowly, letting the wooden frame guide me. In and out of blackness I sank down and down until finally the shingles rasped against my calves and scraped at the inside of my knees. I sat and curled my toes as if I could hang on, monkey-style, to the roof. Blindly I lashed out at my cousin with the barrel of the shotgun. "After a lifetime of screwing me over every chance you got, a few weeks in the afterlife and you're suddenly my guardian angel?"

"Do you see wings?"

I opened my eyes and for just one moment, the pressure subsided. "I see...Bess, I see you."

"I know."

I laid the gun aside. It slid butt-first down the roof and caught on the rain gutter. "How is that possible?"

"You have to ask yourself that." She didn't appear as gaunt as when I had last seen her, but she did have on the clothes we had buried her in. Fawnie's wedding dress, the dress Bess had worn when she married Sterling not so very long ago in the yard below us, sparkled in the moonlight. But then it would, rhinestone buttons and all.

"You look good." I nodded and stretched out one leg in her general direction, hoping it would bring some feeling back into my extremities. "For being dead and all."

"Wish I could say the same for you."

"About me being dead?"

"About you looking good. Charma Deane, you look like hell."

"And you know what hell looks liked because…?"

"What do *you* think?"

"I think Georges don't do the ghost thing."

"Since when? I never met a George yet who didn't believe—"

"Believing is not doing!"

"Well, if my turning up does nothing else but finally help you grasp that simple concept, then it will have been well worth the effort and the output of ectoplasm."

"Hah! You *are* a ghost! I should have known it. You always had to do the opposite of anything the rest of the family thought was the right way to act or speak or handle one's self. It figures you'd be just as big a donkey fart in death as you tried to be in life."

"And with that lovely thought…" She extended her hand to me.

"Are we going to go now?"

"Yes." The voice had changed, gotten lower and the image blurred.

Suddenly I became aware again of my heartbeat pulsating through my veins, of pain and fear and of someone, a real flesh-and-blood someone, taking my hand.

Believing is not doing, Charma.

"Believing is not…" I couldn't form the words. I couldn't grasp the message behind them. I couldn't see Bess anymore.

"Be careful with her."

"Mind that damn shotgun."

I could swear I heard Shug's voice now.

"It pointed right up this way. You kick a stone down that way or knock it off, we have a whole truckload going to the hospital tonight."

"Shug's right, Sterling, honey."

Fawnie?

"Be careful. Be careful with our girl."

"I will, just…you two go on downstairs and get things ready for us, okay?"

"You don't want them to see if this goes badly, do you?" I asked as strong arms urged me to get onto my feet. But my legs would not cooperate. "You don't want those awful, horrible, amazing ladies to watch me pitch forward headfirst off this roof, dead before I come out of the water."

"Shh." His face was so close to mine I felt the rush of his breath on my cheeks.

"That's what they said about my father when he saved me. Dead in the water. He died saving me." I propelled my shoulders up so that I could meet Sterling's gaze and face the naked emotion in his eyes. He was terrified and angry and determined. "Please," I whispered. "Please don't make that same mistake."

"He won't," came the promise in Bess's voice. "But you have to help, Charma. You have to get up and get off the roof. Get off the damned roof now, Charma Deane."

Nothing in my inner being or outer body wanted to comply, but I did, anyway. I pushed with my right foot, because it was the only thing I could feel by then. I raised my head. Or tried. I had no control over my neck. Blood oozed from my scalp. I could smell it and then taste it as saturated strands of hair fell across my lips.

"It's not enough that you just jump in the pond, Charma—"

"I was pushed!" I screamed back at my cousin.

"If you want to save yourself, you've also got to swim."

My arm flailed. It hurt. It all hurt too much and surrender seemed so easy. To go under. To find peace. To give in as Garrett the embalmer had, as Bess and Mama had. To finally stop fighting.

"Don't you give up, Charma. Don't you dare give up." *This* voice was not Bess's.

"Please, Mom." *That* voice was not Bess.

I straightened my legs and moved my feet.

Halfway inside the window I spewed bile and whiskey onto someone's shoes.

I staggered back. A shingle slipped under the ball of my foot.

One last tug, one last push, one last effort and I fell into the room just as a clatter came from the edge of the roof. The clank of the old rain gutter giving away. A crash and instantaneously a shotgun blast from down below.

Then everything went black and I was floating.

"Back away from that mirror, ladies. Charma is *not* dying. I won't let her die. I won't lose her so soon after Bess."

"Bess?" I opened my eyes, then shut them again. I was in Sterling's arms, pressed to his chest like a child. He took the steps hard, jarring me with every footfall and making my limp legs jiggle.

The movement made me sick. Hot, bitter liquid filled my mouth. I spit it out, hoping I hadn't hit anyone. A warm, wet spot on my shirt told me that I had, though.

"Miz Fawnie, Miz Shug, y'all take that robe off that mirror this instant or I swear the first call I make when we meet up with the ambulance will be to have the sheriff come out here and evict your scrawny asses."

I smiled at Sterling's taking up for me like that and I laid my head against his shoulder. "No, that's all right. That's okay. It's right that they should do that. I don't want to get stuck here like…"

"Here's that aspirin."

A handsome face with wavy dark hair came in and out of focus, mostly out. "Boyd?"

"Johnny, Mom. Here, take this."

"Whatever it is, I don't want to take anything right now."

"No one gives a shit what you want, Charma Deane. Put it under her tongue," Sterling commanded as he crossed the threshold into the cool evening and the blinding brightness of the front porch light.

Johnny poked a small orange tablet under my tongue.

I tried to spit it out, but it got caught and I cursed Sterling, my unaccommodating body and St. Joseph, whom I, in my disorientate state, decided was the patron saint of baby aspirin.

"Don't talk like that, lamb." Fawnie rushed ahead of us as fast as her little artificial leg could carry her. "If, God forbid, you should die, you do not want those to be your last words!"

"Right, Aunt Fawnie. It would be a shame if after a totally blameless life God had to boot my ass out of heaven on a technicality because in dying I finally turned into a potty mouth."

"This is not time to try to be funny, Charma." I could hear the crunch of the drive under Sterling's feet.

"This may be all the time I have left, Sterling. If I don't try to be funny now, I will have missed the opportunity entirely." And I meant that. I had lived as an irreverent big-mouthed babe, and I guessed I ought to die like one.

"Only you're not going to die."

Sterling settled me into the passenger seat of my hearse and scooted me to the center.

"I don't want her riding with us." I jerked my thumb over my shoulder toward the back of the hearse, where Bess had made herself far too comfy for my liking.

"It's okay, Mom. It's just me and Sterling here." Johnny slid in beside me. "We're going to meet the ambulance halfway."

"Halfway to where?" If they knew where I was headed, I wanted to know. "Heaven? Hell?"

"The Orla Hospital." Sterling started the engine.

"Aah." I nodded slowly and turned to lay my head on my son's shoulder. "Hell it is, then."

✦ CHAPTER SIXTEEN

"Hospitals give me the creeps," Bess remarked.

"Then leave, why don't you?" Hearing from the dead was one thing, but listening to the dead go on and on and piss and moan about the damned ambience was just not something I was in a mood for at that moment.

The EMTs hit the emergency room door. The gurney jostled over the threshold. They had stuck a chart under my head, a monitor in my lap and probably a half-eaten pizza between my knees to keep it warm. I felt more like a piece of equipment than a human patient. Jerked up, wheeled around, talked over and left out of the entire process.

I reached out my hand not knowing exactly who or *what* had swept along into the crowded corridor with me.

"You want me to leave, Mom?" My son grasped my hand and gave it a squeeze.

"No, Johnny. Stay, sweetie." I commanded my lips to curve into a smile. I have no idea if it came off looking maternal or maniacal, but I made the effort for the frightened little boy I heard inside the man beside me. "I was talking to…"

I glanced at his eyes, and that little boy pleaded with me not to force him out in the open here with all these people watching. "I must have been dreaming."

"We're going to park you here while we see if your space is ready." The middle-aged woman who had identified herself as "Dot" in the back of the ambulance patted my shoulder but did not look me in the eye. Dot did not have a sense of humor. I found that out on the ride over when she had announced her name, issued a curt apology for her cold hands and yanked up my gown and started sticking electrodes all over my boobs.

"That's okay," I said to her. "I've had dates like this before."

Dot didn't smile. In fact she gave me the "I don't get it look," the one people give you when they do get it, don't think it's funny and want to cut you short from making any more similar remarks.

Dot handed me the heart monitor. "Hang on to that. We'll catch hell if we lose track of it."

And she was gone.

I brandished the small tan-and-electronic thingamabob in John's direction. "Sweetie, if you hear an earth-shaking snort from on high and suddenly I get sucked up to heaven in one giant giggle-snort, grab this monitor. Dot will catch hell if she loses track of it."

"Mom, you're not making sense."

"Nothing about this life makes sense, honey. You're old enough to know that now." I patted his hand. Or maybe it was my own hand. I couldn't tell.

Johnny said something, but I couldn't make out what in the din.

All around us people pressed by. Nurses in scrubs. Fresh-faced doctors barely on the job long enough to know how to mask over the abject terror in their eyes. The sick and injured, their loved ones, and I suspect a few of the people responsible for them being sick and injured.

From where they had left my gurney I could see the last few

chairs in the waiting room. There, stuck off to the side, was a Muslim woman I had never seen before, and this being Orla, that in itself was something of a miracle. She had her hand wrapped in a white towel dotted with bright red blood. Beside her stood a young boy who looked like he wanted to bust out crying, but at a glance from her he rallied and calmed down. That was it, just a look from his mother assured him that everything would be all right even though you could tell the voices in that little boy's mind believed the worst.

From beneath the traditional Muslim head covering that the mother wore, her eyes met mine. I smiled at her. We were the same, I thought. Women of faith. Women of hope. Women in trouble. Moms. Two women who knew that we simply couldn't afford to be hurt or worse, because without us the world would fall apart.

Women had certainly held my world together. I mean, I liked men, liked them a whole hell of a lot, but I *counted on* women. I counted on them to make me laugh and to keep me sane, to keep things moving along and to put an end to everything from injustice and pain to bad hair days. And I aspired to be the kind of woman who could be counted on in return.

I loved my gender, and all of a sudden it seemed paramount to know I had instilled in my son the same awe and respect I felt at this moment. "Johnny, honey, if I die—"

"You're not going to die, Mom."

"Just promise me that you will spend some time out at the Aunt Farm, you know, afterward."

"The Aunt Farm? The place where, when I first showed up, you told me to hit the road?" He glanced around us then leaned in to whisper, "Mom, don't worry. No matter what happens, I promise you I will do everything in my power to make sure Fawnie and Shug are taken care of."

"Oh, sweetie, you are so young. And so…male." I patted his

cheek. "Honey, I want you to stay at the Aunt Farm so that Fawnie and Shug can take care of *you*."

His smile went wonky, but under these circumstances, I'd take a wonky smile over that fear in his eyes any day. He forced a laugh. "You really hit your head hard, didn't you?"

"Yeah, maybe it knocked some sense into me."

His expression shouted his disbelief even though his mouth stayed shut.

Another pat. "Those old ladies are tough and they've been through everything. They could teach you a lot."

"It boggles my mind."

"Don't dismiss them out of hand because they're…well, they're the way they are." I waved my hand in the air. How that was supposed to represent the numerous facets of my amazing aunts' personalities and accomplishments, I had no idea. "They are also two of the only people on this planet who will love you, grubby rotten little car thief that you are, no matter what you do. Who will always believe the best of you and want for you…every southern comfort."

His dark eyebrows pressed down over his worried eyes. "The booze?"

I smiled. I think. "The dream. Not only will they want it for you, they will, if they can, help you realize it."

"You think?"

I thought of my whole life and the thread of these women running through it. Weddings and near weddings, babies, bust-ups, breakthroughs and death, they had never wavered. Wobbled a few times, but never wavered.

"Women are wonderful, John. They are resourceful and sweet and wicked and full of every pleasure imaginable. They will save your life, Johnny."

"And wreck it," he muttered.

"Which may just be another means of saving it," I reminded him.

"Okay. Yeah, I got it. Women are wonderful."

"Except that bitch, Dot, who jabbed this IV start into my arm. She must rot in hell."

"That's all I need to know?"

"For now. Oh, and tell your brother."

"Oh, shit! George!"

"You haven't called him?"

"No."

I studied John for only a moment, trying to see in him the softer, rounded face of his younger brother. I couldn't and that was fine. I wanted them to each be his own man, to each have his own look, and for them not to have to share the same experiences, at least not the awful ones. "Well, don't call him."

"But, Mom…"

"I don't want him getting nuts and deciding he has to drive over from Tulsa in the middle of the night. It would just give me one more thing to worry about."

"At this point I think you can let go of whatever crap you've been worrying about and just concentrate on yourself."

"That! There, that. That shows how very little you know about women, son." I pointed at him with the heart monitor in my hand. "Please wait until morning to call your brother."

He didn't get a chance to promise me before an older man came up and cheerfully informed me that they had a room ready and off we went.

They let me climb from the gurney to the hospital bed under my own power, so I figured that meant the worst had passed. One after another people came in and attached monitors and wrist-bands, and, I don't know, maybe one of those radio-tracking devices they use to follow the migratory patterns of penguins.

John tried to stay out of the way, tried to keep his eyes always on me but not to actually see what was going on too close. Sterling came in, and they made small talk. Well, as small as the talk gets when someone you care about is lying in a hospital bed with medical staff working them over.

Finally, I made sure Dot got her portable heart monitor back and that somebody knew to turn on the movie channels for me on the TV. Then everything got real quiet.

"So." Sterling took a step toward the bed, then gave John that look. That man-to-man look that sort of asked permission to make the move closer to me and sort of dared John to try to stop it. Line in the sand and all that kind of thing.

John pushed away from the wall he'd been leaning on, crossed the room and gave my forearm a proprietary squeeze. "Since he's here to sit with you, I think I'll step out for a minute."

I smiled at the damned machismo of it all and let it go. "Tell your brother I forbid him to drive here tonight. He is to wait until he hears from you in the morning."

John nodded, kissed my cheek and left.

"Sorry I took so long." Sterling plopped down in the chair by my bed as if he belonged there at my side, as if he felt at perfect ease in a chair by someone just this side of dying. "I thought that old hearse could probably keep up with the ambulance but decided to stick to the speed limit, just in case."

He looked tired and tested but tranquil. I wanted to hold my hand out to him and tell him that no matter what happened from this point on, he had done good and that I was no longer his responsibility. He would not have listened, so I made a joke instead. "Just in case someone saw you and you earned a rep as an ambulance chaser?"

"Just in case someone saw me and thought it was *you* following a full-lights-and-sirens EMT run. By dawn Chapman's would have to had beaten people back wanting to know when the body of Fawnie—or Shug—or *both* of them would be ready for viewing."

"That's scary."

He shrugged it off. "Small town life."

"Yeah, *that's* scary, too. More scary?" I did hold my hand out to him then and he took it. "That you've already begun thinking like an Orla local."

"Isn't he gorgeous?"

"I thought you'd left," I muttered to Bess.

"When?" Sterling leaned forward, concern all over his—yes, Bess had it right—gorgeous face.

"He's *still* gorgeous," she whispered as if she'd read my thoughts.

"It's only been like six weeks," I snapped.

"Since I left? You mean since I moved to Orla? It's been a lot longer than that. Lived here a year before I got tangled up with your family."

Back on track, I smiled and curled my fingers around his. "Before you got tangled up with them but not with me."

"But not with me," Bess mocked. "You think you are so hot because you dated him first."

"You ever had a serious relationship with a man I didn't date first?" I looked around the room for the source of the taunt but I had only sensed her presence, not seen her, since that one moment on the roof.

"Charma, honey. Should I call a nurse in?"

"I know you kissed him." Bess again.

"Nothing. It was nothing." I put my hand to my eyes and answered them both, then met Sterling's gaze. "Thanks for thinking about my family first, Sterling. That was…" *Totally unexpected.* "Nice. Real nice."

"Least I could do. Uh, I also took a minute in the parking lot to make some phone calls."

"Okay." I glanced over at the tan phone sitting by the bed, thinking about who did and didn't know by now.

Sterling flipped my hand over in his so that both our palms turned upward. He traced the lines there with his one fingertip as he spoke. "Abby had called Inez for your aunts, but I wanted to give her my number and, you know."

"Let her know that you trying to literally steal the foundation right out from under me wasn't the thing that drove me onto the rooftop with that shotgun?" I dipped my head to try to catch his gaze.

"That was something," he said. He chuckled. I guess that's what it was, and he jerked his head so that I couldn't see into his eyes.

"Something *idiotic*." Bess muttered. A ghost that muttered, she would manage to pull that off.

"Why didn't you stay inside and just point the barrel out the window?" they both asked together. Or maybe just Sterling asked it. If Bess had really joined in, there would have been more swearing.

"I didn't think of it." Suddenly I could feel the weight of the gun in my hands again. The shingles under my feet. The moon and the throbbing of my heart. I rolled my head to watch the monitor *blip-blip-blipping* quietly away. "I wanted to get everyone's attention."

"And in that household a shotgun blast out the window just wasn't going to be enough?"

"Hell no." This time I know Bess spoke when I did, and it tickled me enough to make me laugh, which made me sick to my stomach again.

Sterling closed in to come to my aid.

I looked down past the plastic container he held under my chin. "Sorry about your shoes earlier."

He brushed my hair back. "I've had worse."

I spit.

"There at the end with Bess." He set the container aside as if he'd just finished offering me an hors d'oeuvre. "You remember. Blood, vomit, whatever."

"You were very good with her."

"I loved her. And I love you, Charma Deane." He took my hand again and rubbed it between both his palms. "Except, you know, not in the same way."

"I should say not," Bess said.

"Shut up." I closed my eyes.

He laughed. "I had that comin'."

He did, so I let it go without trying once more to make somebody else aware of the unseen presence in the room.

"Anyway, Inez is heading to the Aunt Farm. Abby is calling her parents, uh…"

I stared at the ceiling. "Did anyone call Guy?"

"Was I supposed to?" Sterling played it cool. Usually he and Guy had gotten along fine. In fact he'd pushed me toward restarting the relationship, so this attitude was new. And yet, since that kiss and his moving into my house, it didn't surprise me.

"I'll call him." I don't know when Johnny had slipped back in. "He should hear it from someone in the *family.*"

And he was out again.

"When did Johnny and Guy gets so pal-sy?" Bess asked.

Or maybe it was Sterling.

I couldn't tell anymore.

A nurse popped in. The TV lady. Someone with a menu for breakfast, which she snatched from my hand the second she realized they didn't have an order to feed me.

I sighed and Sterling shot up from his seat.

"This is nuts. No one is telling us anything."

"Tell him this is normal," Bess urged.

But I didn't follow her command.

"I'm going to go see what I can find out," he said.

"Thanks." I couldn't see Bess so could only guess that she was shooting darts from her eyes and standing all slack-jawed at my not rushing to do her bidding. Tough. I was the one lying here not knowing what had happened or what might happen next. There were worse things in a case like that than having a lawyer who loved you ready to take up your cause.

I shut my eyes. I didn't think I'd fallen asleep. I didn't dream. I just zoned out for a while when a deep voice called me back.

"You had a heart attack."

I opened my eyes. "Guy?"

"God, Charma Deane. You had a heart attack." He stood at the foot of my bed. "A heart attack," he repeated, as if he thought I needed convincing.

I reached out to him. "I believe you."

"God," he whispered again and came to me. Careful of the wires and electrodes, he wound his arms around me and drew me up to him.

"Safe at last." Bess hissed both *s*'s, sarcasm dripping like acid from every syllable.

Maybe *I* put that sarcasm there. Maybe Bess wasn't there at all. All I knew was, I didn't feel safe in Guy's arms. I didn't feel…anything. No sense of relief, no rush of emotion, no longing for him to hold me forever and never stop. None of that shit that you are supposed to feel toward the man you have promised to share your body, soul and bathroom with for the rest of your life, amen.

With one hand Guy cradled my head, and a sudden searing pain made me suck air between my teeth.

"What?" He eased away, just a little.

"Bumped my head."

"When?"

"Just before I went out on the roof and carried her to safety."
Sterling stood in the doorway.

"God," Guy murmured again, more prayerlike than curse. He
touched my head, my cheek. He took a long sideways look at the
heart monitor. "Shit. This afternoon I thought my life was in the
crapper because we're going to lose the business and now...are you
all right?"

"Had a minor cardiac event." A doctor I knew only by name
strolled into the room with his eyes fixed on the chart in his hands.
"Going to keep you here a few days, run some tests. Don't want
to overlook anything."

"What's the preliminary assessment?" I asked, turning loose of
Guy and pulling my knees up.

"Actually, it looks good." The doctor flipped another page, his
head shaking.

"But?" I knew doctors. There was always a "but."

At last he looked at me. Looked at me long and hard, his expression this weird blend, impassive yet troubled. "You shouldn't be
here."

Guy swore again.

Johnny turned away and disappeared into the hall.

Sterling stepped forward. "We acted fast to get her to the ambulance, but we didn't take any extraordinary life-saving measures.
Are you saying her being alive is some kind of miracle?"

I listened for Bess to chime in and hog the glory for saving me
from certain death. She didn't.

"I don't mean she shouldn't be alive. She shouldn't be in the
hospital." The doctor pressed his fingertips to the top page of the
chart. "She shouldn't have had this happen. She has no history.
She's too vital. She's too young."

I swear, if the man had tacked on "and too thin" I'd have ditched both Sterling and Guy on the spot and become his love slave for life. "So that's a good thing, right?"

He frowned. "I don't know."

"Damn doctors." Bess was back.

"I just can't help thinking…" He chewed his lower lip and stared at me. And I could tell it wasn't because he was envisioning that whole love-slave aspect, either. "You might be the one."

"The *one?*" I croaked. Given that I had a personal-savior complex and had recently begun communicating with the dead, the exceptional designation concerned me more than a little.

"Yeah, the one they always warn us about. The one every doctor dreads."

I looked at Guy and then at Sterling. If I could have seen Bess, I'd have looked at her, too. The *blip* of the monitor picked up slightly.

I clenched my jaw and waited for the man to finish pronouncing sentence on me.

He met my eyes in a way that made me think he wished he could see something more there, something that would give him some clue, some hope. He shook his head, just barely. He let his breath out and looked and looked and at last he said softly, "The one we send home saying she's fine and she drops dead a day later."

❧ CHAPTER SEVENTEEN

Go home and die.

That was the hex that doctor put on me.

This…this…*thing* happened to me. This breach. This fickleness. This vandalism of my body—*by* my body. Further compounded by the objectification of said body by an entire hospital's worth of people.

Oh, and there was another royal pisser—who would have known I'd object to my body being objectified? I mean, wasn't that exactly the kind of thing I'd worked so hard to accomplish since the first time I figured out that if you got onto a swing in a full skirt, every boy in the schoolyard would want to give you a push?

After I sent everyone home so I wouldn't feel guilty about them waiting around while I got wheeled from machine to machine, I proceeded to lift my shirt to more strangers than a drunken co-ed on a *Girls Gone Wild* video. I should have been proud. But I had been hexed. Voodooed. Or is it hoodooed? I had been prophesied over by a medical man and heard it confirmed to me by every nurse and tech and even another patient waiting in the post-MRI hallway: "You're the kind who goes home and dies."

Dies, damn it! It's one thing to be ready for it in the midst of the event, but to have it flung out into the universe like that to lurk around gathering power and probability?

"Shitfire," I whimpered to Bess the first minute the two of us were alone. Or, in point of absolute fact, when I was alone but thought maybe Bess was hovering nearby close enough to hear me. "I have got to get my life squared away. Minnie will have spoken to Abby by the time she gets here, and to Shug and maybe to Guy and… You aren't off talking to Minnie right now, are you?"

An alarm went off at the nurses' station just across the hall from my room. I waited and listened, half expecting them to burst into the room and try to resuscitate *me*. That's what this had all come to—even my most basic instinct to think of helping other's first now failed me. My whole world had been reduced to me, me, me.

"Maybe I've stopped hearing from Bess because I'm turning into Bess," I mumbled, my eyes pressed shut.

"Oh, you *wish*." The voice came from no particular direction at first, then settled on the left side of my bed. "Do you honestly think that if I had the ability to inhabit the living I would choose someone who not only hasn't showered for a day, but has a bad heart and pasty-white flabby thighs?"

"*Fleshy* thighs," I corrected the presence I could feel like a weight against my calf. "Hot, sensuous, fleshy thighs."

"Hop up, whip around and get a glimpse of those saddlebags in that hospital gown and say that."

I gave a random kick.

The weight I had sensed, as if someone were perched on the bottom left side of the bed, lifted.

"I only know that if I had thighs like yours…" The sheets rustled, and the inexplicable heaviness settled on the bed again. "Man, if I had any thighs at all, I'd wrap them around that firm, adorable better half of my ex-better half."

"Ex?"

"Former? What should I call him? We're not married anymore. The vows were honored. The marriage bond is no more. I can highly recommend him though, you know, if you ever want a creative way to work off some of that, uh, flesh."

"You cannot be suggesting... Me and Sterling?" I considered confronting her about how jealous she'd seemed over our one kiss. Then the bizarre likelihood that I was, in fact, holding a conversation with no one but my own subconscious pulled me up short.

Me and Sterling. Bess and Sterling. Me and Guy. Bess and Guy. The interconnectedness of these relationships and trying to sort out the whys behind them all could keep a therapist busy for years. I didn't have years.

At any moment now I could drop dead. Or one of my relatives could show up. Either way, there was a distinct possibility I would end up in hell.

"Bess, the only ex of yours who will be getting close enough to me to determine whether my thighs are flabby or fleshy is Guy, and he was *my* ex before he was yours—*as was Sterling.*"

"You just cannot stand the competition, can you?" This voice—this accusation half ballyhooed in jest, half bellowed in anger—did not come from some disembodied presence but from across the room where the door was simultaneously opened hard and banged against the wall.

"Minnie!"

Damn, I was happy to see that girl—that gray-haired, middle-age-spread-inflicted, fat-pad-under-the-chin-and-still-grinning girl I had loved forever. I should have pulled back, I suppose, knowing what I knew. More to the point, knowing what she *didn't* know. But here was Minnie, my cousin and oldest friend, the only human being left on earth who heard the music of my soul, the music Mama said no one else heard. Min had flown from halfway around the world to my side, and as things stood at this exact moment in time, she still loved me. How could I not celebrate that?

"You just couldn't stand the idea of Bess hogging the big old spotlight of death all to herself, so you had to go and stage a little dead-dog-and-pony show of your own!" Unlike the men in my life, Minnie did not linger in the doorway or stop at the foot of the bed or take a seat beside it. Within seconds she had climbed onto the mattress and had her arms wrapped around my neck and shoulders like a kid wrestling with a rag doll.

"A dead-dog-and-pony show? Sheesh, Min, that is one sick image."

"You should see what I'm looking at right now," she shot back at the same time that her fingers swatted back a tangle of hair stuck to the side of my head with blood and vomit.

Even in that awful shape I could be pretty vain, so I looked in the direction of Bess's ghost, just in case Min could see her, too, and had been referring to Bess as "what I'm looking at right now." I confess I wasn't sure which I wanted more, to share my haunting with Min or to gloat over the fact that my fleshy thighs were not the only notable imperfection between my dead cousin and myself.

But Min's gaze stayed fixed on me. "I'm only giving you crap because they say you're going to be fine, you know. If you were really in trouble, you can bet I'd pretend that I really cared about you. At least to your face."

"Thanks." I laughed. Tough love, southern comforts—they are pretty often the same damn thing.

She kissed my cheek.

"Don't try to make up with me now." I pushed her face away gently.

She sat back on her heels, kneeling on the bed, and studied me a minute, beaming.

If only she knew what I knew about Abby and my role in what was happening—in what was *going* to happen—I doubt she would be so pleased to be here.

"You scared me," she finally whispered, this time taking only my hand in hers, which between Min and me was more than enough. "Tell me now, are you really okay?"

"I have never been 'okay' a day in my life."

"Fine. Then tell me the truth—are you still fabulous?"

I primped a bit, pinching at the almost threadbare fabric of my gown, trailing one fingertip along my cheek, fluffing up the side of my hair not plastered down with bodily fluids. "Fierce and fabulous."

"And fleshy," Bess tossed in.

"I'm okay," I said, my teeth clenched. I gave Min's hand a squeeze. "How about you? The trip must have exhausted you."

"I'm spent." She lay down on her back beside me.

I scootched over, mindful of leaving Bess some space—though I didn't think she deserved it. But here we were, the three of us together again, and why ruin that by crowding Bess's spirit and sending her ass spilling onto the floor?

"You didn't have to come right here. I'd have understood if you wanted to go to the house first," I lied.

"Liar," Minnie said, calling me on it. "You'd have pitched a fit if I had gone there first. Probably woulda started looking for a shotgun, climbed out onto the ledge and started shooting."

"Heard about that, did you?"

"It's a great story, Charmika." She laced her arm around mine. "Wish I'd thought of something like that."

"You have a reason to climb out a window with a gun?"

She raised her shoulder and met my gaze. "Do I?"

What do you say to a question like that? I could have spilled everything, but I didn't *know* everything. I only had unconfirmed suspicions as of yet. What if I told Min about the baby with two daddies and it turned out that Abby had a pelvic infection instead?

"Or a cyst," Bess added.

Or a cyst. Never had I ever thought those three words could feel so much like a lifeline to me.

"Lifeline? Hey, you were grabbing at straws, I was just giving you another one to reach for." Bess again. "You know I'm just letting you get in deeper, don't you? Just giving you a little push so you will face your fears and…"

"Minnie, what do you want me to tell you?"

She sat back again. "Nothing."

"No, I mean it. If you have a specific question, ask it, but I want you to know right now, I don't have any specific answers. Just some semieducated guesses, a few burning spiritual convictions and, you know, bullshit."

"I don't want to know anything right now, Charmika. Just that you are okay. That you are not going to leave me the way Bess did, the way Abby has."

With that she asked me to go right on deceiving her, at least for a while longer. Oh, and not to die.

"I promise," I said, wondering if that was also a lie.

She exhaled the way you do when you've just finished a good long cry, or set down a heavy load, pushing the air out hard and all at once. "Travis went on out to the house to try to get some rest and make sure Abby is okay."

Blip, blip, blip, the heart monitor ticked off my concern. "He's going to talk to Abby?"

"Charma, it's Travis."

"Oh, yeah."

"He'll hug her, sort of. And kiss her on the head and tell her that we love her no matter what, and if she opens her mouth, he will throw up his hands, step back and say, 'Maybe you should save that girlie stuff for your mom.'"

"Girly stuff?" I shifted in the bed. The red numbers of my oxygen monitor fluctuated, dropping momentarily before stabilizing again. Maybe Travis and Minnie knew more about the possible pregnancy than I suspected.

"Yeah, romance and why she chickened out on meeting her boyfriend's family. Girlie stuff. He doesn't want to know about that. He doesn't want to think of her as having real feelings for this—or any other—boy."

"You two just live in your own little world, don't you?"

She smiled, catlike, sly and slight. "I learned from the masters."

Now, how the hell could I refute that?

Minnie rolled her head to rest on my shoulder even as she scooped up the TV remote and depressed the power button. "Do you have the movie channels?"

"Didn't you watch movies on the airplane?"

"I *slept* on the airplane." She flipped from one channel to the next. *Click, click, click.*

"Really?" Maybe she was taking this whole Abby thing with more composure than I expected. "I thought you'd have been too anxious and/or pissed off about what your daughter did to you to sleep."

"I was." Another *click.* A pause for the punch line of a car insurance commercial. *Click* again. "That's why God gave us little pink triangular-shaped pills."

"Now they've worn off and you're all geared up."

"Now I'm all geared up and exhausted and jet-lagged and I still haven't seen Abby to get any kind of explanation out of her." Groaning, she wedged the toe of one shoe against the heel of the other and her simple black pumps plopped to the hospital floor. She found a romantic comedy on TV and set the remote aside. "There."

The room fell silent except for the predictable dialogue about some kind of merry mix-up of the couple keeping them from recognizing the inevitable nature of their impending happily-every-after.

I opened my mouth, not sure what I could or should say to provoke the conversation I thought the situation called for, but Bess cut me off. Bess or my own inner voice that sounded just like Bess.

"She's in hiding."

I studied my cousin's—my living cousin's—profile and saw the truth in my dead cousin's pronouncement.

Minnie hated conflict. She had arranged her entire life in such a way as to avoid it. Between Bess and me she always played the mediator. She minded her mama and strived to be the teacher's pet in every class from kindergarten to college. She'd married a man who never raised his voice, ever, for anything.

Then there was Abby.

"Your daughter is everything you struggled not to be, Min," I said softly. "That has to wear you down."

"Her choices wear me down" was all she said, never looking my way.

Choices and having the self-confidence and risk-everything wherewithall to make the tough ones, that was a huge deal to Minnie. Not choosing, that was her style. It was her saving grace. Her best hope of holding her world together.

Less than two years away from home, Abby had embraced all aspects of her heritage and chosen what she wanted from each— Japanese, American and heathen. Only Minnie still didn't know it had gone way beyond an embrace.

"I don't know where she gets it from," she grumbled.

I nudged her shoulder. "Yes, you do."

Min smiled. "She is a bit like you, girl."

"Or Bess," we both said at once.

"Or me," Bess chimed in one beat behind.

"Mostly, you know, she's like Aunt Shug." I braced myself for a blowup at the mere suggestion.

I loved my mother more than I could ever express, but she had kept me at a distance. Whatever her reason, she had never allowed me to get close to her. Min did the same with her mother, set clear boundaries. It was all that *not choosing,* that trying to keep everyone happy, that did it. It was like performing magic, I supposed—you had to keep people from getting close enough to see how you did it to keep up the illusion. Min could not allow herself to get close to Shug. Now Min's daughter had pulled a stunt that required her mother to perform the ultimate magic trick—pulling from herself the fearless intimacy of trusting her child to make the right choice.

And I had gone and pointed out that Abby was just like Shug, that if she worked things through with her child, she would have to face things down with her mother.

"I know," Min whispered. "Now hush. I don't want to talk about this anymore."

"You can't just hide from your own daughter," I murmured.

"Not if you keep trying to drag me out into the open, I can't." She snatched the remote again and turned up the volume. "Now, shut up and let me watch this movie."

"And hide," I tacked on.

"And hide," she agreed.

The deal was struck. "Okay. We won't discuss Abby. Not now."

For now we would sit and just be, trying not to think beyond the time when we would go back to the Aunt Farm, where I would wait to die and Min would have to deal with the realities of life.

"Considering the realities of *your* life, Charma Deane," said Bess, or whatever, hovering close. So close, I swear I felt a chill work over my whole upper body as she concluded, "I think you may have the better bargain there."

❧ CHAPTER EIGHTEEN

"Did we treat you like this?" I hadn't thought that Bess would come home with me, but then again, where else would she go?

"Like what?" she asked.

I fixed my eyes on the white ceiling both to help me focus my thoughts and because I couldn't keep talking to empty chairs and the open doorway in the sheer hope she might materialize in one of them. "Like Minnie sinking deeper and deeper into denial. Guy standing at the foot of the bed, staring and sighing. Sterling sitting in a chair sighing and staring. And all the damned patting."

"Patting?"

"Fawnie and Shug. Every time they get within an arm's reach, they start up with it. Patting my legs, patting my back, patting my cheeks." I demonstrated with a hand on my face, my body, the furniture. "Did they do that to you?"

"I think they thought I was too frail for patting."

I smiled. "I think they thought you would bite them."

"I think that *you* should bite *me*." I don't know if ghosts laugh, but Bess did. Laughed at her own damn joke, which wasn't all that clever, and then before I could come up with a witty comeback she said, "No, Charma Deane. No one treated me like that. But then again I had the common decency to have a disease that people could interact with, that made them feel useful. I needed things."

Tempted as I was to make a remark about her having any kind of decency, common or otherwise, my deep-seated desire to wallow in self-pity overcame it and I whined, "I need things."

"The things you need are things you have to get for yourself."

I sat up, ready to challenge that, but she didn't let me.

"Why compare your situation with mine, anyway? Minnie was right. I'm dead two months now, and you are still making everything between us a competition."

That was because it *was* a competition. All our lives it had been the two of us, neck and neck, tooth and nail, heart to heart. It wasn't the kind of thing that ended with death, and she knew it. She had to have known it, or she wouldn't have willed *my* house to *her* husband. No, the bittersweet struggle between us was still on—and right now Bess was winning.

If I had doubted it, I had it reconfirmed for me when I got home and found where my family wanted me to recuperate. Not in the main parlor that everyone habitually walked toward when they came into the house. Not that small but cozy book-lined room with the marble fireplace we called Grandpa's parlor. Not the special space where Bess had spent her last days and where I had gravitated when I couldn't sleep.

No, on the evening when I finally got released and brought back to the Aunt Farm, they tucked me away like some fragile antique in the other parlor. The fancy company parlor, as Guy liked to call it, on the far side of the entry. With Fawnie and Shug leading the parade, Sterling directed the way, and suddenly I found Guy helping me down onto a couch covered with floral chinz and surrounded by cut crystal vases and gilded plaster statuettes of naked cupid babies holding rose bouquets and water jugs.

"I'd say I was in hell, but even the devil has to have better taste than this."

"Kill me. Kill me now. Don't leave me in here with those cupids, they scare me.

"There's too much damn sheer curtain fabric in this room. Come dawn, it'll be flooded with the blessing of first morning light, and you know how much I am going to hate that."

One by one I registered my complaints with my loved ones, and one by one they planted kisses on the appropriate places about my head and neck, then told me to get some rest. And then they left me there with only my ghost and my curse to keep me company. For that they would have to pay.

Ding. Ding. Ding-ding-ding-ding-ding. Bright and not so early the next morning I tapped a silver butter knife from my breakfast tray against a crystal vase to summon my lady-in-waiting, Inez. Only as she blustered into the room with a martini glass in one hand and a framed aerial photograph of the farm some guy had conned Shug into buying a few years back it did it dawn on me that Inez might not consider herself a lady, nor was she particularly interested in waiting on me.

Too bad.

"Where is Minnie?"

"Getting Travis off."

"Oh, my word, Inez, that is too tacky to announce, even to me." I made my most disapproving face. Okay, I don't actually have a disapproving face, since there is—no surprise here—so very little I actually disapprove of. Certainly not enough to have rehearsed a facial expression just to condemn it. So I made my "what is that smell?" face, which I thought would be a more-than-adequate expression of contempt to a woman already drinking at ten in the morning. Then I leaned in, lowered my voice and added, "How do you know? Were you listening at the bedroom door?"

"I'd tell you to get your mind out of the gutter, but this is the first time in a week you actually sound like yourself, and I've missed you. So I'll just keep to myself any thoughts about that hoochie whore-dog mentality of yours and how you apply it to way too many things that are perfectly innocent and you know it." She tossed back her drink, then dabbed at the corner of her mouth with her pinkie. "Minnie is taking Travis to the airport so he can fly back to Tennessee."

"Airport?" A two hour drive there and back plus time to see him to his gate. Or to the closest security checkpoint that Minnie could broach without risk of a strip search or embarrassing wanding incident. Something about Min puts those security people on edge—they stop her every time. Maybe they sense that as a child our nana Abbra often accused her, along with Bess and me, of being no better than a heathen. It's hard to live long enough to get ahead of a reputation like that.

Anyway, a trip to the airport gave Inez and me the good part of the day without Min around to interfere. Of course, for what I had in mind I couldn't risk that Min and Travis had just run to the store and would pop in directly. "You sure they went to the *airport?*"

"Travis said he had to fly home. Now, maybe he planned to sprout wings and self-propel, but I doubt it."

"After all that man has gone through at the hands of the females around here, he deserves wings and a halo and nice turbulence-free flight back home for a few days of steak and silence," Bess chimed in from across the room—or under the coffee table, I couldn't really say which.

"Anyway, speaking of getting back to work…" Inez turned around and began to prance out of the room.

"What kind of work are *you* doing?"

"God's work," she said.

"With a martini and a photo that shows every tree, hill and meadow on this property?"

She raised her glass. "God works in mysterious ways."

"So do Yankees and loony old women. What are the three of you up to?"

"Why do you care?"

I cared because I felt like I had taken a turn out while the carousel of life around here had kept on spinning, and that maybe I wanted to get back on. And I cared because it looked like fun and I hated that they had left me out. Yes, I'd asked to be left out, but now that they had actually started to get up to some good mischief…"I care because if Minnie is out of the house for the day, we have to act quickly."

"*We?*"

"Yes, didn't you know? I am using the royal 'we' now."

She arched her eyebrow. And that was impressive given it was already overarched by the outdated pencil-and-plucking method. But she managed to inch it up on one side really well.

"Oh, don't get all snooty on me. I'm just joking." *Sort of.* "But with Minnie gone and you here, it's the perfect time."

"For what?"

"Abby."

"Abby? Oh, you mean…"

I'd left the child hanging. Not by design but that didn't change the fact of it. And while some part of me had genuinely hoped the girl would confess all to her mother and Minnie would have taken on this responsibility, experience told me that was just nuts. Minnie didn't want to know. But Abby *had* to know.

So that left only me, Inez and a home-pregnancy kit to get the job done. "Today is the day we pee on the stick."

"That better be that royal 'we' thing again, because, girl, I am *not* squatting over no stick." She gulped back the last of her martini, then huffed off.

I had to ding for a good three minutes before I could get Abby awake and downstairs.

"Maybe someone should bring me my cell phone so I can call people when I want them down here," I said as the girl dragged in rubbing her eyes and moaning that I hadn't even given her time to get to the bathroom.

"Maybe you should just haul your ass up off the couch and get your own damn cell phone." Inez popped in, sans the glass and photo, and dived with one hand into her slouchy canvas purse. "Or better yet, climb the stairs and tell people what you want in person."

"I'm supposed to take it easy for a month."

"Your coming home with a boatload of information about proper diet and an outline for a comprehensive exercise program, and taking it easy for a month—which applies to not overdoing it and trying to reduce stress—is the only thing you latch on to?"

Latch on to? I had found nothing to latch on to in that hospital. I came away feeling cast adrift and doomed. Latching on to perfunctory advice was not a priority here—tying up loose ends was.

Inez tugged free some receipts and a crumpled dollar bill along with a bright pink box. An earring dangled from a gash in the dented corner. "Here. I've been carrying this around since you let me know you needed one."

"It's okay, isn't it?" Abby asked.

She opened the top and peered in. "The inside packaging is fine. Let's see what's in here—"

"Here." I snatched the box from her. "You keep an eye out for Fawnie and Shug."

"I don't have to."

"Why not? Where are they?"

"On assignment."

Abby and I shared a look, but neither of us followed up with the obvious question. I dumped the contents of the box out and hurriedly handed the plastic gadget with the silver tip, single button and little dark screen that had tumbled into my lap to Minnie's suddenly wide-eyed daughter. "Okay, take this—"

"And give it to me," Inez intercepted.

I grabbed for it, but didn't stretch or strain myself. "She's supposed to pee on that."

"Well, she can, but that would be a waste of good urine, not to mention what it would do to my digital thermometer." Inez depressed the button, the thing *bleeped* and she showed me the numbers on the screen.

"Why is there a digital thermometer in your purse?"

"I put together my own little first aid kit because some of my patients don't have even the basics when I do home visits. The thermometer must have fallen out of the kit and ended up in the box. I told you it's been jostling around in there for days."

"Fair enough. Just one more question."

"What now?"

"Did you just say *waste of good urine?*"

"Yes, it's the kind of thing you have driven me to, Charma Deane." She clicked off the thermometer and jabbed it back into the bunched-up sack she called a purse. "Putting together words like that and having them actually apply to real-life situations."

"Fair enough." I gave a queenly "Carry on" wave.

"Here, Abby, sweetheart, follow me and I will tell you exactly how to do this so you won't mess things up. You can't leave this kind of thing to chance, or to your aunt Charma. She never reads the instructions, just jumps in and—"

"I am *not* her aunt." It was the only part of the accusation I could refute.

Inez returned a minute later, and we waited.

"How long do these take now?"

"Two to five minutes according to the—"

"Yeah, yeah, the instructions. Big deal. Honestly, Inez, how bad could she have messed it up? If she just opened the box and let her go, she'd hit the mark."

"You're right. They make them pretty simple these days. I believe she could have done just fine without our help."

"I wouldn't go *that* far."

"People have managed to muddle through without your vigilance and supervision, girl."

"So *you* say." I attempted the eyebrow arch and, I swear, got a charley horse in my forehead.

"I don't just say it. I believe it. In fact, I'm positive."

"Good. Because so is my pregnancy test," Abby informed us.

If that came as a shock to Inez, it sure didn't show in her face or her posture or the way she sighed, rolled her eyes, cocked her hip and gave the most pained-faced and borderline-sarcastic rendition of crossing herself I had ever seen. I'd like to say that made me feel morally superior, but as someone who planned to nab my son's laptop later to locate a *kokeshi* to assuage my own guilt, I understood the ambivalence of a blessing for something I didn't dare allow myself to think of as a baby.

"Okay. Okay. At least now we know—step one." I rubbed my eyes. "On to step two. You need to see a doctor."

Abby sniffled. "Can we take care of this without involving my mother?"

I still did not look directly at the girl. In fact, I was looking directly in front of me, willing Bess to materialize. I needed her strength now more than I ever had before. "You can do this without involving your mom."

Abby sank into the nearest chair and hugged a ruffled floral pillow to her belly. "Thank God."

"But *I* can't."

"Shit."

"And that pretty much sums up my life as well." I reached out and gave the girl a pat. Even knowing how annoying the gesture would be, I couldn't help myself. "You need to see a doctor and, uh, well, from that point on you are going to have to make your own decisions."

"But, Charma—"

"*Butt* out, Inez. This is a family thing, and as my friend, a person I have brought into our family in a position of trust and affection, what goes for me goes for you."

"Charma, I didn't say a word." Inez studied me, her back to the wall.

I wanted to curse Bess, but then realized she'd take too much delight in that.

Abby made a sound, deep, guttural, juicy.

I had to swallow hard to keep down my reaction, a sudden rush of bitterness rising in the back of my throat.

"I'm going to be sick." Abby covered her mouth and ran from the room.

"Charma, what's going on here?"

I lifted my gaze to Inez and blinked, wanting to make sure she had spoken those words.

"Charma?" she asked again.

"We're going to get Abby to the doctor, then we are going to step away from this, Inez."

"That don't sound like you, Charma."

"You never did know when to jump and when to stay put and watch and wait." This time I knew who had spoken.

"Shut up, Bess."

"It's *Inez,* Charma." She moved in and sat on the edge of the couch.

"No, it's Bess." I looked my friend square in the eye.

"She's...well, maybe it's just the memory of her, but she's here, Inez. Pointing out my missteps, as usual."

"If I can quote Abby—shit."

"Yeah. But it's not for you to worry about."

"Only you can see her?"

"Hear her mostly. I take it as a portent." I had first seen Bess on the very brink of my own death. The fact that I could still sense her presence had to mean I couldn't have put much distance between myself and the afterlife. "Like I said, Abby to the doctor and then we remove ourselves from this. It's not our call, not our choice."

"What does Bess think?"

"I don't want to know," I told both of them, speaking loudly and with complete finality. "I know what Min believes and I think I know what Abby really wants, or what she doesn't want. She doesn't want to have an abortion before she's really thought it through."

"You honestly believe she hasn't thought about this nonstop since she first suspected?"

"Worrying over something and thinking it through are two different things. Not to mention talking it through. She hasn't told the father." *Whoever he might be.* "She hasn't talked to her mother or grandmother or even me much. She has stewed about it but she hasn't dealt with it, and I can't help her take this kind of leap without knowing she's considered what lies ahead. I thought you of all people would understand this, Inez."

"Because I'm Catholic?"

"Because you're someone who wants women to make the best choices for themselves without getting pushed into things. A midwife, a mother-earth type, a safe-port-for-a-woman-in-a-crisis type."

"No ports for women in crisis, not here." Sterling, going through a stack of mail, strode by the door. "No ma'am."

"Asshole," Inez called after him.

"Meddler," he called back at her without missing a beat. His footsteps moved along the hallway until he reached his office door, having just passed by the side door to the kitchen. "Miz Fawnie, Miz Shug, I saw you two creeping around in the side yard."

Moments later the pair appeared at my doorway, red-cheeked.

"I better not find so much as a single blade of pink or orange or black grass out there."

And caught red-handed each with a can of spray paint in her hand.

"We didn't spray nothing." Shug shook her head and crinkled her nose.

"Speak for yourself." Fawnie lifted her skirt to reveal a blob of hot pink paint dripping down her artificial leg and a light dusting of the stuff over her cane.

"When you do that?"

"When you told me I was holding the can wrong. I was trying to hit you in the butt, but—"

"You was holding the can wrong."

"You moved."

"Come on, old woman, we clean you up."

"Look what that lawyer has reduced those sweet elderly women to." Inez shook her head.

"They were always like that."

"Why are you letting him do this, Charma? It's your house."

"It's *his* house," that voice reminded me.

"Bess says it's his house," I told Inez.

"What do you say, Charma?" Inez folded her arms. "I have more cans of spray paint."

Tempting but not enough. "It's one more battle that I can fight."

"Are you crazy? You have more fight in you than anyone I know—except maybe your aunts."

I shook my head. "I have fought my way through this whole

last year. Death and loss and love and all the fragile ties between them, I have done my best. I flung myself at every crisis, hunkered in and…and…and gave it everything I could."

"And now you don't think you have anything left to give?"

"I no longer think it's my decision."

"What are you saying, Charma Deane?"

"I'm saying I jumped in the water to baptize myself. I made a deal with God, and I got a heart attack and a haunting in answer to my prayers. I am done thinking about the next stage of my life. I am done fighting."

"You never even tried fighting," Bess admonished.

"You don't look good, girl. Here. I have a cuff and stethoscope in my purse." Inez whipped that baby out before I could even come up with a smart-ass remark about it, and perched on the side of the couch, wrapping my arm in the thick black band. "Sit there and relax and let me take your blood pressure."

"Sit and relax? What happened to get up and fight?"

"That comes after. Right now just shut up so I can hear your heartbeat."

I let her do her work, not really caring what she would find. "You know, every third person in that hospital told me that I was the one who looked like nothing was wrong. Who shouldn't be there. Who had every reason to live, then went home and died."

"Oh, Charma, you've been a nurse long enough to know that's the kind of crap that gets said in hospitals all the time. It doesn't mean anything." She let the air out of the cuff and frowned.

"Maybe not, but I think this means something—my dead cousin appeared to me as my heart stopped beating, and she is still keeping close. I believe that means the doorway between this life and the next is still open. What are my numbers?"

"One-fifty over ninety-five."

She could have just said "not good." I had more meds than a

busload of senior citizens returning from Canada running through my veins, and still the pressure had not subsided.

"And since I don't know when I will be walking through that life-death portal for good this time," I finished up even as Inez reached for the phone to call my physician, "the only thing left for me to do is to get my ducks in a row and pray to God they know how to paddle."

❦ CHAPTER NINETEEN

"Hey, look alive in here! You have a customer with fistfuls of money and one foot in the grave." I pushed through the front door of the funeral home. The foyer was dark, the place still. My voice really carried. So I tipped my head back and announced, "Maybe one of those Chapman boys should wiggle his butt out here and sell me one of those prepaid package deals."

"Mom!" Johnny closed the door quietly behind us.

"Which one?" Loyal stuck his head out of the office.

I slipped off my sunglasses in my best movie star style and smiled horizontally, which is to say without letting the corners of my mouth lift. Bess read that in a fan rag when we were kids—to avoid wrinkles, smart stars and starlets smiled horizontally. So I tried it out on Loyal, knowing I had nothing to lose. "Five days and four nights in some steamy Caribbean island, cold drinks and hot men included."

"If you could get one of those deals around here, I'd book it for myself."

"Mom, there could be mourners here." Johnny grabbed my elbow.

Nothing stirred around us. The lights in the visitation rooms were off. Even the perpetually opened guest book on the pedestal by the door had been shut and the pen laid down instead of planted sticking upright out of the elegant brass-and-marble holder. "Any chance of that, Loyal?"

"What?"

"That there could be mourners here."

"Well, *I* am feeling pretty blue. But if you mean loved ones of the recently deceased, then no, not a chance in hell." He vanished back into the office. "You never answered my question. Which one?"

"Loved ones," I shot back.

"I meant which Chapman boy did you want to see wiggling? Because if it's me, I need a few minutes to warm up, and if it's my brother…seek psychiatric help."

I craned my neck to try to peer around the doorway and into the living quarters. My stomach lurched a bit at the thought of seeing Guy, wondering if he would walk out, see me and get that weird, sad face and start sighing. Creeped me out.

In the hospital and in the house, I hadn't thought about it so much. But here, in this place that had held so much history for Guy and me? In this place beyond the safety of soft beds and scores of well-wishers, it hit me. This heart attack business had changed things between us.

Maybe it gave him second thoughts about striking out on a new life even as he was losing his livelihood. Maybe it made him think about his own mortality, and he wanted to keep some distance from that. Maybe, and I certainly could empathize with this, this whole damn year had overwhelmed him. He had cremated my mama, helped us nurse and bury Bess, dealt with Loyal's lover committing suicide. Maybe with all that in his recent past, he found it hard to look at me and see any kind of future.

I got that. I totally got that. Up until the minute I walked through those doors I had not let myself dwell on it, on what was going to happen between Guy and me, but standing here it came at me all at once, and I knew what I had to do.

"You quarrelling with your big brother, Loyal?" I asked, still searching for any sign of my once and present fiancé.

"No more than usual." The voice carried from the next room. "But I don't have to have a beef with the boy to know that anyone who would derive any kind of enjoyment out of watching him shake his groove thing is one sick puppy."

"Do men have groove things?" I asked my son.

"The men I know do." Loyal popped up in the doorway again to give me a wink, then his eyes moved past me and his demeanor shifted. He stepped into the hall with his hand outstretched toward John. "Jiminy Fricassee, aren't you Boyd Parker all over?"

If you live in a small-enough town long enough, you know everybody. And if you know everybody as well as the George and Chapman families knew everybody, you knew everybody's secrets, but not necessarily their children. "Loyal, have you ever met my eldest boy?"

He gave my son's hand a firm shake and announced, "I should have been your uncle."

He did not gush or gay things all up like some people might have expected him to do. Now that everyone knew for sure, now that the unspeakable had been not just spoken in Orla but printed in the police records, Loyal could have burst out of the closet in full flaming regalia and not caused any further scandal. But he didn't. If anything, his public outing and impending professional disgrace had driven him deeper into the quiet, gentlemanly persona his mother had cultivated and adored.

It touched me to see him transform like that right before my eyes, because it reminded me of all the necessary deceits that had taken place in this house. People pretending to be something they were not, something that everyone else wanted them to be. It had taken the worst thing possible to give them an opportunity to change at last, to be free of it all, but it hadn't worked; nothing had changed at all.

"Johnny, this is Loyal Chapman. Loyal, this is my son, John Parker."

"Nice to meet you, son."

"Yes, sir." John muttered the way young men do when meeting someone who, with the first words out of his mouth, had overstepped all boundaries. John did not want to hear that he should have been Guy's son any more than he wanted to be told he was Boyd Parker all over.

John had come to the Aunt Farm for one reason, I understood then, standing there between these two men. And I had done nothing to help him realize his heart's deepest desire—to just be himself.

I took Loyal's hand in mine to guide him away from John and turned to say to my son, "I'll just be a minute here."

He nodded.

"There are cold Cokes in the fridge, right through that door." Loyal pointed. "Help yourself, son."

John rankled at the word, as if Loyal had intended it as a pejorative. Not for one minute, of course, did Guy's brother think that. He'd have loved to have had nieces and nephews he could watch grow up, children who would have loved him despite his faults and maybe a little bit because of them. Johnny was still too young, I guess, to see that Loyal wanted the same thing he did, to be accepted for himself. So he walked away, kind of bristling and smug.

Loyal watched him, and the minute the boy moved through the door, he relaxed and took my hand. "Boyd Parker all over."

"He doesn't want to hear that."

"Why? Boyd Parker was one fine, sexy bastard."

"Still is," I said, smiling a bit. "A bastard, that is. He called me, you know. In the hospital, just to tell me he was glad I hadn't died."

Loyal looped his arm in mine and led me toward the front office. "And there you just called him an ugly name."

"Bastard? You said it first."

"*I* meant it as a compliment."

"You didn't let me finish, though. Called me to say he was glad I hadn't died before I could get my affairs in order."

"Affairs? You have more than one?"

I swallowed. If Bess had come along with me, this was the point where she would have gotten in a dig about me and Sterling. I waited, then figured there were some places too dull for even dead people, and tagging along on a trip to see my doctor and my mortician was one of them.

"Boyd didn't mean *affairs* like men, he meant my will. With all the changes this past year, who owns what, what was left to who, Mama's estate and her belongings, none of that is yet settled even now, and he didn't want me to die without getting it in order." There. I'd said it aloud and in so doing added yet another thing to my list of things I needed to get taken care of.

Abby. Guy. Johnny. Mama. I rubbed the bridge of my nose and waited for the pain in my chest to come over me like a wave. It didn't, so I exhaled and raised my gaze to zero in on Loyal again. "Where's Guy?"

"Bank." He pulled out a chair for me.

I took it. "Bank?"

He moved around to sit on the edge of the desk. "Charma, honey, I don't know if you know it, but your little trip to the here-after—"

I held up my hand. "I didn't make it nearly that far, Loyal. Only over to the hospital in the next county."

"That's not the story your aunts are putting out."

"Oh?" Yes, I wanted to hear this. I mean, if God had it in for me and I wasn't long for this world, I wanted to hear now what kind of stories would be shared about me after I was gone.

"Your aunts are saying that this Sterling fellow literally snatched you from the jaws of death. Pulled you in off the rooftop just as you fell into a death swoon and grazed his gorgeous blond head with a bullet from Miz Dinah's shotgun."

"No, that's not..." I looked around me at this place where nothing was what it seemed. Hell, why not? Bess had written a book that she would always be remembered for. Guy and Loyal had the legacy of this business and its downfall. Why shouldn't I do some storytelling of my own? "You know, Loyal, if I had meant to shoot the man I'd have blown his head clean off. I only wanted to make sure everyone knew I wasn't just fooling around out there."

"Well, you scared the shit out of a lot of people."

"Did I?" Okay, I smiled, and a cocky smile, too, none of this horizontal movie-star stuff would do. Scaring people, having big tales told about me, I liked it. Probably more than a middle-aged mom of two should.

"Yes, everyone's talking about it. Scared the shit out of a whole lot of people. My brother included. Only you did more than scare the shit out of him, you also scared some sense into him."

My smile faded. I drew my feet up under my chair and laced my arms over my body. "How so?"

Loyal fidgeted with his tie, smoothing, jiggling the Windsor knot, brushing at something unseen amid the tiny pattern. "He's gone to the bank to lay all his sins on the altar of the Orla Chamber of Commerce."

I sat straight-backed. "*All* his sins?"

"Gay brother with dead criminal lover, lying frontman for his black mortician and all."

My hands fell open. "They will crucify him."

"Yes, but maybe out of that Chapman's will rise again."

Never going to happen. I knew it. Loyal knew it. Guy, even as he went to humble himself before people who had once held him in such high esteem that just his name kept his business running, knew it. In the space of a few days the world had changed, and he couldn't put it right with words or eleventh-hour actions. He should have let this fall away and be done with it.

Still, Guy probably felt a responsibility to Dathan and Dathan's wife and the staff Dathan had personally hired to run the place, and so he would at least make one reckless grab at trying to set things right again. When he made up his mind, Guy could be scary-fierce in his loyalty to someone or something. His father's business. His long-ago pledge to love me forever. Bess. Even after all the years of bitterness between them, when she had sought him out to share her secrets, he had been there for her, even when in doing so he knew that he was hurting me. I loved that about the man, and despised it, too.

"He's looking for partners, a way to reenergize the business with good will from the community."

"And if it doesn't work?"

"I'm still holding out for that going-out-of-business sale."

I suppose I smiled at that. Politeness would have dictated that I smile. So I probably did even as my brain shuffled through a thousand bits and pieces of thought and emotion. The world had changed. Nothing had changed. Guy was a man moved by obligation. I had failed my son. It was too damn late for me to avoid wrinkles by smiling horizontally.

Too damn late. I checked my watch. "I don't have time to wait for him then."

"You got a date?"

"With the lab. Blood work."

"Everything okay?"

Nothing is okay! I wanted to scream at him. Don't you understand? Coming here today only made me realize it more than ever. You are looking at a person drained of all her hope and a good damn deal of her faith. Here I am, this mom, this cousin, this friend, this lover, who has let down everyone she loves in one way or another. I did not love enough, I did not know enough, I did not have enough to extend myself far enough to make a difference. I am broken. I am ruined. I cannot fix anything. I jumped in the water and I wish I had never come to the surface.

I met his eyes and knew that if I breathed a single word of my true feelings to him we would both dissolve in a shower of tears and self-pity. Who would that help? How would that set anything right again?

I stood and took his hand, trying to seem reassuring. "Inez took my blood pressure, and it's not going down the way they hoped, is all. So I'm going to have some numbers checked, maybe change my prescription."

Like any of that would change anything.

"I'll say a prayer for you, darlin'," Loyal said. He kissed my temple.

I know he expected me to say the same right back at him. He coveted my prayers, as my aunts would say. I could see it in every fold and crease of his worn expression.

I kissed his cheek. "Tell Guy I came by."

I called for Johnny, and we stepped from the cool dim funeral home into the brilliant November day.

An hour later, driving home, I still could not slip off the heaviness that had overcome me at Chapman's. "That took a lot out of me."

"Like three vials."

"Not having blood drawn. This whole adventure."

"Adventure?" Johnny sneered, but it was the cutest sneer, not mean-spirited at all. "Mom, you are not old enough to think of a trip into Orla as an adventure."

"An expedition, then," I said. One where I had discovered a few things and realized I had to realign my course. And I had to start with my son.

I slipped off my shoes and put my bare feet on the dash of my lovely old Cotner-Bevington. I wriggled my toes. "There are all kinds of adventures, kiddo."

"I suppose." He handled the old hearse well. Well enough that if Chapman's wasn't totally in the crapper business-wise, I'd have suggested he consider asking for a job.

"They are going to change my prescription, and the pharmacy won't have the higher-dosage pills until four. Can you go back into town to get them?"

"You're not afraid I'll steal your car and run off?"

"It's not my car." What the hell else could I have said? The kid was baiting me. Hey, what goes around comes around—he might as well learn that now. "And since you'll be headed for the drug-store, you can drop off the rolls of film you've taken so far."

"Or not."

I waggled my leg a bit, the way you see an old fisherman do when he feels that first tug on the line but doesn't want to give away that he knows he's got something. "Don't you want to see what you've caught on film?"

"*Caught* on film? You know Aunt Shug was only joking about the paparazzi work, right?"

"Stop evading the question." I made a motion with my hand, turning the reel.

Johnny had walked away from his job. He had purposefully misunderstood the deal between us about my car in order to buy himself time—also food, booze and dinner for a date or two in hopes of getting laid—but mostly time. Now he had taken to futzing around the Aunt Farm with that damned camera, and if somebody didn't force him to do something with it, even if that something was to toss it in the pond, then he might not ever do anything, really, ever again. "Do you not want to get your film developed?"

"Maybe I don't."

"Why?"

"Chicken."

"Again, *why?*"

"Because, Mom, I really like doing it. Enough that I could totally see pursuing it as a living."

"And that's scary to *you* because?" There was a whole raft of reasons it was scary to me, but then I might drop dead tonight and this was his life, so I pressed on. "Johnny?"

He was quiet a moment. I knew that kind of quiet. Boyd Parker quiet. Had to come from that side of the family because no one on the George side ever shut up long enough for that kind of brooding mood to set in like a dark fog over the exchange.

Finally, he moved his palms against the steering wheel and said, softly, "What if I stink at it?"

Then you'll go back to work, apply to law school, get on with your life. If I felt like I had another forty or fifty years of that kind of hardheaded butt-kicking to get through to the kid, I'd have said it. I'd have said a lot more. I'd have gone off on a tangent about everything the kid had ever started and never finished, going all the way back to his first-grade science project. He was supposed to collect eight examples of different leaves. He collected at least eighteen—then, when it came time to catalog them in the black-and-white composition book we'd bought for that purpose? He told me the wind had blown them all away, and he'd just pick up some leaves and stuff them in a regular notebook on the way to school.

When I cleaned out his backpack on the last day of school there was the composition book, all eighteen leaves taped inside and notes in kid writing.

"The guys said only sissies and girls did that project" was his only defense. I'd let him slide on that then and on every other project and undertaking in his entire life, right up until he stole my car and didn't have any way to pay me back for it.

When I heard him talk about this newfound love of photography, I couldn't help it, I saw those leaves and knew I no longer had the luxury of telling myself he'd do the right thing on his own. "If you look at what you've done so far and decide you stink…then you work on getting better. And if you really love the work, you keep getting better and better and you don't give up because it's hard or even hopeless. Got it?"

He nodded. He stared straight ahead. He made the turn toward the Aunt Farm. Then, still not making eye contact, he set his jaw and cast his own line, quietly but with no less purpose. "I will if you will."

My quiet didn't come from some deep genetic need to make everyone around me utterly uncomfortable. I just didn't know what to say. Tough love. Butt-kicking. I had expected it from Bess. I accepted that from Minnie. I took it and dished it back with Inez. But from Johnny? "My doctor is pleased with my progress."

"Your doctor was pleased that you had bothered to keep your appointment." He pulled into the drive and up to the front of the house. "The man has treated you so long he doesn't exactly have high expectations."

"I had a heart attack."

"Yeah, I know. A heart attack, not a couch attack." He cut the engine.

"What's that supposed to mean?"

"It means that since you've been home, I haven't seen you get off your ass, outside of this trip, to do anything but go to the bathroom. Sometimes I check on you and think that damn couch is trying to swallow you whole."

"Don't you get onto me, too, Johnny. Please?"

"Too?"

"Inez is pissed that I'm too passive. Abby wants me to give her permission for something I don't have the power to even pass judgment on." And my dead cousin was riding my ass. That part I decided to leave out, as well as any reference to Guy or Sterling, because of that whole he-who-tries-to-sleep-with-my-mama-ain't-no-friend-of-mine thing. "Oh, and Fawnie and Shug want an ally in another one of their evil plans."

That got a chuckle from him. "Women are wonderful. They nurture. They nourish. They are the axis upon which our world turns."

I dropped my feet to the floorboard and inched my nose in the air. "There are exceptions."

Another chuckle. "Maybe you should keep a list."

"Maybe I will."

"Get you a Big Chief Tablet like Aunt Fawnie uses. Only on the front, instead of, 'Things I Have to Do Before I Die,' you can write 'Women Who Have Let Down Their Sex by Not Buckling to My Demands of How They Should Behave.'"

I narrowed my gaze at him. "If I kept a list, it wouldn't just have women's names on it."

He laughed, but I had to admit I liked his idea. So when I sent him back into town to get my pills, I stuffed his pockets with the rolls of film and told him not to come back without receipts from the photo shop for himself and a brand new Big Chief Tablet for me.

❧ CHAPTER TWENTY

"**I** want to hire you to update my will." I slapped my Big Chief Tablet smack in the center of Sterling's bare desk.

He stood and stared down at the red cover with the bold black lettering. *Things to Do in Case I Die.*

"Get thee behind me, Satan." He formed a rudimentary cross with an expensive gold pen and a plastic letter opener. "You are possessed by your aunt Fawnie."

"I am not. Her list is *Things to Get Done Before I Die.*" I pronounced every word hard and slow, emphasizing them each with a tap of my finger on the tablet cover. "This is not the same at all."

"So yours is a proper life list? The kind you and Minnie and Bess used to complain your aunt's list *wasn't?*" He lowered the pen and letter opener slowly, clearly not entirely convinced that I hadn't been corrupted by some otherworldly, or in Fawnie's case, way-too-worldly force. "See Paris? Sleep with a major political player high enough to have the FBI run up a classified dossier with the name Charma Deane George Parker slapped on it?"

"Done and done." I made invisible check marks in the air. "So, you see, I have no need for that kind of list at all."

"When?" He took a step backward, away from the desk and my

list, and folded his arms over his soft charcoal-colored sweater. "When did you see Paris?"

I liked that sweater and the way that man looked in it. Hell, now that I had decided I was dying and that things with Guy and me were never going to come to any real fruition, the whole self-denial deal seemed a big waste of precious time. I tipped my head to one side and sort of cooed my answer. "Boyd took me."

He narrowed one eye, his head sort of cocked, too. "To Paris?"

"Yup." I plunked one butt cheek on the desk and let my leg swing. I wished I had been in a soft, fuzzy sweater, too, and a tight straight line skirt like some 1940s film noir bad girl trying to get the hard-boiled detective to do her bidding.

He glanced down at my behind, just as I had hoped he would, then leaned in.

I wet my lips.

"Paris, France?" He yanked free the file folder I had unknowingly been sitting on.

"Paris, Texas," I confessed, a bit deflated but still plenty defiant.

"Shee-it." He stretched it out the way someone from our Lone Star State neighbors might do. "That doesn't count."

"Does so. You said Paris. Not my fault you didn't say which one." I laughed then. Partly because getting the best of Sterling made me feel a little like my old self and partly because seeing the best of Sterling kept me from feeling old at all. "You want to do my lawyering, you better learn to get down to specifics better than that, too."

"Okay, what about the other thing?" He stuffed the file he had taken from under my behind into a dark brown faux-wood box on the floor. "Major political player? FBI dossier?"

"None of your beeswax." I looked right and left for a better place to park my fanny and, finding nothing, whipped my head around and gave him my most queenly glower. "What kind of law office is this, anyway? Where are your chairs? Where are your lawyer bookshelves? Where are your fancy oak filing cabinets to stash a bottle of really good hootch in?"

His head still bent down, looking through the files in his little box, he said, "You're not supposed to drink, Charma."

"Hey, I can't let a little thing like dying make me stop living." I flashed a fabulous grin his way.

His lips clamped down into a tight, thin line. He frowned, mostly with his eyebrows and the set of his jaw. During our brief season of dating, he had never hesitated to call me a hypocrite when the occasion called for it, which was, oh, you know, daily. Now he held his tongue and his ground. A sign of maturity on his part? Or a hard-won acceptance of just how stubborn my own immaturity would be on this subject?

I lived in a world of my own making, where time, history and the motives of others all fell subject to my whims. No man was ever going to change that. Especially not now that I had so little time left to suffer fools, or foolish realities.

I tapped the tablet lying between us on the desk. "My list is both things I need to get done in case I die and things other people need to do in the event of my demise."

He glanced down. "Trying to control things beyond the grave?"

I spread my fingers, spiderlike, and using just my fingertips, swiveled the pad around so that it faced him. "It's a family tradition."

"I'd argue, but Fawnie's list did come in pretty handy." He brushed the pad of his thumb over the edge of the tablet's red cover. "Some days if I hadn't had some pressing chore waiting for me from those pages, I might have set down at Bess's bedside and drunk myself into a stupor."

That pricked at me a bit, having made that stupid joke about him hiding booze in here. Sterling was no alcoholic. I knew alcoholics. Sterling was just a man in a world of hurt who wisely knew that there wasn't enough liquor in all the distilleries of Kentucky and Tennessee combined to wash away his guilt and grief.

For one split second I thought of inviting him down to the pond for a proper rebaptizing. But why? What good had immersing myself done me?

He flipped open the tablet and ran his finger along the first item on the list, written in all caps, tall enough to fill up two lines just the way we'd done it in first-grade penmanship class. "Update will," he said softly.

"It's not a bad idea, is it?"

His shoulders rose and fell. "No."

"Well?"

"Well?"

"Are you my man?" I hadn't meant it to sound that way but once it was out there, I didn't backpedal or hem and haw or even play it up big, in case he would then feel he could make a big joke of it.

"Your…?" He dipped his chin; his eyes honed right in to mine.

I swear you could almost feel the pop and sizzle of an electric arc between us. *Sszszzsszz.*

Then quiet. Not just quiet. The sudden quiet of something having been extinguished.

He looked away.

I dropped my gaze to the desk, my fingers nudging the tablet ever so delicately in his direction. "Will you help me get these things done—starting with my will?"

"Oh, yeah. I'd be happy to." He picked up the gold pen and rocked it between his thumb and forefingers. "I guess."

"You *guess?*"

More messing about with the pen with one hand while the other smoothed down his chest, his fingers splayed against the subtle weave of the gray wool of his sweater. "It's going to be a lot of work."

"I'll pay you."

His head jerked up. "The hell you will."

There was my old Sterling again. I smiled and batted my eyes, big flirty stuff, big enough to let him know it was all show, or *mostly* show. "I'll give you my house."

He grinned a little.

I wanted to see him turn loose and grin a lot. I leaned in, one hand on the desk, the other reaching to still the twiddling pen in his hand. "Unless you want my firstborn son?"

"No, thank you." He interjected his words with a breathy smart-ass chuckle. He retreated a step again, then a half step back toward the desk. He ran his hand through his hair, the one not maneuvering the gold pen over and under his knuckles like a magician keeping his fingers nimble.

It all seemed so clear now, watching him, seeing his hesitation played out so clearly. I laid my hand on the pen again and ducked my head, trying to see into his eyes. "You don't even want my house, do you?"

He dropped his gaze, and it fixed on the page in front of him. He ran his finger slowly down the list.

"That's what I thought."

He twisted around and leaned against the other side of the desk, his broad back to me, his arms folded. "Bess wanted me to take charge of this place, and I—"

I put one hand on his shoulder. "You don't want to let go of Bess. Not just yet."

He rubbed the back of his neck with his left hand. He kept his face to the undecorated wall for a minute before he glanced back at me. He opened his mouth, then shut it and adjusted his shoulders.

"You don't have to confess it, kiddo. I can see it in your eyes. And your hand."

"Hand?"

I touched the fingers curved at the base of his neck. "Still have on your wedding ring."

"Oh, yeah." He brought his hand around and looked at it first from one angle, then another. "I know we were only married a short time, but I feel naked without it."

"Awww, and he looks so good naked." I could imagine Bess saying it, but I did not *hear* her saying it. Not like before. In fact I hadn't heard from Bess all day. It made me hesitate to mention my encounters with her to Sterling.

That and the fact that he would have thought I was nuts. Even in a world of my own making, I know that you should avoid saying things to the man making out your will that have him questioning your being of sound mind.

His hand fell into his lap. He stretched his legs out and lifted his head until the curls of his dark blond hair fell over the collar of his soft, warm sweater. "You know, Charma, that we can't really proceed with any of this until you deal with a few issues."

Like my talking to the dead? I cleared my throat to keep from blurting out the question. "Like what?"

"Your inheritances, for starters." He pushed off from the desk and turned to face me.

"*Ezz?* More than one inheritance?"

"Your mother's belongings. What Bess left you."

"Bess?"

He bent down and picked up a box just smaller than the cardboard box he had stuffed the file in earlier. He chunked it onto the desk. "Here."

I backed up a good three feet, one hand out in the classic "stop in the name of love" move, the other groping around in thin air trying to find the doorknob. "Oh, no. Uh-uh. That's yours."

"It shouldn't be. Her personal belongings?" He shook his head.

He flattened his hand over the lid. "Guy's brother said he came across these when he was cleaning things out. I debated what to do with them, but I can only guess they were things she had on her when she got to the funeral home."

"You haven't looked?"

"Can't."

"I know what you mean."

"What if there are gold fillings in there, or something…I don't know."

"Something you don't want to know about?"

He nodded.

That's when I knew he had not just loved my cousin, he had known her and accepted her faults and all, lies and all. I loved that girl myself, but I knew better than anyone what she was capable of—the betrayals, the self-serving choices that could cripple the people she loved. Anything could be in that box. A letter that confessed she'd never loved the young man she had married. A key to a safety deposit box where she'd hidden a manuscript about a vain young lawyer. Another man's love letters. Sterling had worried about finding a gold filling, but it was his own undoing he feared he'd find in his late wife's belongings.

I stared at the box, my mind running through the possibilities, through the names too numerous to mention of people who might be hurt by one final blast from Bess. "There's another possibility you are entirely overlooking here, you know."

"What?"

I swallowed hard, trying to force down my apprehension, then approached the box and trailed my hand over the roughened cardboard top. "That's Guy's handwriting."

"Yeah."

I raised my eyes to his. "These things could be left over from all those years ago."

"When they ran off together?"

"They did a lot more than run off." *They ruined my life. Well, sort of. A little.* Actually, not at all, but that didn't mean I didn't like people thinking they did. "They lived together for almost three years."

He scratched the side of his head. "Did I know that?"

I had no idea. As open as Bess could be about everyone else's shame and skulduggery, she could be pretty damned evasive about her own. Slanting things this way and that. Casting them in just the right light. A regular Houdini at making herself look good, especially when held in comparison to others.

I nodded slowly. "It's Guy's handwriting. Maybe we should let him deal with it."

Sterling may have nodded at that, I don't know. I do know that the room went quiet again. I could hear the man breathing, and that made me feel I could hear that he was thinking, debating. He wanted to say something. But he didn't want to say too much.

Being, among my many nearly deified roles, the queen of not knowing when to shut up myself, I did not press him. I just stood there, studying the box a moment longer, waiting to see if the man would decide to express himself or if he would suddenly pounce on the box and rip it open with his bare hands, laying bare the contents for him to devour with his eyes. Lucky box.

"He loves you, Charma," Sterling—who obviously hadn't gone along to steamy-love-scene-sexual-energy-sublimation land with me in his thought process—said softly.

I cleared my throat and buttoned my mind back up a notch. "Does he?"

"You know he does."

I blinked and thought that through. "I know he *did*. But does he? Really? He hasn't said it, or if he has, he said it in passing, you know?" I gestured as I spoke, hands waving off Guy's actions as if

I considered them no more significant than gnats, maybe a bit pesky. "Not the big profession, not the looking-deep-in-my-eyes-and-telling-me-he-can't-live-without-me kind of thing."

"Maybe he says it in other ways." He sat on the other side of the desk again and reached for my hand. "You know, the way he tried to protect you from that corpse and from his family's funeral home scandal. The way he brings chicken innards to your aunts. He let you have his vintage hearse. He keeps your mother's ashes in his house."

"Listen to yourself, Sterling. Corpses, innards, hearse, mother's ashes?" I withdrew my hand from his and touched his cheek. "Such things are not involved in professions of love for normal people."

He smiled. "When did you ever strive to be a normal person, Charma Deane?"

He had me there.

"He loves you," he assured me again, only this time with less emotion, more like a lawyer laying down the perimeters of his case.

"That's not for you to decide, Sterling."

"You must have agreed with me. You accepted his engagement ring." Again, more like a plank in a legal framework than the defense of another man's feelings.

I couldn't fault Sterling for his pragmatic approach. I felt the same way. Like we were arguing case law, not building a case for Guy being the great love of my life. "We've only been back together a little while, and suddenly he wants to rush into marriage."

"It didn't take me long to know with Bess."

I wanted to point out to him that at best his commitment to Bess was a finite thing. But I couldn't be so cruel.

Finally I looked at my hands and drew a breath. I let it out and said aloud the conclusion I had drawn earlier at the funeral home. "I'm thinking of breaking it off with Guy. Giving him back his ring."

Sterling put his finger under my chin and raised it so he could see clearly into my eyes when he asked, "Really?"

I fiddled with the impressive, fine diamond. "I can't say I'd feel naked without it."

It wasn't just his finger under my chin now but his hand, which he opened up and laid along the side of my neck, the blunt fingertips reaching downward, brushing the sensitive skin so lightly that it made me shiver. "You could take it off and let me be the judge."

"Sterling." I did not pull away or sound overly shocked.

He touched my chin with his thumb, angling my head up, and moved in close to me. "Take off your ring, Charma, and I'll take off mine, and we'll be naked together, just for tonight."

I should have shoved him backward off the desk, but I didn't want to hurt his feelings. Oh, bullshit—I didn't want the kiss to end.

The man was handsome and young and lonely. And if I gave in to him, I could chase away the loneliness for a little while. And maybe he could do the same for me.

I wanted to feel him over me and in me. To press myself to his hard chest and, while I still had some heat in the fleshy, soft thighs, to wrap myself around a firm young man and feel alive.

He ran his hand down the length of my body, cupping my bottom and pulling me under him. Still kissing me on the lips, the neck, lower and back up again, he raised his knee to the desk and—

Crash!

"Oh, shitfire! Bess!" I rolled away from my cousin's widower, careful not to step on the now-busted-open box and its contents, spilled across the office floor.

Sterling sank to his knees on the floor and laid his head against the desk.

I shut my eyes and listened for the ghost to sneer and snarl at me for my betrayal. Silence. Only Sterling's steady, heavy breathing.

"Are you okay?" he asked, and I could hear him getting to his feet.

I rubbed my eyes when what I really wanted to do was to wipe my mouth to try to take away the dampness and heat still lingering there. The evidence of my guilt.

That, or take a running leap at the man, rip off that body-hugging sweater of his and have crazy, hot sex with him right there on the floor. For a second, it could have gone either way. Then my eyes landed on something small and wooden and painted that had rolled against the baseboard of the old linen room.

"Shitfire," I said, almost in a whisper this time.

"What is it?" Sterling asked, even as he tugged his sweater back into place.

"Bess's *kokeshi*." I moved toward it on my knees, reached out and scooped it up.

"Her what?"

"Her soul. I thought this was buried with her."

"Her *soul?*"

"Obviously it's symbolic, but…" But maybe not. Unlike any George before her, Bess had come back as a ghost, and now I sat on my knees with her former husband, holding my cousin's soul in my hand. "I have to go now, Sterling."

"Go? *Now?* Where?"

I pushed my way up from the floor. My head spun for only an instant, then I felt my legs grow strong. I threw back my shoulders, eyes ever on the doll in my hand. "You just work on the will. I have my own unfinished business to take care of."

❧ CHAPTER TWENTY-ONE

"Ollie, Ollie Oxen free!"

That's what Min and I had always shouted to end a game of hide and go seek. When we played with Bess, she insisted we use her version. *All the, all the, all the outs in free.* That made more sense but wasn't nearly as fun to scream at the top of your lungs all over the Aunt Farm. I used my version today because I am a big girl and make my own rules—and because I figured it might piss Bess off enough to bring her spirit out to correct me.

Now, *that,* that right there, does make a compelling case for a George to forestall the hereafter—the opportunity to go right on bossing your loved ones around. And them not being able to do a damn thing about it.

"One, two, three on Bess in the parlor!" I peeked under the coffee table in the spot where I thought I'd last heard from her spirit. I shoved aside stacks of unopened mail and piles of magazines flopped open to pages where I had lost interest in looking at them.

I flipped on a light. Not dark yet, not really, but twilight, dim and hard to see into corners and behind chairs and curtains. All the places an obstinate little ghostie might try to hide.

But Bess wasn't hiding. Not here. I could not sense her presence as I always had before. This room where my family had laid me up, in hopes I'd heal my haggard heart all by myself, was empty.

I studied the crumpled sheets on the comfy couch. The feather pillow punched and wrestled and folded into just the right shape to fit into the hollow along the side of my neck and cradle my head. I could curl up right here and wait for Bess to come to me. She would…maybe. She'd have to, wouldn't she? After all, I thought as I gripped the elegant *kokeshi* in my hand, I had her soul.

The gentle curves of the carved wood fit into my palm. The painted eyes smiled up at me. The head wobbled slightly. My nose tingled, and I sniffled. Fat tears clung to my lashes. It had felt so right to bury this little doll with Bess, and finding it had not gone with her to her grave made me sad. And frustrated. And more than a little bit relieved.

I had Bess's soul. And she had my sanity.

Somebody had to have it. I certainly didn't seem in possession of it anymore. Jaw clenched, I pressed on and moved from the light and airiness of my personal recovery room to the dark parlor where Bess had died, determined to ferret out the voice that had guided me these past few days.

My grandfather's parlor, where he had escorted men come to the house to discuss business and to smoke pipes and big cigars, stood in perfect silence. The clock did not even tick as it had for so many years. Stopped on the day and hour of Bess's passing, we had never wound it up again. Dark paneled, lined with books, the windows shielded by layers of heavy fabric, the room had both an oppressive and protective feeling to it.

It gave me the creeps. It never used to, but walking into it with only some natural light seeping in around the curtains and barely penetrating the darkness from the arched doorways, it felt different now. Different but not occupied. Bess's spirit was not here.

"Where are you?" I called out. "I know you're still around."

I said what I wanted to be true. I wanted Bess to still be here, but deep down I didn't even know for sure that she had ever been here at all.

"I have to talk to you," I said.

No answer. No sense of eyes watching. No Bess.

I could press on through the downstairs, wind my way around and find myself either at the back porch and on the path that led to the pond or even back to Sterling's office.

Bess was not in Sterling's office.

Bess was not at the pond.

Bess had already done her worst...um, her *work*...at those places.

What are you waiting for, God Almighty to kick you in the butt?

All our lives Bess had done whatever it took to get me to act in my own best interest. A kick, a shove, a betrayal of epic proportion. It was all the same to her if it accomplished what she saw as her ultimate objective—to bend me to her will and, yeah, make me a better person in the process.

"Shitfire," I muttered in a mix of reverence for the setting and angst over what I had just realized. Bess was in the last place I would ever want to go. If she could not push me, she would pull me, drag me, trick me if she had to, into crossing that threshold and facing my anger and my fear. Bess was in my mama's room.

Before I could think on it overmuch, so was I.

"Bess? Hello?" The door creaked. I stepped fully in and leaned against the wall. The light switch prodded my shoulder. I moved aside. I wasn't ready to see this room bathed in seventy-five-watt radiance. I waited and my eyes adjusted to the light, or rather to the lack of light. I could see just fine. I could see all I wanted to see.

It had not changed in the past year. Why I expected it to have changed only spoke to the power and mystique of Dinah McCoy

George. Behind the door I had commanded to stay shut I had imagined her going about her daily business, making her bed, doing her hair and makeup, plotting out world domination. Her world, of course. *My* world.

It smelled like Mama, here. Like her perfume and powder and stale cigarettes and expensive clothes. Fine things have an odor, you know. The leather, the fabrics, the linings, the boxes and bags and even the crisp white tissue paper that everything comes wrapped in, that Mama kept to protect her things even long after they had gone out of season.

"Good taste never goes out of style," she would remind us. Often as she slid a pair of hand-made snakeskin shoes into a box and wrote on the outside the date she had bought them. Some-times, if they had been part of an ensemble that just loads of people would have seen her in, she also wrote where she had worn them last and maybe even a few words that described the reaction they elicited. "Envy of everyone in the room." Or "Great for legs." One time, "Ghastly!"

I glanced toward the closet. It warmed me to think that Johnny had gone in there as part of his quest to find himself. He had known with some kind of instinct that being part of this family was not something he could separate himself from. In order to understand himself, he would have to understand us.

"Smart kid, I murmured.

"Smarter than his mother. He must get that from me."

"You?" I spoke to the doll in my hand, hoping to pinpoint the voice without searching the seemingly empty room for a form I suspected would not appear. "Since when did you ever try to be a part of this family?"

"When I realized I wasn't going to beat cancer twice and I came home to you."

I touched the *kokeshi* on the cheek. "And I let you down."

"Yeah?" My game had worked, the voice drew near to me, nearer than it had ever been since the night of my heart attack. "I didn't feel let down."

Deep breath, don't look. Not yet. "Sterling says…"

"Sterling isn't one of us, Charma. Don't get me wrong. I loved him and the sex was through the roof, but then I suppose you kind of surmised that by now."

I pressed my lips together. I pressed my back to the wall and crossed my legs at the ankle.

Bess did not seem to recognize the flash of modesty and embarrassment in me, she just went on with her thought. "But Sterling doesn't know squat about us."

I wanted to believe what she had said, but…"He said I let you carry my pain to your grave."

"If that's what you needed from me, Charma, I was glad to do it."

I wish she had denied it. I shut my eyes and waited for the wave of pain or anguish to overcome me. But instead I felt at peace. An awkward peace, at best, but maybe that was just because the feeling was so foreign to me. Finally, I turned the doll over in my hand and opened my eyes. "I have your soul. Or maybe it's just a cheap, tacky souvenir."

"Why can't it be both?"

I laughed at the very idea of keeping my cousin's soul as a tacky souvenir even though it really did hold a certain kind of appeal for me. "Maybe I can glue it to the dashboard of my hearse."

"You think Guy is going to let you keep driving that hearse once you give him his ring back?"

"I didn't come here to play games, Bess."

"Then why did you call all the outs in free?"

"I called the oxen free. Maybe that was just my way of proclaiming a bullshit-free zone."

"Maybe I did the same by luring you up to Aunt Dinah's room."

"You didn't lure me. Once I thought about it, I knew where you'd be and came of my own free will."

"Then maybe you should come on in."

I hung back, one hand still on the door frame. "Maybe I am just fine right where I am."

"All right, if you're going to be that way…"

"Bess? Bess, don't go." I stepped in but did not turn loose of the door. I inched inside a bit more. "I wanted to…don't go. Ollie, Ollie, Oxen free!"

"Outs in free." Minnie pressed inside the door, bumped into me in the darkness, and before I could even cry out, flipped on the light.

Too much. The light stung my eyes. I bowed my head and covered my face with my hands. "Turn those off, Min, please."

"What? Why?"

"It's just that…" I couldn't face looking at my mother's things just yet. If I told her that, I'd have to admit I had gone an entire year not dealing with Mama's death, and in doing so would, in fact, be dealing with Mama's death. A no win situation? Not in Charma-world. I held my hand up and made a show of swallowing, as if I had to catch my breath and steady myself from the sheer shock of it all, and then launched into a lie that, fortunately for me, was also the truth. "The doctor just upped my meds, and he said there might be a period of adjustment when I'd have an increased sensitivity to light."

"Sorry, sweetie." The lights went out again.

I took a deep breath and turned to leave.

Min did not budge. "So what did you want?"

"What?"

"Sterling said you flew out of his office saying something about talking to your cousin. I find you in here calling the outs in—"

"Oxen," I corrected.

"Free," she finished. "So here I am. Home free."

"You wish." I had expected Bess's ghost to say that, but from the look on Min's face and the fact that my hand immediately shot up to slap down over my open mouth, I knew. I had just said exactly what I thought to my cousin.

"I know, Charma."

Pretty much if she had said anything but those two words, I'd have had a comeback, but "I know"? What did she know? About me and Sterling? About me and Bess? About me and Guy? Or worse yet, something that wasn't about *me* at all—about Abby?

This situation had the term *conundrum* written all over it. Damn, I hate that word.

Where was Bess when I really needed her? I looked away from Min, and a light caught my attention. A small light, what did they call them on those Halloween reality shows? An orb. There out in the yard beyond the balcony, an orb danced and beckoned.

"Let's get out of here, Min." I pushed her backward and out into the upstairs hallway. I had held off dealing with my mother's passing this long, what could another day, or week, or the rest of the time I had left on this earth, matter? "Let's go outside. I have something important to show you."

❧ CHAPTER TWENTY-TWO

"Look there." I pointed to a light bobbing and drifting and weaving in the high weeds at the side of the house. We had gone out the front way to avoid passing by Sterling's office, then went around to the side of the house and toward the back. There, under a tent of tree branches, we walked among the broken sidewalks and the bathroom fixtures that decorated our backyard. We stopped and I finally showed Minnie the treasure from the box. "And now look at this."

"Bess's *kokeshi?*" Minnie took it from my hand. "Where did you get this? I put it in her coffin myself. They buried her with it."

"Apparently not. And now her restless spirit is wandering all over the countryside." I glanced out at the light again. It seemed to see us, whirl around wildly for a moment, then begin the trek back in our direction. "But mainly just hanging about the house, getting into my business."

"*Unfinished* business." Of course, if Bess were in earshot—do disembodied spirits have ears?—and I said anything, I knew she would zoom in as fast as she could to correct me. "That's what holds a spirit to a place, you know."

"There." I looked heavenward, feeling this time the voice had come from on high, and found myself staring at the moon. "Did you hear that?"

Minnie dutifully looked up, too. She had on a long-sleeved pajama top, a big one that looked like it might belong to Travis, and orange sweatpants. And standing there against the backdrop of bare trees and blue-black sky, she looked as lost and out of place as I felt. "Is sensitivity to light the only side effect of your meds, girl?"

"Actually it has shitloads of side effects," I confessed. So many, it filled up two pages front and back in tiny mice print. *May cause sleepiness, restlessness and heart attack with sudden discontinuation of use* and on and on with various threats and consequences. Of course, threats and consequences have never worked on me. "And while I did not commit all of them to memory, I think I can say with some measure of assurance that not once did it cite communicating with the dead among things to watch out for."

"What about impaired ability to communicate with the living?" She wriggled around in her oversize outfit and her feet crunched in the dry leaves. "Because I am having a hell of a time understanding what you are trying to tell me here, girl."

"Look." I pointed out at the field and the light bouncing along.

"Yeah."

I leaned in, putting my head almost on her shoulder to make sure she had the spherical glow of Bess's essence in her line of vision. "You see that?"

"Yeah."

I waited for her to ooh or aah or at least say "what the hell is it?" When she didn't I moved in close to whisper in her ear. "It's an orb."

Her expression got all pinched and a little bit pissy. She leaned toward the light, then pulled away from me. She crinkled her nose. "It's a flashlight."

I squinted. "You think?"

"I *know*. As I was heading upstairs to find you, I crossed paths with Mom and Fawnie and Inez. They had flashlights, garden stakes and a big old library book. And they were headed off in that very direction."

"You thought that was *me?*" The ghostly voice conveyed both disdain and humor.

"I thought that was Bess," I told Minnie, heaving a sigh.

"Bess?" She actually stepped away from me this time. Clean away. Then she tucked her silver-streaked long black hair behind one ear and winced. "*Our* Bess?"

I had come out here to reveal Bess's presence to Minnie. If the only way I had to do it was with words, well, then, that would have to do. "That night on the roof, she appeared to me."

"Really?" Min rolled the doll over in her own palm. She brushed it with her fingertips.

"Really," I said softly. I took the doll from her again. "Or maybe not."

She looked at me.

"That first night, when I was…my heart was about to…" I put my hand to my chest and pressed, hard. I tried to conjure it all up again, to remember moment by moment, breath by breath, but it did not come. "I *think* I saw her. Since then it's just been her voice. But it's been *her* voice, you know what I mean?"

"I wish I did." Minnie's shoulders sagged. She folded her hands together and looked up into the bare limbs overhead again. "Is she here now?"

"Yes," Bess said.

"Yes," I repeated for Min's benefit.

"And no," Bess said, way more softly this time.

That wasn't meant for Minnie, so I didn't repeat it.

Min did not look at me, just kept her gaze fixed in the trees, or maybe beyond, to the stars. "I wish I could hear her, too."

"What would you want her to say?" I raised my own gaze. "If you could hear her?"

Quiet greeted me. Then more leaves crunching underfoot. Min cleared her throat, stepped back, folded herself tightly into Travis's nightshirt and laughed a wavering, fake laugh. "Okay. Second thoughts. I'm actually glad I can't hear her."

I blinked and studied her face to see if she really meant that.

Min wiped her brow, playing up the "whew, glad I dodged that bullet" angle of the blessing of *not* having Bess nearby to point out your shortcomings. "Especially right now. You know with all this stuff with Abby and all."

"She knows," Bess whispered in a kind of verbal push to urge me to say or do what needed to be said or done.

Where Min was concerned, though, I didn't need Bess. Why else had I tried to manipulate the situation between Abby and me? Because I knew that between me and the cousin who was only six months younger than me, there could be no secrets. I opened my arms to Minnie. "You know, don't you?"

"That my baby is going to have a baby? Yeah." She met my embrace in kind, laid her head on my shoulder and sighed. "How did that happen, Charmika?"

"Happen same way it always happen." Shug reached the backyard first, and being the torchbearer, turned to shine a light on the path for the others behind her. "Same way happened since Adam and Eve. Same way happened when you have her, and when I have you."

"Mom! *You* knew?" Min grabbed blindly for me and snagged my sleeve at the shoulder.

"Sure she knew. We all knew. We're women, ain't we?" Fawnie batted away Inez's outstretched hand in favor of lunging along in her uneven gait to stand beside Shug, facing me and Min. "This is a situation women have been dealing with since even before me and Shug were young."

"All *that* long ago, huh?" Inez shook her head. She shook the flashlight in her hand, the way you do when you think that might jar the batteries into the right position to start working again. Then she muttered in Spanish and repositioned the thick book under her arm.

"What were you all doing out in a field after dark?" I asked Inez.

"I could ask you the same," she shot back.

"We were ghost hunting," Minnie said, giving me a smile.

"What?" Fawnie frowned.

"Why didn't you bring flashlights?" Shug pointed hers to jab the light at our feet as if she thought it would make us dance to escape the beam.

"You have them all," Minnie said, even though we all knew that neither she nor I would have been industrious enough to have actually gone looking for flashlights.

"Only one works, though." Fawnie gazed down into the dark lens of the flashlight in her hand. "Mine doesn't even have batteries."

Shug clucked her tongue. "Why is it in this house we all the time run out of batteries?"

Inez opened her mouth.

"I think you've worked this pair up enough for one evening, Inez." I was actually kind of glad they didn't have lights just then, anyway, because they might have caught a glimpse of the guilty flush on my face. "Spare us your vivid conjectures about what sort of small appliances might be sucking up all the batteries around here."

"Interesting choice of words," Inez muttered.

A tart reply died on my lips when Min pushed forward, put her hand on her mother's shoulder and demanded, "Mom, if you knew about Abby all this time, why didn't you say something?"

Shug shone the light under her chin as if she were about to

launch into a ghost story of her own, then said simply, "Not my business."

"Not your…?" Min yanked the flashlight from her mother's hand and snapped it off. In the dark, still night we could hear every nuance of anguish and bewilderment in her quivering voice as she whispered, "Mom, she's going to have a baby. It's—"

"Not my business. Not *your* business, either." Shug snatched the light back and flipped it on again. "That between her and God and, if she lucky to have picked a good one, between her and her man."

"Men," Bess corrected.

I held my tongue.

"Not for you to decide, Minami. Not for me. Not for this crazy family." Shug threw up her hand with the light in it and practically blinded half the gathering. "This is her choice. We can't make it for her. We can't stick ourselves into it all or it will always be all gummed up with us and what we did. I come from a place where they drown babies they say they don't want. I don't believe that. I think they want those babies, but they drown them because they don't have a choice. Abby has choices. We have to trust her to make good ones and not get in her way, not force her to make the choices we want."

"Hooray for Shug," Bess said. "Finally someone in the family with the balls to tell you all to mind your own business."

"Mind *your* own business," I muttered to the opinionated spirit.

"Yeah, that's right. Mind your own business." Shug nodded.

"But, Mom, this is a big thing. This is something she will need a lot of help with."

"Then we help her. When we ever not help a woman who needs us?"

"Never turned one down since *you* showed up pregnant on the arm of my husband."

"This is no time to dredge up the Fawnette-and-Sugi who-did Kel-love-most? debate, Aunt—"

"No, no, this perfect time." Shug patted the air with one hand.

"But not the perfect place." Inez slid the book from under her arm and shivered. "Ladies, shall we adjourn to the kitchen?"

No! I wanted to scream at them. *I came out here to deal with Bess, not with all this. I came to try to put my cousin's soul to rest.* I didn't want to go all girlie and gushy and wise-women-rule-the-world just now. God only knew what kind of life lesson they'd try to work into this. I didn't want life lessons. I wasn't planning on using my life so much longer that I'd have cause to apply them. I wanted...

"Minnie." I tugged her hand. "What about Bess's *kokeshi?* What about her spirit?"

"It's just a doll, Charmika." She tugged my hand in kind and made her move to follow the others to the house. "Can't you see that? Abby, you, me, Mom. Bess is gone, but we're still here. We have other spirits to tend to now."

She slipped away from me.

Bess had gone, and now Min, in her own way. Min was going to be a grandmother. I could see that now. Shug knew what I had sensed. If we let Abby know we loved her and would support her in making her own decision, she would choose to nurture the new life inside her. Min was going to be a grandma. But first she was going to be a daughter, and to try to be a better mother.

"One thing to cross off your list." I mouthed the words but heard Bess speak them.

In a matter of ten minutes Inez was making hot tea in the coffeemaker carafe. We had grabbed extra chairs from the porch and now sat at the chrome table that held so many memories for us all.

"I hope you ladies aren't meeting here to plot a way to overthrow the generous benefactor of your home." Sterling stood in the doorway, his shirt rumpled from what looked like a hard day at work.

I knew better, of course. And when I met his steady, cool blue-eyed gaze, my hand went to my own clothes, tidying here and straightening there. My fingertips brushed the skin of my neck. I swear I blushed.

I must have blushed, because he smiled at me as if I was standing there buck naked and maybe even a little bit bent over.

"Get on outta here." Fawnie waved her hand. "There's going to be woman talk, and we don't need some bull man stomping around trying to trample on it."

"You can't fool me, Miz Fawnie. You want me out of here so you can smoke."

She reached for the perpetually fresh pack that could always be found on the kitchen table.

"I'm leaving." He threw up his hands and stepped back at her attempt at intimidation. Another step put him in the shadows with just enough light for those of us sitting nearest to Inez to see him point at her when he said, "I meant what I said. No plotting. Y'all behave."

Shug let out a cackle.

Fawnie joined her, her laugh so hard and fierce it brought on a shower of short, sputtering coughs.

"You hear that, old woman? Some sweet-cheeked man-child think he going to tell you and me how to behave in *this* house."

"Go on to bed, Sterling, sugar," Fawnie called out. "But you best lock your door when you do."

"That a threat?" he asked.

"No, just fair warning," Fawnie said, still coughing slightly.

"Yeah, us weak little womenfolk might get all liquored up and succumb to your animal magnetism." Inez pulled the carafe from the burner.

"Animal magnetism? You mean we all going to go wild and try to get in bed with him?" Shug held up her mug to be the first filled.

"No. I mean if he keeps on insisting on acting like a donkey, we may just have to keep riding his ass." Inez topped off the cup, then clinked the carafe against it.

Even Sterling laughed at that and bid us good-night.

Min had gone to check on Abby, and she returned with the report that the girl had finally fallen into a restful sleep.

As for where John might be, well, I left the door open and shut it after Sterling left. Heard a car in the drive not long after that, then later another one, and I could only guess that John had gone out. Or come back from being out. Or maybe he was taking advantage of our distraction to systematically steal everyone's cars.

Whatever he was up to, he was on his own. For now.

After all, he *was* on my list.

"Forget the list for a few minutes, will you?"

I looked down at the *kokeshi* in my hands, wondering if that was where Bess's voice had come from. Damn, I was a mess. Talking dolls and flashlight orbs aside, I had lost control of my libido, my aunts and my place as queen bee and/or Goddess of Beeswax for the whole George family.

That didn't seem right at all.

Looking around to see everyone finally settled in, I opened my mouth to tell them all just that very thing, knowing it would both play on their sympathy and get them riled up enough to fix all their attention on me and what I wanted to talk about. Except I didn't actually have anything to talk about because, as I had noted earlier, I was out of control and a mess.

"So you were telling us about Kelvin George showing up with a second wife, Miz Fawnie?" Inez edged in between us with the hot tea and cut me off before I could make a sound. "And about how y'all never turned any woman away from this house who needed your help."

"Oh, since when did you earn the right to use 'y'all,' Inez Conchita Maria Señorita High-Hair Orla Jersey-Girl Calaveras?" I demanded, because my mouth was already open there and *something* had to come out of it. Or go *into* it, and since no one had thought to bring out snacks and the only real man in the house had left the scene…

Inez bumped my shoulder with her plentiful hip. "Ignore her, Miz Fawnie, she's not herself."

"I don't know. That sounded an awful lot *like* her." Minnie pushed my hair back off my shoulder.

"It's her." Fawnie coughed in my direction, which I took as a sign of affection. "She's still with us, our Charma. She's just…" She looked at me a minute and her eyes got misty, then she coughed and turned to Inez again. "You know about the sacred self, don't you, Inez?"

"That what you tried to tell me about the night we found that jerk's body in the bushes?"

I shrugged, my mind still fixed on what Aunt Fawnie had seen when she looked at me that had touched her so.

Fawnie waited for Inez to stop pouring before she whipped out her flask and added just a dash of whiskey to the brew—"to ward off the night chills," she said when she offered to pass the good stuff around.

"We all got one," Shug reminded us, taking the flask but meaning the sacred self.

"That part of us that we would die to preserve. The way a soldier will die for a cause or a parent for a child." Fawnie stirred her tea, then tapped the silver spoon lightly on the edge of her mug. "Your sacred self is the person you want more than life itself to be. It's the idea of who you are that, if you can find it, will define you and guide you all of your days."

"Wow," Inez murmured.

Fawnie shut her eyes and seemed to inhale the aroma of her tea in an almost trancelike state. "For me it was to be a member of this family."

"For Dinah, too, to be your daddy's wife, to be the head of this family, that was what she sacrificed everything for."

Even her relationship with me. I did not say it, of course.

Fawnie leaned over and put her hand on my leg, as if she had heard my silent sadness. And she probably had. She was the one who had told me about my mother's sacred self, about the choices she had made in order to protect that inner being, even knowing that it all came with a high, high price.

I put my hand on Fawnie's frail fingers, gave them a squeeze, gently, then looked at Min's mother. "And Shug wanted to be an American."

"With all my heart. I'd have done anything to get here, to have my baby here."

"There was never any jeopardy of not being born here, Mom. You and Daddy were already married—"

"Married?" Fawnie squawked, then without so much as looking at Min or any of us, picked up her tea and took a dainty sip.

"As far as you knew, you were married," Minnie corrected, and she, too, took a sip.

Shug took a sip.

Fawnie looked into her cup.

I decided to forgo the whiskey and passed it to Inez, who took it but didn't do anything with it, just stood there with the flask in one hand and the carafe in the other, looking at Shug, then Fawnie, then Shug.

"My life began as music," I said a little too dreamily. "I always knew my parents weren't married when Mama got pregnant."

"Hmm." Inez kept shifting her gaze.

Shug sat back in her chair, then forward again.

Fawnie swirled her tea and whiskey, raised it to her lips and muttered something I don't think was a prayer of thanksgiving before taking another slug.

Minnie edged her chair forward, the legs groaning over the old floor. "Mom?"

"None of your business." Shug held up her hand.

"Is there something you need to tell me, Mom?"

Shug looked into the distance, or as distant as one could look in an old brightly lit kitchen filled with a bunch of faces staring right at you.

"I wasn't, either, though."

Inez finally looked at me. "What?"

"Married. When I got pregnant with Johnny. I'm surprised I didn't have a baby with Guy, you know, because we went at it like rabbits fed a steady diet of Spanish Fly and Oysters. But he was careful, I mean, he always had rubbers, and if he didn't, then we didn't…" I folded my hands under my chin and thought about that. At the time it had all seemed sweet and that he was thinking of me, protecting me, but now I wondered if even then he had known he didn't want children. And that I did. That part of who I was, who I wanted to be, sacred or otherwise, was a mother. Maybe that as much as anything helped him run off with Bess on the eve of our wedding. "Of course, it doesn't matter now. I mean, we use protection now because I could still get pregnant, I suppose, but…"

"Oh, you two *should* get pregnant. You make nice babies with that man." Shug gave my arm a shake.

Minnie rolled her eyes. "We're not talking about Charma, here, Mom. We're talking about you and Daddy."

"Talk, talk, talk, that's all you two ever do around here. What happened to the times when this house full of women who *do* things, not just sit on their butts yakking?"

"Here, here!" Inez raised her cup.

Fawnie, who had retrieved the flask from Inez, raised it as well. "Here's to the ladies who get things done!"

"Mom!"

"What?" Shug snapped at last.

Min sat up straight. She pressed her lips closed. She shut her eyes, clenched her jaw. I could see she didn't want to do this. It would have been so easy, too, to just go right on pretending everything was as she had always thought it was. To keep those old mother/daughter boundaries in place a little longer, maybe even until...

"Aunt Shug, you can't start something like this and then just expect to shut it down. Not you. You're a better mother than that, you're not..."

Dinah.

Or me.

I wasn't sure which I would have said or which one each woman in the room supplied for herself.

Shug reached out to me, her hand open, and no words were needed for me to know she wished my relationship with my mama had been different.

I blinked. Tears. Not a flood, just that wash of dampness on my lashes, a tingle, then they were gone.

Shug released my hand and turned to Min. "What do you want to know?"

"I can't believe I am asking you this, but..." She chewed her lower lip, then took a deep breath. "Was Kelvin George my real daddy?"

"Yes."

I think everyone in the room exhaled at once. I could tell from the sound and sudden draft that smelled of tea and whiskey.

I picked up my drink.

Inez freshened Fawnie's tea.

Minnie held her cup up to be next.

Shug cupped her hand around the mug on the table before her and cocked her head. "I just ain't sure you're his real baby."

Clunk. I set my cup down.

Clunk. Inez plunked the carafe down.

"Shit." Min hung her head. "You just said he was my real father."

"He was. He real daddy to you. I just can't say you real baby come from him. Maybe you are. *Probably* you are, but maybe…not so much *his* seed, you know?"

Min cursed again, but with her head in her hands I couldn't hear it real clear.

"You knew about this, of course?" I turned to Fawnie, and not for the first time this past year saw that sly old broad in a totally new light.

"'Course." Another sip. She didn't meet my eyes. She reached out for her cigarettes and got one out but didn't light it.

"Incredible," I murmured.

Fawnie shrugged.

Shug took up the lighter and flamed it up for her old nemesis and, apparently, the woman she owed the very reality of her very sacred self to.

"Why didn't you use it to get her out of your house?" I asked quietly, the way you ask something you know deep down you shouldn't really ask at all.

Fawnie took a long draw and blew it out. "I don't know. She was already here, and Kel had his head in the clouds over the idea of being a daddy."

"Head in the clouds or head up his ass?" Min scooted back in one sharp screech of metal chair legs. "Mom, how could you have pulled something like this on him?"

"You don't remember your daddy much, do you, child?" Fawnie had the gleam of a good story coming on in her eyes.

Min didn't say anything.

Truth was, neither of us remembered our fathers much. Me, it was just a few mental snapshots, a holiday, him kissing Mama, him teasing Nana Abbra, and then that brief golden moment at the pond just before I jumped and he stayed true to his sacred self, Charma's daddy, and saved me. Before that I had very few memories of John "Jolly" George.

Min was the same way, she'd been even younger than I'd been when I lost Daddy. When Kel has passed, I knew for a fact she mostly remembered him for the shenanigans at his funeral. Whether or not the man had supplied the seed that became the middle-aged woman she was today didn't really matter all that much to her.

"This isn't about Daddy, Aunt Fawnie," Min said. "It's about Mom. It's about all the years of lying and—"

"I didn't lie. You just didn't ask the right questions until now." Shug put her shoulder to Min's and hid her face behind the guise of drinking more tea.

Min blinked. "If all this is true, I'm probably not even a George."

"Don't ever say that, sweetie." Fawnie's hand shot out to take Min's. "One thing we all know, you *are* a George. We're all Georges here."

"I'm not," Inez announced.

"You help us get our house back, sugar, and you can be an honorary George," Fawnie said through a stream of smoke.

"There're two words you don't often hear together, honor and George," Bess shouted out. No, not shouted, but for once her voice seemed to come from a great distance. I looked around for the *kokeshi* and realized I'd let it fall to the floor—where I left it.

Inez wriggled her fingers, took the cigarette from Fawnie's hand and had herself a big old drag. She held it a sec, as if she was thinking it all over, then blew it out and handed the thing back to the old lady. "I was married before I got pregnant—does that disqualify me or should I make up a story about a baby I put up for adoption and how I heard it got shipped off to Arkansas with its new parents and that's why I came to Orla?"

The ladies laughed, even though I thought that kind of story might prove useful at some point in time.

"I never got pregnant, Inez, honey." Fawnie flicked off an ash. "Giving birth doesn't make you a member of a family any more than giving blood makes you a damned vampire."

"Vampire," I echoed, looking at the pale old gal and knowing just what Bess might have said. But she didn't. Not from under the table. Not from the *kokeshi* doll. Not from inside my head.

"So, that's the way it is." Shug lifted her mug. "Dinah pregnant before she marry. Charma pregnant before she marry. I pregnant before I marry. Now Abby pregnant. So we now know."

"What?" Min asked, just a tinge of surliness remaining in her tone.

Shug grinned at her daughter and raised her cup. "We all just a big bunch of whores."

"And Georges," Fawnie reminded us all.

"And Georges," I echoed.

Inez followed.

Then Shug.

Min hesitated.

I nudged her.

Shug smiled, meekly.

"And Georges," Min finally joined in with a sideways glance at her mother. "This does not mean I'm over being mad at you."

"You wouldn't be so mad if you knew your sacred self," Shug said.

And Min looked at me.

I knew exactly what she would have said if we had been alone.

"How did this happen to *us?* We're of the lineage of the lesser gods and goddesses of Orla, of Sugi and Kel, of Jolly and Dinah, of Abbra, who made this family, of Ruth, who had the nerve to get out and who gave us Bess, and even of Fawnie."

"We come from a long tradition of women who make too big a deal out of everything," I'd have agreed with her. "Who appreciate their southern comforts but will sacrifice anything to preserve their sacred selves."

"We are of the women who get things done."

"Then why are we such cowards?"

I saw it all in her eyes. I knew it all in my heart just as I knew I wasn't going to find my answers in Sterling's bed, or in marriage to a man I no longer really knew. No ghost or wooden souvenir doll was going to give them to me, nor would I find them in a hip flask duct-taped to an old lady's prosthetic leg.

Bess would not have had these feelings. Bess had always known her selves, sacred and sacrilegious alike. She wouldn't have had all these conflicts, all these fears and doubts. Bess didn't need anyone to push her. And right now I hated her for that.

I bent down to retrieve the *kokeshi,* wondering if I should go throw it into the pond now or wait until morning. Or maybe I should take it to Bess's grave. Or give it to Sterling, or maybe even to—

"I know it's late, Charma." The dead-serious voice jerked me upright.

"Guy!"

He strode in through the back door as if he'd been in the house for a while now, and held out his hand to me. "We have to talk."

❦ CHAPTER TWENTY-THREE

"How long have you been in the house?" I followed him into Sterling's office. The things we had knocked off the desk had been picked up. The lid placed back on the box. My list was gone. I tried to make sense of it all. "Why didn't you let me know…"

"What the hell is this?" Guy held his hand out to me, his palm cupped.

I pulled up short. I had Bess's doll in both hands, practically in a choke hold. "My ring."

"And?" he asked with this kind of quiet dignity that told me he didn't want to ask but he had to.

I blinked. The simplicity of what he held there broke my heart. "Sterling's wedding band."

"I found them together on the desk here." He moved around and put the heavy piece of furniture between us.

"Why are you in his office?" I asked.

"He called me and told me to come by and get this stuff out of here. Said he didn't care what time I came. I let myself in, and when I saw you and your aunts having a grand time in the kitchen, I thought I'd just slip out again, call you in the morning. Then I saw these."

"I thought maybe you came to see me." I flirted, a little. I couldn't stop myself. It was Guy. I think I'd have to have been dead a long time not to want to catch his eye and try to make him want me. Again I twisted the doll in my hands. "Didn't Loyal give you my message?"

"He said you came by. I wasn't in a mood to talk, though, so I figured we'd see each other later. Your turn. Answer my question. Why are these here?"

I had no answer. If I told Guy that I had encouraged Sterling that it was time to take off his ring and move forward with his life and that I had simply slipped my ring off to show him how easy it could be, he would have accepted that. Hell, if I had said Sterling was using hand lotion with his ring off and shared the excess with me so I took my ring off, too, Guy wouldn't have made a big deal out of it. There was that fierce loyalty of his.

I could have taken advantage of it. In the past I might have done just that. It would have taken only a slight shift to blur the line between the leniencies I thought I deserved and the right to know too damn much about me that Guy had not yet earned. But looking into those eyes now, with the warmth of gold and the ice cold glitter of diamonds between us, I couldn't do it. So I resorted to the last refuge of the weary, the cornered, the guilty. I told the truth.

"I kissed Sterling."

"Okay, then."

"Okay?" I stepped back. Had I just heard right? "That's all you have to say?"

He didn't look at me. His feet shuffled over the floorboards. His shoulders rose and fell. "Hey, I ran off with Bess. Lived with her for three years. You kissing Bess's widower doesn't really shake the foundations of my existence."

"Bess. Bess. Bess." Hell yes, he struck a nerve. Maybe his foundations hadn't been shaken today, but *mine* had, time and again and all too often, and that same person was there at the center of it all. "Why does everything in my life have to be so intertwined with her?"

"What are you talking about?"

He had a right to ask that. It did come out of the blue to him, I'm sure, since he didn't have her voice in his head, her name on the lips of everyone who mattered to him or her soul in his hands and on his conscience. "Guy, I have had a dozen conversations today, and all but the one with my doctor involved Bess in one way or another."

"One way or another?"

"Yeah, talking about her, talking about relationships with her, talking to her."

"*To* her?"

I exhaled hard, then thrust the doll practically in his face. "How the hell did this, which was supposed to get buried with her, end up in a box of Bess's personal belongings? And don't try to tell me you didn't know it was in there—I recognized your handwriting on the top flap."

"I don't know how it got there." He took it from me but did not look at it. Clearly it didn't mean a damn thing to him. Not like finding my ring and Sterling's. It was just a thing to him. And despite all my trying to make it mean more, I knew he was right. "Sometimes the family asks that everything be removed from the casket before the interment. It was a big-ass funeral, Charma, lots of people left mementoes. I can only guess it got mixed up with the ones we took out."

"You can only guess?" I knew he was right. That didn't mean I was going to let him know it.

He handed the doll back to me. "If you want a better answer, maybe you should ask Bess."

I set the doll on the desk. "Don't give me crap, Guy."

His smile came slow, but sweet and sincere all the same. "If we don't give each other crap, Charma, what will we have to talk about?"

"Bess," we both said at the same time.

I lifted my head and groaned. I listened, thinking she might be there with us and have something to add. At last there was nothing more to do but what any woman of my family would do, I asked about something I knew damn well I should have let be. "Did you...did you love her?"

He shook his head. "I don't know. Yes. No. *Hell, no.*" He looked me in the eye, his expression wry and a little bit wounded. "Damn it, Charma, you know how she was. You *had* to love her."

I nodded. "Do you *still* love her?"

"She's...she's dead."

The words came like a shove. Not to push me away but to say "Back off a little on this one." I couldn't, of course. "That's not an answer."

He curved his hand over the edge of the cardboard box, possessively. "It's all I've got."

And all I had was one simple question. "Do you love me?"

He chuckled. Not like I was ridiculous to ask but like he had known what I was going to say next and I had proved him right and he was proud of himself. "I just humbled myself in front of the Orla Chamber of Commerce on the slim chance I can keep the doors open on a business that I despise, because it's here and *you* are here." He found my gaze and held it. "And I can work anywhere, but I can't live anyplace if you aren't there, too."

"Guy..."

"I am holding in my hand your engagement ring and the wedding band of a man I know has wanted to bed you for at least a couple years and pretending it doesn't chap my ass to know he kissed you." He dumped both rings onto the desk again, then picked up the one with the huge diamond setting. "Because I know what I did and who I was and that I lost any chance at righteous indignation years ago."

"But do you love me?"

"More than life itself."

Say it. Just say the words and take me in your arms and...

"Okay, then." I moved to the door and held it open for him. "Thanks for coming by."

Obedient as ever, he came to the door and put his hand on the knob, his fingers barely brushing mine. "Charma?"

I pulled my hand away and tucked it behind my back, never meeting his gaze.

"You forgot to take your ring." He held it out to me.

I turned my face away. I took a step toward the desk and then another and another until I had put half the room between us. "Maybe you should keep it awhile."

Ghostly and fleeting as my encounters with Bess, I heard him leave but did not see it.

"Go," I whispered, unsure if I meant the word for him or for myself.

I rubbed my forehead. I stared at Sterling's ring. I shut my eyes and tried to think of a proper prayer for probably having just screwed up two lives, or perhaps saving them.

"Please, God please," was all I got out.

Then the phone rang and scared the living daylights out of me.

"Hello?" I practically barked the greeting into the receiver. Phones have never scared me much unless I thought maybe Fawnie was on the other end of one. That's more angst than apprehension, and rightly so. That woman can talk and carry on and make you wish Bell had channeled his inventive industry into something less pain-inducing, like a bicycle-powered dentist drill. But the phone ringing out of the blue in the evening like this doesn't send me into a panic the way it does some people, who fear they are about to get bad news. Probably because most of my life, my bad news has had the balls to march right up in person and slap me square in the face, bypassing the phone lines entirely.

"Charma Deane? This is your uncle Chuck. Is that you girl? Did I dial the wrong number?"

"Well, I don't know what number you meant to dial, Uncle Chuck, but this is the house."

"Is it? Damn. I thought I dialed Sterling's office."

"Sterling's office is in…" Then it dawned on me. The man had had a private line put in for his office. "Damn indeed."

"What, honey?"

"He has really moved in. He actually plans on making this his home."

"Yes, but I didn't *want* to call his home, honey. I thought I dialed the number he gave me for his office."

"You did, Uncle Chuck. You want me to look around and see if I can find him?"

"If he's not there, don't bother him. I can give you the answer to his question if you'll give him the message."

I stared at the ring in the middle of the desk. "Uh, why don't I let you—"

"Tell him to go ahead and pack up whatever Dinah left Ruth and the boys and send it on down here."

"Dinah?" I realized then that Guy had not taken the box with him. Maybe Uncle Chuck had meant these things. He certainly couldn't have meant…"Mama?"

"He said y'all were trying to get things cleared away up there, and that your mama had left a few things to Ruth."

"She did?"

"Nothing too personal or sentimental, I don't think. Her fur coat, some jewelry that's been in the George family awhile and some antiques. Not sure where we'll put them. The boys already checked out the going prices for some of the stuff on the Internet."

"They want to sell off Mama's belongings?"

"No, no, of course not. A few. Yes. Probably. 'Course, if there's anything you want of your mama's, Charma, you go right on and keep it."

"No. No, if Mama wanted y'all to have those things, I want you to have them, too." Sterling had moved in. He had moved forward with Mama's will in order to begin work on mine. It all had a strange finality to it. Strange, but not distressing. Comforting, almost.

At last Mama's death would be dealt with, tied up. And after I died, it would be the same. My belongings would be packed and shipped to my sons and my cousin's children for them to cherish and sell off in small lots on eBay bid by bid.

"How you doing, darlin'?"

Strange but not distressed. Comforted. "Fine," I said instead.

"What they got you on?"

"Hmm?"

"Beta blockers? Baby aspirin?"

"Um, yeah. All sorts of stuff." I didn't want to get into a game of prescription poker with my uncle. I see your two heart meds and raise you a Lipitor and a painkiller. I rattled off a name or two, then downplayed it.

"Oh, I was on that awhile. Wish they'd put me on it again, really improved my golf game."

"What?"

"You know they use that same drug to help golfers overcome the yips?"

"Yips?"

Talk turned entirely to golf at that point, my uncle explaining the finer points of putting versus the long game and what kinds of medications all his golfing buddies took as opposed to Aunt Ruth's bridge buddies.

"'Course, in bridge they don't get the yips, you know. More like the yaps!" He laughed.

I may have also laughed. Or made a feeble attempt at it before finally promising to relay to Sterling Uncle Chuck's love and packing instructions and saying goodbye.

"Yips? Damn it. Damn it all to hell." In a few pounding steps I made my way from the office to the kitchen, to the place where John had brought my new prescription and had stood by while he watched me take it.

May Impair Ability to Drive or Operate Machinery. Use with Care Until You Become Familiar With Its Effects. The pharmacy had printed it out like the title of a textbook, and like a title by itself it didn't really teach me anything. I whipped my head around, and my gaze fell on the trash can.

"Where is it?" I muttered, flipping off the lid.

The old house did not have a disposal, and the evening's dinner scraps had pretty much permeated everything I had to search through. Photocopied pages from some book. The receipts for the film I'd insisted John drop off—proof John did not intend to pick them up. The paper sack from the pharmacy.

"What the hell are you doing?" Inez came in.

"I thought you went home," I said even as I pulled my food covered hand and a dripping piece of paper from the depths of the garbage pail.

"I got sidetracked talking to Sterling on the porch."

"You mean you stopped to bullshit Sterling, trying to throw him off the scent of whatever you're up to?"

"He's not an idiot. If he is being bullshitted, it's because he wants to be bullshitted."

"He didn't try to, um…" I placed my finger to my lips, and that's when I remembered the plate scrapings on my hands. I spit the bits of tea and something I couldn't name back into the can and swore, just a little.

Inez laughed. "What the hell *are* you doing, girl?"

"I wanted to read about the side effects of my medicine."

"You didn't read all the materials that came with your medicine?"

"Don't get all high and mighty with me, Inez." I shook the worst of the food off the long, almost-tissue-thin paper with the information about Uncle Chuck's yip-busting meds and began to read. "You are wearing makeup and using a whole skin-care regimen bought from black market vendors and their flea market compatriots that contain more chemicals and additives than anything I have ever put in my body. And I know for damn sure you didn't read any warning labels before you slapped it all over your face, neck and thighs."

"Yeah, but that's for beauty. You *have* to suffer and take risks for beauty like mine, otherwise just anyone could look this good."

I read on, ticking each side effect off in my mind, thinking things like, I can live with it, I can live with it, I might *like* that and so on. "Go home and get your beauty sleep."

"Not until you tell me what's going on. I saw Guy storm out of here. Frankly, when I saw him in your house, I just assumed he had come to spend the night."

Bingo. The drug they were using to regulate my heart rate was, in lay terms, a happy pill. My doctor, who had known me long enough to know that I did not want anything to do with the whole better living through a chemical-enhancement kind of life, had given me a damned happy pill!

"From the look on his face as he left, I think Guy had thought the same thing about spending the night and was not too pleased about the change of plans."

"Damn, girl, I had a heart attack. I'm not supposed to be having sex yet." It made a better excuse than admitting I was scared and confused and angry and jealous of my own dead cousin. I mean, I like making a big deal out of things as well as the next person, but there is a time when it loses its luster. Standing in the kitchen heartbroke, up to your elbows in garbage and "happy" whether you want to be or not is one of those times.

"What is it, Charma?"

I handed her the page and pointed out the passage.

"It's all the pills, Inez. The sense of purpose, the comfort in things that really shouldn't hold any comfort for me at all. The highs and lows. Damn it, even Bess. Maybe even hearing Bess is just…"

"Oh, Charma." She wadded up the paper and threw it in the trash again. "You're reading too much into this. You are going to have mood swings, honey. You had a huge thing happen to you. Depression is part of that, and all sorts of new emotions and—"

I pulled away from her. "Just go home, Inez."

"I wonder if I should."

"What does that mean?"

"Let's see, your house is in turmoil. Your relationship is screwed up. You are haunted in more ways than one, and you are suddenly way more curious than normal about your meds. If there was ever a time for a friend to stay close by…"

She had a point. If I had one iota of sense left in my drugged-to-the-gills body, I'd have hugged this woman and hung on for dear life. Instead I put on my sweetest smile, shook the goo from my fingers and held my hands up in surrender. "I'm just going to go to bed, honey. I'm just going to get some rest and think about it all in the morning."

"And you won't do anything crazy?"

"Crazier," we both said at the same time.

"No." I took the two steps to the sink and rinsed my hands off. "I'll even sleep downstairs in the fancy company parlor, so if I do get a mind to crawl out a window, I won't have far to fall. Okay?"

"Okay."

She bought my act, kissed me on the cheek and said goodbye.

I watched her walk away. I listened for her to go out the door, onto the porch, and for her car engine to start. Then I curled the small brown bottle of pills into one hand and tossed them with the soiled paper and the refuse that had become my life right into the garbage.

❧ CHAPTER TWENTY-FOUR

I woke up with the midmorning sun warming the parlor and reflecting through all the cut-glass vases to send rainbows bouncing off every surface all around me.

"Oh, shit! Oh, shit! Oh, shit. Oh, shit, shit, shit!"

"Never were much of a morning person, were you?" Min sat a tray with juice and oatmeal down on the end table nearest my head.

"What time is it?" I demanded.

"Ten." She stole a triangular-cut piece of toast from the ornate silver rack on my breakfast tray and bit off a corner.

I rubbed my aching head. "What day?"

"Wednesday."

"Is it still November?"

"For another ten days."

"So that's…" I tried to calculate how many hours since I had stopped taking my meds. My brain rebelled. Hey, my mouth had been rebelling almost since birth. My hormones had staged a revolt the first time Guy Chapman kissed me. My ass and thighs and belly had declared outright war on my ego the day I hit forty. It was about time my brain got in on all the fun. "How long ago was it that we sat up and talked? In hours?"

"Hours? Um, twenty-four plus…" She made the motion of the hands of the clock moving around and then around again. Then she reversed the movement, her lips moving to count out the numbers before she finally threw the toast on the tray and said, "I don't know, Charmika. It's been more than forty-eight and less than seventy-two, if that helps."

I nodded. Even that small motion made my stomach churn.

She sat on the edge of the chair across from my couch, eating my breakfast and staring at me. "Why?"

Why? Because I felt like crap. Because even with those despised meds I hadn't been doing all that whippy-skippy, and now without them I felt like death on the crapper. Or death at the doorstep, for a more delicate image. Or death the day after a bar fight, waking up with a hangover. I didn't know exactly, but death played a prominent role. Which made me think of my list. That made me think of how much I really had become like Aunt Fawnie. Since that revelation didn't bother me as much as it would have a few days ago, I didn't actually, physically snarl when I demanded of Min, "Have you talked to Abby yet?"

She tucked one leg under her and hugged the other knee to her chest. "Inez got her a doctor's appointment. She needs to leave in about an hour, and I offered to go along, so she knows that I know."

"In other words, you have *not* talked to her."

She threw her hands up. "Mama says it's not my business."

Damn it, I was never going to get my list completed facing this kind of resistance. "Not your business to tell her what to do. But to tell her what you *know?*"

"I just want everyone to be happy, Charma." Min rested her chin on her knee and gazed at me all sad-eyed and pouty, which coming from any other human on the planet would have royally pissed me off. From Min, well, it just nearly broke my already beat up heart.

"You can't give anyone happiness. Not even your own child," I said in barely a whisper.

Of course you could go to a doctor and see if he'd prescribe something. I waited to hear Bess sound off. She didn't. She hadn't since…

"Damn," I muttered. I probably owed her whole "existence" to those damn pills. "You can't *make* anyone happy, Min. And you can't make anyone bend to your will and still have the same kind of relationship with them you had before. You can only love people and hope…" I raised my head to listen again. I listened for Bess, for John, for Inez or the aunts, for Sterling. No, not Sterling, for any hint that Guy was here, had been here, might show up here. Nothing. I hadn't expected anything, of course, but I had hoped. "You can only love people and hope they love you back enough to stick around, even when you've both realized you don't have the power to make each other happy."

I looked around me. The sunlight stung. I shut my eyes.

"You should call Guy," she said softly.

"You should talk to your daughter," I shot back.

The room grew still. Not just quiet but still, as if time itself had stopped and nothing, not even the breeze, could stir.

I opened my eyes, expecting to find myself alone, and saw Minnie sitting there, just looking at me.

"You didn't leave."

"Of all the people you have ever loved and irritated to within an inch of their lives, girl, you should know that I am one who will stick around. Even when I know you not only don't have the power to make me happy but that there is a very distinct possibility you will make me very, very cranky."

"I love you, girl."

"You look like shit," she said.

"Do I?" I stared into space, my head nodding. "Good. Then I look a hell of a lot better than I feel."

"Do I need to call the doctor?"

"Yeah, Abby's." A heaviness came over me. I wanted to lie down then and bury myself in my blankets. "Tell him you'll be coming along for moral support."

"Maybe you should come along, too."

"What for? To provide the *immoral* support?"

"Actually, I was thinking of asking Mom to come along for that."

"Good idea," I murmured. And it was. The three of them facing this together would provide the perfect balance. "Why don't you go and get ready? I have things to do here."

"What things?"

"Well, for starters, I did have a list."

"You're scaring me, girl."

"I gave it to Sterling. It was…" I glanced up. "Where is Sterling?"

"Cataloging."

"Shopping my mail?" So that's how he always looked so great without monthly out-of-town buying trips.

"No, cataloging the things Aunt Dinah left to Ruth and the boys, and I don't know what all. He's had everyone marching around this place the past few days gathering things up. Don't you remember, Charma? You pitched a fit yesterday when he said it was time to go into Dinah's room and go through her personal items."

"Oh, hell, Min, I've pitched so many fits in my lifetime, how could you expect me to remember any one specific one?" I didn't remember it, of course, and that fact scared me. Not enough to make me admit my shortcomings, but enough to make me wonder what else might have gone on that I now had no recollection of.

"Well, for starters I'd think you'd remember it because this fit was just yesterday and because it was a doozy." She dropped both her feet to the floor and leaned in my direction. "Charmika, are you okay?"

Okay? I opened my eyes then and made myself take in my surroundings. Stacks of mail clustered around empty plates on the coffee table. Small yellow squares of paper stuck to every surface, phone calls missed, things that needed my attention yesterday and the day before that and the day before that.

My chest ached. My head hurt. My mind had not just rebelled, it had run off and left me here to deal with this mess without any idea of where to start or what to do. My happy pills were in a landfill, and what was left of my life? "My life is a dump heap, Min. A stagnant swamp. I...I haven't even begun to deal with things after Bess's death. Or Mama's, if you want to hear the hard-core truth."

"I don't have to hear it."

"I know, you knew it all but didn't want to say anything to me about it." I smiled. Well, my mouth twitched and I intended to smile, so I am counting that as a gesture of goodwill no matter how it might have come out looking. "I probably owe Chapman's a bundle for Mama's cremation. I know I owe the hospital and doctors and the ambulance people."

"That's what you have insurance for."

"I don't think I have insurance, Min. I quit my job after Mama died, and I never tended to the most basic stuff, and then Bess came back and...I can't say for sure that I saw to keeping up with my insurance after that." I reached out and began to shuffle blindly through the unopened envelopes. "This is serious trouble here."

"You can work it out, Charma. We'll all help."

I glanced up at the sweet face of my cousin and in that instant saw the child she had once been. On the day Bess had pushed me into the pond to try to force me to face my fears, Minnie had taken my hand and offered to make the jump with me. She had promised we could do anything together.

My daddy had also made that kind of promise. And then he wasn't around any longer to keep up his end of the bargain. I wouldn't risk that with Min.

No, some leaps you have to make alone. Stripped to the bone and bare naked to the soul. And no one can make them with you, no matter how much their love makes them want to stay.

"Go with Abby and your mom, Min. That's where you belong. This will all be waiting when you get back."

She left.

I lay back and stared at the ceiling.

"Now, God," I said, "I've had all of this nonsense I can stand. Do that snort thing and suck me up now. Quick and painless and without a lot of folderal and ceremony."

But God has never taken orders from the likes of me.

And once again my heart made the leap I was unable to take with Minnie, or with Bess or even with my mama, and everything went black.

❧ CHAPTER TWENTY-FIVE

"Am I going to die?" I opened my eyes when the gurney hit the doors of the ER.

"Not unless someone kills you." My doctor met me at the door and took my chart from my old friend Dot. "But I heard your family talking in the waiting room, and apparently that's not entirely out of the question."

"So my heart…?" I felt around for the monitor.

"Is fine." He read the chart, flipped a page and double checked the information. "Your head could use some adjusting, though."

He pointed toward the last room at the end of the hallway and murmured something to the EMTs and a man on staff in periwinkle-colored scrubs to indicate that he planned to release me within the hour.

"That's it? My heart starts beating like a son of a bitch. I pass out trying to get help. Dot jabs a needle in my arm, and you send me home?"

He glanced down and handed the chart to periwinkle guy. "You can remove the IV start."

I turned my head to tell him to be gentle, but the damned thing was already out. I sighed. "You ever thought of becoming an EMT?"

"No. You ever thought about taking a job at this hospital?" He gave me a look that said, 'Yeah, I know you.' Since he could have known me from anything from a professional conference, a one-night stand or my having put a bandage on the young man's knee when he was in grade school, I didn't ask him about it. "We could use you around here on days like these. We're understaffed."

"Maybe I *should* come to work here. At least I know better than to tell a crabby person in ER something like that."

"You know how to treat ER patients and yet you don't know enough to take your *own* medicine?" The doc had already began scribbling away on the prescription pad he'd pulled from his pocket. He showed it to the man pulling off latex gloves after taking out my IV. "See if you can get me a couple of samples of this. I want to watch her take it before she leaves." He tore off the page and handed it across to me. "Nurses make the worst patients."

"Second only to doctors," I grumbled.

The male nurse chuckled on his way out the door.

"Okay, let's have it." My doctor wheeled a stool over and plunked down by my side. "What else *weren't* you doing?"

I sat up, still feeling pretty damned confused and crappy. "The list is endless."

"Following the diet?"

"You know me better than that. I'm a leader, not a follower."

He didn't laugh. "Taking steps to reduce stress?"

"Asks the man who says he just spoke to my family. What do you think?"

"Okay, then." He held his hands open. "Getting exercise?"

Does ghost-chasing, hissy-fit pitching, tongue wrestling horny lawyers, throwing the love of my life out on his ass or playing hide-and-seek with reality count as exercise? I decided to answer that with an awkward shift of my shoulders and a sudden intense interest in the state of my nightgown.

"Well, what have you done?"

I met his gaze. I had to say something. I had done something, after all. I hadn't just sat on the couch and…wait, yes, that's pretty much exactly what I had done. Sat on the couch and felt sorry for myself. I hadn't actually done any huge physical activity, aside from some spectacularly limber for our age sex with Guy, since… "I jumped in a pond once."

"You what?"

"To start a new life." I made the "Keep up with me here" gesture, then went on talking as if mine were the most perfectly normal and understandable actions in the world. "I jumped in a pond."

"Then what did you do?"

I jumped right back into the comfortable old life I had always known. I jumped into a living arrangement taking care of my aunts in the house where I grew up. I jumped into an unfinished and maybe a little unhealthy relationship with the man who had jilted me two decades ago. I jumped every time anyone I knew was in trouble, or in pain or even slightly inconvenienced.

"I moved a dead body," I said, because of all those things I had done, that was the *one* thing that sounded most like it would have made me break a sweat. "And I climbed onto the roof. And I…I…"

He shook his head and rubbed his eyes. "Did you swim?"

With a dead body? I blinked and chose not to ask that. Because, honestly, if that's the kind of thing people suspect I am capable of, I really don't want to know that. "Beg your pardon?"

"When you jumped in that pond to start your life over. Did you swim?" He pantomimed a classic stroke.

I shook my head, and not just a simple shake. I gave it the kind of energy you expend when you want someone to know you think that they are just loony.

His eyes narrowed. "Then how did you get back to the shore?"

"I, uh, kicked a few times and pulled myself up." I went over it in my mind. Got naked. Jumped in. Got out. Got dressed. Got on with things. "I didn't actually jump very far out."

The male nurse returned with a small box and a can of caffeine-free soda.

My doctor opened up the box, then twisted off the cap and dumped the flat round tablets into his hand. He held them there a minute, looking at me. "You should have."

I stared at the pills that I did not want to take but knew I could not do without. "Jumped farther?"

Jump out, Charma, jump way out beyond your fears. That's exactly what my father had told me just minutes before I went into the water.

I took a breath. Then another. "What am I supposed to do?"

"Take these." He started to hand the medication to me, then withdrew. "Were there any side effects you haven't told me about?"

I wet my lips. So many things I might have said, so hard to know which came from the pills. Finally, I drew in the smell of antiseptic, blood, sweat and latex. Then confessed, "I think they mellow me out too much."

I thought for a moment he'd ask me if I really thought that was a bad thing. He didn't, so I decided that whatever he said after that might just be worth hearing.

"Fair enough. We can make adjustments." He broke one of the pills in half with his long, strong, scrubbed perfectly pink fingers. "Let's back it down a bit and see how you do. But you have to take them, and you have to keep your appointments, and you have to let me know if you have any problems."

I accepted the compromise. Me, compromise? Who knew I had it in me? I swallowed the medicine and a big swish of soda before asking, "Then what?"

"Then I want you to rest awhile here and I'll check in on you before I let you go home. My take is that you're going to feel a whole lot better once this stuff is in your system again."

Well, it wasn't a guarantee that I'd have a long and happy life, but then again it wasn't a hex that I was going to go home and die.

"Then what?" I asked again, a bit more persistently.

Go home and die. He still had a shot at saying it.

"Swim, Charma."

"Swim?"

"Yeah. You can jump all you want, but how will you ever hope to get stronger if you don't swim?" He gave my arm a squeeze and got up and left me alone in the room.

"He's right, you know."

"Bess!" I gulped in some air and pressed my hand to my chest. "I can see you!"

She gave me that look that only Bess could give. It said she knew more than I did and liked things that way. "Can you?"

It was a fair question.

"Guess you weren't just a figment of my medicine, then." She'd come to me before the meds, of course. But I'd thought my nearness to death had allowed that. Or maybe my need to have her close, or because I had looked to God for guidance. Or because I had asked Loyal's lover to send my family to help me. Something I had done had brought her here: the meds, I thought, had only allowed her to overstay her welcome. I looked over at the quiet monitor, then at my cousin, who had now been dead almost two months. "Why are you here?"

She sat on the counter next to the discarded latex gloves and the torn box my sample pills had come from, still in her wedding dress, her burial dress, still smiling. "Maybe I'm still here because you won't let me go, Charma Deane."

"I thought maybe it was because we didn't bury your soul with you."

"My soul?"

"The cheap souvenir."

"Aah, the *kokeshi*." She shook her head and I noticed she was wearing a delicate pearl necklace. "That's not my soul any more than my body was me, and I think you know that."

I brushed my fingers over the hollow of my throat. I hadn't thought of that necklace since the day of Bess's funeral—of how I had to take it off in order to jump into the pond. And now Bess's ghost was wearing Mama's best pearls. "I don't know anything anymore."

"I believe they call that simple statement the beginning of wisdom."

I held my hand up in a pose that must have looked more like I didn't want John to take my picture than it looked like I wanted to ward off any further spiritual enlightenment. "Great, just what I need—*another* beginning."

"Dead to the old ways. Reborn in the new."

I said it with her, only soundlessly. Then I sat there and tried to conjure up the feel of the sun on my bare back again. The splish of going in, the murkiness, the water overhead, the rising again. "I wanted that to be true so badly."

"Wanting is not doing."

I opened my eyes, half surprised not to find myself on the dock. "I thought *believing* was not doing."

"*Nothing* is doing but doing."

"Can you say that again?"

"Nothing doing."

"I miss you, Bess."

"Not half as much as you miss yourself, Charma."

"Let's not speak in riddles anymore." I put my head in my hands. It still hurt, but the throb had begun to subside. "I feel like we're on a merry-go-round, or worse yet, plodding step by step along the circles in that labyrinth Inez drug me out to walk through."

"Why didn't you walk it?"

"Because to do that, to put your feet on a path, to surrender to something more than yourself? It was asking too much."

"Too much?"

"To stop fixating on the far-flung things you knew you could never really plan for or protect against and instead to set your sights on nothing more than what happens in the next footfall, then the next, then the next?" I shook my head. "To be deliberate about life and where you want it to take you instead of just getting up each day and jumping into whatever comes at you? That's some scary shit, girl."

"Your daddy told you to jump all those years ago, and you still haven't stopped."

"I jumped at everything, and away from everything. I never stuck to it long enough to reclaim my house or build a solid relationship with Guy."

"Or Sterling."

"Or Sterling." Is that what I wanted? *Really?* He was awfully sexy but he wasn't…Guy. He wasn't Guy. And I wasn't Bess. I'd pegged it back in the funeral home. Guy had always thought the love he could never win was the only love that would ever save him. Maybe Sterling *not* being Guy was a good thing. "Whoever."

"Whoever," she echoed.

I lay back and stared at the ceiling. "So is that it, then?"

"What?"

"Telling me to figure out when to jump and when to stick and just to do something in general? Is that the unfinished business that brought you back?"

The lights overhead buzzed. Footsteps and voices carried in from the proceedings beyond the door.

"Bess?" I raised my head to look where she had been sitting and saw nothing.

"I don't have any unfinished business, Charma." Just a voice again, and growing faint. "You do."

"*My* unfinished business caused you to manifest yourself to me?"

No answer.

I sat up and spoke to the wall where a chart of the respiratory system hung. "If it worked that way, then why isn't my mother haunting me?"

"'To everything there is a season and a time for every purpose unto heaven.'"

"'A time to embrace and a time to let go.'" And I knew. Just as much as I needed to let go of Bess, I needed to embrace my mother, shotgun, eBay-bound fur coat and all. I needed to let go of everything that had held me hostage and embrace…my sacred self.

"Charma?" Guy stood in the doorway.

I blinked. "What are you doing here?"

"Sterling called. I came. I hope it's all right."

I smiled. "It's a hell of a lot more than all right."

I tossed the covers off and started to climb out of the hospital bed.

Before I could swing both feet down, he was at my side. And just as quick I noticed Sterling had come in and taken a step toward me. Johnny, too. "Where're Min and Inez and…uh…they're at the doctor's with Abby, right?"

"Soon as they knew you hadn't had another heart attack, they headed off." Sterling had my other arm and helped me steady myself on my feet.

"Life goes on," I said. "Rightly so."

I took a weak but steady step, one foot then the next.

Johnny planted himself in front of me. "What are you going to do, Mom?"

I met my son's eyes, took a deep breath and made a promise I had every intention of sticking to, "I am going to swim, son. I am going to swim."

❦ CHAPTER TWENTY-SIX

"Well, what's the big news?" I tilted up onto the back legs of my kitchen chair.

Fawnie took a long drag with her lips pursed and gave me such a look.

I blew her a kiss.

"I got prenatal vitamins," Abby said, holding up a bottle of huge pink pills. "And a lot to think about."

Min made a face, a comical grimace that said she couldn't believe they were going through with all this. But her eyes sparkled, and I knew that deep down she was hoping for the best and ready to deal with her child, however things turned out.

Of course, as the mother of John Parker, I knew that sentiment exactly. Not that Johnny would ever turn up pregnant and unmarried himself. Though if it were possible and he knew how much it would drive me crazy…naw, he's got too much of his daddy in him to suffer childbirth, even with the bonus of finally driving me over the edge. And, of course, having put my own mama through the same thing…

For the first time since Abby came to the Aunt Farm, it dawned on me. I had done the same thing, been where she had been and fallen into such deep denial about it and what had gone on between Mama and me even all those years ago, that I had completely blocked it out. I raised my eyes, not to the heavens but to the room above us. Mama's room. A sacred spot in a house just crammed to the brim with them. And I smiled and said a little prayer of thanksgiving for Ms. Dinah McCoy George, walls that kept me out and love that kept me safe and all.

"So, what's the plan now?" Inez had not gone to the doctor with the others but had been called away to attend a birth and had arrived back at the Aunt Farm just a few minutes earlier. She was whooped but on the baby-high she gets every time she goes off and plays midwife. I guess bringing new life into the world can do that.

"When your time gets close, you should come back here. We should have a birthing center up and operating by then." She took the vitamins from Abby's hand and read the label carefully.

"Sterling said no businesses." Fawnie glowered and blew a long stream of smoke in the general direction of the rooms Sterling had claimed.

"A contract he violated himself by putting in a law office," I reminded them, and everybody's eyes lit up.

"Birthing ain't a business," Inez protested. "It's life."

"This house should be filled with the business of life." Fawnie took another draw on her cigarette and held it in.

Inez opened her mouth to say something, but I waved her off.

No use pointing out the incongruities of Fawnie puffing away on one of the leading causes of death in our country while proclaiming this house a monument to the power of life. She wouldn't get it and she wouldn't change.

"We'll work around her," I muttered to Inez, who gave me a startled look that all but jabbed me in the shoulder and said, "Does this mean you're on our side now?"

I rocked back on the legs of my chair. I smiled and motioned for Min and Shug to get themselves into the room fully, to have a seat, and then, with a wink, I even suggested they tip their chairs back the way mine was.

"Thanks for the offer." Abby took the pills back from Inez. "But I really can't make plans that far ahead right now."

Silence fell over us. Clearly things were not settled about the baby, not to mention the daddies.

Min let out a big sigh as she sat down.

"One step at a time," Shug assured her grandchild.

Abby nodded, her round face impossibly sweet and her eyes filled with concern. "That's just it, the next step is the scariest of all. I have to go home and tell Daddy. I'm just so afraid of what he's going to say."

"Your daddy?" Fawnie huffed, and smoke escaped her lips in a forceful cloud.

Min scoffed and rolled her eyes. "Trust me, honey, Travis Raynes is not going to say a word."

There was a second when everyone contemplated if they should laugh about poor Travis and perhaps risk making Abby feel even worse. But, hell, we are Georges. We broke up.

"So what next?"

"Then I'm going to tell the baby's father." She looked at me.

Not my business. Trust the girl to do the right thing and be there for her no matter what.

I nodded.

"And for you?" Min asked as she stroked my hair as if she thought I just might say I was going to bed and stay there forever.

I thought for a moment, or rather I put on the appearance of mulling it over. I'd already made up my mind. I made it up when I hopped off that hospital bed and decided not to die just yet. "I am going upstairs and throwing open all the windows in Mama's bedroom."

"You?" Min gathered my hair and in her surprise pulled it back a bit too hard. "In Aunt Dinah's room?"

I batted her hands away to avoid her snatching me bald-headed when I let out this next tidbit. "Yes. Because if I'm going to move in there, it will need to be aired out first."

Everyone murmured for a minute or so, all of them teetering between shock and pride at my decision. Finally, Fawnie, the one who seemed to understand the most about Mama and me, snuffed out her butt, then turned her discerning eye on me. "You going to start going through your Mama's things, then? You want us to plan on helping you later on tonight?"

"Plenty of time for that." I wet my lips and waved my hand to brush aside the task I knew I would now be able to face and accomplish one step at a time. "Tonight?"

I plunked the legs of my chair down and reached beneath the table. "Tonight, ladies, we are going to take back our home."

I pulled a grocery bag filled with spray paint and that library book Inez had checked out and plunked them on the table.

"What are you going to do?" Abby's eyes were big as dinner plates.

"We are going to make a labyrinth," Inez said, actually rubbing her hands together in glee.

I smiled as a confirmation.

Fawnie's eyes glinted, and not-kid-on-Christmas-Day style, either. Teenage-hoodlum-on-Halloween style.

"Shh. *He* might hear you," Shug said.

"I sent *him* to get more boxes and bubble wrap so we can mail the stuff to Aunt Ruth that Mama wanted her to have." I'd created jobs for all the men. I'd asked Guy to look over all my mail and bills and try to figure out just how bad things were for me. And I'd sent John to Chapman's with him, to pick up Mama's ashes and bring them home at last.

I needed the time to make these plans, but more than that I needed to come home to the women who had held my life together, who had held one another's lives together and would keep right on doing so, generation after generation, friend by friend, woman by woman.

I held out my pinkie as Inez had in Sterling's office not so long ago. "So it's agreed. Tonight, we make our mark. Ten o'clock. The side yard."

Each one pledged to be there, and they kept their word.

Those of us staying in the house pleaded weariness from the busy day, and who wouldn't have believed that? We'd worn Sterling himself out with errands and carting things up and down the stairs and taping up boxes. He must have spent a good two hours searching for my mother's best pearl necklace, which we never found despite the fact everyone recalled my having worn it to Bess's funeral.

One by one, just after ten, we each snuck down and out to the meeting place where Inez waited, having brought the hearse around so we wouldn't have to depend on flashlights with mysteriously dead or missing batteries to guide us.

It took an hour or so of stepping off and we knew our result would be rudimentary at best, but there it was in neon orange. Circles within circles. A path. A plan. An enigma. A symbol of faith and heathenism that said here, on *this* little bit of Arkansas dirt, the George women have taken a stand and done something. Sugi and Fawnette. Minami and Abby. Inez and Charma Deane. Bess in spirit, her place held in our group by a little wooden *kokeshi*. And Mama in an urn that I planned to bury on this spot before we brought in tons of gravel to make it permanent.

"Now what?" someone asked.

"We should try to walk it." Inez held up her hands, as if she was really the one in charge.

But Inez was not the queen bee here, she was not even a lesser goddess of Orla, though I have no doubt she was some kind of royal deity-lite in her own family and circle of influence. And when she was standing in *their* yards at midnight, *she* could call the shots.

But not here. Not on my turf. No, this was not a night for prayer and reverence. This was a night to howl at the moon. To say welcome to the world, Charma Deane, and to the second part of a truly amazing adventure.

"I have a better idea." I held the library book aloft. "Back in the time when the Christian faith was young and the heathen urges strong, they found a way to satisfy both the drive toward the divine and the desire for the down and dirtiness of the human experience. And on the night of the solstice they did not walk the labyrinth, they danced in it."

"It's not the solstice," Inez felt compelled to point out.

"It is in *my* little universe." I slung my arm around her shoulders.

She conceded the point with a nod and laugh. "Well, then, I definitely think we should dance."

"Why?" Abby blinked

"To celebrate," I said simply.

"To ask for blessings," Inez added.

"For plenty and fruitfulness." Min put her hand on her daughter's still-flat belly.

"For all the southern comforts," Fawnie summed up for us.

Shug thrust her fist upward. "For the right to bear arms!"

"You tell them, Shug!" Inez laughed.

Abby turned and looked at what we had created. "This is really going to piss Sterling off."

"What do we care? It ain't his house." Shug wrapped her arm around her granddaughter.

"How can we dance if we don't have music?" Abby asked.

Sometimes I worry about the young and their total lack of imagination.

"Who says we don't have music?" I set Mama's ashes on the top of the hearse, so she'd have a good view, you know, then leaned down inside the passenger side door and flicked the radio on full blast.

I cannot say that I had resolved every issue between my mother and myself. But just having her ashes here with us now and knowing I was not going to let this house she loved so much pass away from us made me feel closer to her than I had in most of the years we spent together before she died. I would work through it. Piece by piece, kid glove by kid glove, shoe box by shoe box…and then I would let it go. I would let her go. Just as I had let Bess go. And I would embrace my own sons and try not to choke the life out of them when they made me crazy mad, which I just knew they would.

"C'mon, Charmika, show us what to do." Min motioned for me to join them at the center of the circles. "I don't think I know any heathen-Christian-labyrinth-initiating dance moves!"

"Oh, I do!" Abby shouted, and took her mother's hands.

"Us, too!" Fawnie and Shug chimed in, already swinging around, albeit slowly, with their arms linked.

And so we danced the dances of our foremothers—the shimmy, the jitterbug, the twist. And passed onto the new generation the sacred steps of our own youth—the pony, the bump, the electric slide. Abby showed us a move that would have made Nana Abbra roll over in her grave and we joined in with joy—dancing, not rolling in our graves.

And when we were sure we had insulted and invoked just about everyone and everything possible, we brought out the sacred shotgun of Miss Dinah McCoy George and blasted away at the mother moon—just to get Sterling's attention.

And it worked.

EPILOGUE

"I can't believe he didn't call the cops on y'all."

"And tell them what? A Puerto Rican, a pregnant girl, a one-legged southern belle and his in-laws were in his side yard dancing in the headlights of a hearse to the delight of the ashes of the queenliest queen bee to ever grace the face of Orla society?"

John granted me that point with a most gracious nod of his sweet little pea-brained head. Pea-brained for not thinking like a George, of course, not because he's dumb. Then my boy looked me in the eye, smiled his daddy's most bedeviled smile and asked, liking the idea of troubling Sterling a bit more than was decent, "So what *did* he do?"

I leaned my elbows back on the step behind the one where I had plunked my butt and gazed out the open front door of the Aunt Farm. "Stuck a white hankie on Fawnie's cane and waved it."

Johnny leaned against the banister and stared out the door as well. "Maybe he's not such a jerk after all."

"Maybe not." I stood up.

"I thought you weren't jumping to conclusions anymore." Guy came down from Mama's room, where he'd been taping off the doors and windows to help me paint. He passed by me close enough to press the whole front of his body against my backside, and I have to admit, it made this old heart flutter more than my meds should have allowed.

"And from what I heard, you're taking up where I left off." I brushed a cobweb away from the back of his work shirt.

"How so?" he asked me over his shoulder.

I folded my arms. "Heard you hired a kid with no experience to drive your hearse."

I stopped at the foot of the stairs and started rolling up his sleeves. "Hey, we have big plans for Chapman and Daniels Funeral Home."

Chapman and Daniels. It was a bona fide miracle, was what it was. And here I'd thought Orla was fresh out of them, but it seemed that once again people had fooled me. I could get used to being fooled like that. Of course, I knew that a whole lot of people were backing this deal just hoping to see the high and mighty fall on their faces, but still... "I can't believe you talked the bank into covering your debts and giving y'all another shot at burying a good portion of the town."

"Hey, we have a George on the team now."

"Parker," Johnny corrected.

"I know your name, kid. But don't fool yourself. They didn't loan us the money because of me and Loyal or *our* names, they loaned it to us because of our father's name, and your grandfather's."

John nodded.

"*Us,* they want to see fall on our asses. Then they get to be the ones who brought down the finest families in Orla."

"Or hooked their own names to them and improved their own social and financial standing," I offered.

Guy slapped John on the back, not hard but somewhere between "I'm your boss now, don't fuck with me" and "we're all in this together." "I know how it is. You want to be your own man. Well, you will be. You'll also always be your father's son."

John took that well. It showed in his eyes—and the fact that he didn't take a swing at Guy.

It was so clear now. Guy had not wanted to be that father to John or George or any child. His own family relationships, or maybe his father's line of work, had soured him on the idea of children. I knew that now, and in a funny way, he gave me my sons by leaving me at the altar. Knowing that, it made it pretty damned easy to forgive him.

No, he would never be like a dad to John or George, but I thought, watching him now, he might just be a friend to them.

I came down a step, but not all the way to the floor. "I guess all this means you're staying in Orla."

Guy began rolling up his other sleeve. "I never planned on leaving. Not as long as *you* are here. I told you that."

"Then I gave you your ring back," I said softly.

"I still have it in safekeeping. In case you ever want it again." He raised his eyes to mine.

I all but melted right there. But I didn't, because my acting-on-pure-emotion days are behind me now. For the most part. "Ever?"

"Like I said, I'm not going anywhere."

Another step toward him. "Oh, you're going somewhere, pal. On a date with me, next Saturday."

He cocked his eyebrow. "A date?"

"Yeah, maybe you've heard of them? Dinner that doesn't come out of a bag? Conversation? It's a way for members of the opposite sex to get to know each other and find out if they want to take their relationship further."

He leaned in and spoke all quiet and growly. "What if they've already taken their relationship all the way?"

I ran my finger along his cheek. "All the way? Oh, Mr.

Chapman, if you think that was *all the way,* then you have got a lot to look forward to."

"Hey, hey!" John retreated from the banister, his hands up in the air. "Offspring in the room! Ix-nay on the ex-say talk."

I shook my head. "I wasn't talking about ex-say."

"You weren't?" Guy asked.

"I was talking about our relationship and how far we still have to take it." I reached out and grabbed him by the shirtfront. "It's not the kind of thing you can do in a couple weeks. You can jump in that fast, but if you want to get strong, you have to swim."

He moved in again, and when he was almost nose to nose with me whispered, "I've got some swimmers for you—"

"La-la-la." John stuck his fingers in his ears.

Guy laughed and pulled back. "Okay, we'll work on our relationship. We'll date."

The sound of a U-Haul backing up to the porch made him lift his head, and I had no doubt it prompted him to also ask, "But it will be an exclusive kind of dating, right?"

I glanced out through the open door toward the truck that Sterling had rented for the afternoon. He hopped out of the front cab, caught me looking and paused, all faded T-shirt, low-slung khakis and sensuous, sleepy-eyed smile.

I sighed. "Nope. Can't promise exclusive."

"Okay, then give me this much. No dating little boy lawyer as long as he still lives under the same roof as you."

Sterling bent and seized the handle on the back door of the truck.

"Deal." My whole life I had shared Guy with Bess. I didn't *plan* on starting up anything romantic with Sterling, but I also didn't mind Guy thinking that maybe, just maybe, *he* might have to share *me* for a change. I smiled. "'Course you know he's taking possession of his new house this afternoon?"

"Not soon enough for me."

"His office is still going to be in the Aunt Farm," Johnny, ever the helpful child, said with a gleam in his eye that I swear was the devil in Boyd Parker incarnate.

Guy cleared his throat.

I laughed. "My favorite lawyer there realized he'd never keep his hold on the whole Aunt Farm, but he does still hold the deed. One room doesn't seem too much to concede to the man who loved Bess and made her happy in her final days."

Guy made a man sound, something between a grunt and a "huh." Then he moved in close to me, up on the stairs, and spoke over my shoulder, like a big bear staking his claim, "And no sleeping with him until I'm dead."

"My luck, I'd wait that long and you'd come back and haunt me like Bess did."

"*Did?*" He glanced around us. "She's gone now? For sure?"

"What's for sure?" I laced my arms over my chest. "I think she's gone, I *let* her go. But *for sure?* I'm not even for sure her spirit was ever here to begin with."

"Did you find those pearls?" John asked.

I shook my head. "We went through everything in Mama's room and never came across them."

"They're probably in your room," Guy suggested. "Isn't that most likely where you would have left them?"

"Maybe. But then we left Bess's *kokeshi* in her coffin, and right now it's riding in a suitcase to Tennessee along with all the rest of Abby and Minnie's baggage."

"Yeah, that dumb doll and Grandma's camera, too."

I blinked at my son. "What?"

"I gave it to Abby. You know, to take pictures of her kid."

"What about your becoming a photographer?" I asked, not sure if I was sad or relieved at this news.

"Turns out I wasn't any good at it."

"What makes you say that?"

"Every other picture has a…I don't know…I must have screwed up with the aperture setting or something." He pulled a packet of photos from his pocket, handed it to me then headed out onto the porch to help Sterling haul in empty packing boxes.

"Here. This will go faster with three of us working on it." Guy let his hand trail over my back as he hurried off to join them.

I flipped open the envelope and pulled free the photos my son had taken. The day we made the pinkie swear. Me at the pond at night. Me in the hospital. The women who get things done, standing in the beginnings of the labyrinth the morning after we had reclaimed the Aunt Farm.

I studied the images one by one, and then went back to the one made on that night at the pond, the night that I had first felt Bess's spirit. There in the darkness hovering right next to me—a beautiful light. An orb.

Johnny could play it off as a flaw in his technique, but I knew better.

"Well, I'll be. She really *was* here."

"Charma? Can you get out here and settle something for us?" Sterling hollered from inside the truck he'd rented to help him move on with his life.

"No," I shouted back. "But I can come in there and help you work it out."

That's how you get strong, you know. That's how you claim your life and keep from going under forever. You can't just jump— you have to swim.

QUESTIONS FOR
THE SOUTHERN COMFORTS

1) In the opening chapter, Charma Deane feels she must leap into the pond she had feared for a lifetime as a catalyst for her to move on. What do you think about using a symbolic act (for example, doing something you fear, writing a letter, burning a memento) to mark the ending of one stage and a hopeful readiness for what lies ahead? Have you ever done such a thing? What effect did it have on you?

2) Charma realizes that when she takes in and counsels Abby, her cousin Minnie's daughter, that this may impact on the cousins' relationship. What would you have done in this situation and why? Would you have kept Abby's secret? Would you have wanted to keep your distance, feeling this matter should involve only parent and child?

3) Early on, Charma considers the significance of finding her own path to God. Can you see how the other characters help to direct her in her seeking? Do you think any characters try to trip her up or stop her? At what point did you feel that she had finally gotten on the right path, even if she had not actually found everything she was looking for?

4) Which character did you most identify with? If none, or even if all of them, which one would you most like to have dinner with?

5) Have you ever had a life-altering experience or illness, such as Charma's heart attack?

6) After her heart attack, when Charma began seeing Bess, what was happening? Was she projecting her own emotions onto her dead cousin? Hallucinating? Actually interacting with a spirit? Other theories?

7) Do you believe in ghosts? Why or why not? Have you ever had an otherworldly or paranormal experience? Talk about it.

8) Do you have your own "Things To Do Before I Die" list? What's on it? If you don't have one, what would you put on one?

9) *The Southern Comforts* is a celebration of the things that women do that make a difference—bringing laughter, guiding, nurturing, sharing of themselves to their circles of family, friends and community. What women in particular enrich your life? The characters all also have very special men in their lives. These men in particular provide a framework for them and love them even when the women aren't being lovable. They are ordinary heroes. What men are the ordinary heroes in your life?

10) Can you apply Charma's conclusion—that it is not enough to just jump into the pond; to get stronger, you have to swim—to a situation in your life? Do you think, given where Charma is at the end of the book, she will follow through and make more significant changes in her life? Do you think she will ever marry Guy? What would you do with the Aunt Farm if it were yours?

A Book Sense Notable Book by

MARY ROURKE

Seeking to restore health to her lungs, Joanna, wife to
Herod's chief steward, approaches her cousin Mary, mother
of the healer Jesus. Though their families were estranged when
Joanna's parents adopted Roman ways, Mary welcomes her
graciously. Jesus indeed heals Joanna's body…and her soul
blossoms through her friendship with Mary and with her work
as one of his disciples. But as word of Jesus' miracles reaches
King Herod's court, intrigue, treachery and murder cast
shadows onto Joanna's new path, changing her life forever.

TWO WOMEN
of
GALILEE

"In the spirit of *The Red Tent,* Rourke has pondered
the lives of the women of the gospels, and…
has skillfully evoked an entrancing world."
—Geraldine Brooks,
Pulitzer Prize-winning author of *March*

Available wherever trade paperbacks are sold!

MIRA®

www.MIRABooks.com

MMR2432TR

NEW YORK TIMES
BESTSELLING AUTHOR

SANDRA BROWN

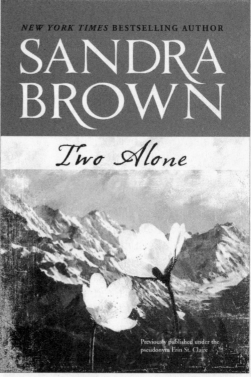

Two Alone

They didn't trust each other. But after a plane crash stranded
them in the remote reaches of the north, the strangers had no
choice but to depend on one another.

"A master storyteller."—*Newport Daily News Press*

Available wherever hardcovers are sold!

THE EXTRAORDINARY DEBUT NOVEL BY
DEANNA RAYBOURN

A PSYCHOTIC MURDERER IS ABOUT TO MAKE HIS ONE MISTAKE. UNDERESTIMATING LADY JULIA

SILENT *in the* GRAVE

Available wherever hardcovers are sold.

MDR2410TR